The Graffiti Killer

The Graffiti Killer

by

David Milnes

First Edition

First published by what tradition books in 2025

British Library Cataloguing in Publication Data available

ISBN 978 19 16183 21 6

Also from what tradition books:

The Ghost of Neil Diamond by David Milnes
The Whores of Coxcomb Hall by Egg Taylor
To Have Nothing by David Milnes
The Pathology of Graphology by David Milnes
Way of the Infidel by David Milnes
An English Airman Foresees his Death by David Milnes

All hail The Ghost of Neil Diamond

"Ghost is a beautiful cathedral - at the risk of sounding effusive you should make a pilgrimage. It's that superb."

dissidentbooks.com New York

"some of the most meticulous prose I've ever read"

the novel blog Canada

"A dark comedy stemming from the howling despair of a man who is out of his element in every way . . . a book that subtly plays with the tropes associated with its subject matter to raise some interesting questions about what represents the real, and what constitutes the fake"

"A thoroughly enjoyable and idiosyncratic story that holds your attention until the rather brilliant end."

bookmunch.co.uk Manchester UK

"I highly recommend The Ghost of Neil Diamond if you're tired of reading the same old shit and want to check out something truly unique."

alternativereel.com Florida

The Graffiti Killer

by

David Milnes

what tradition books
whattradition.co.uk

Before dawn lifted its greasy lid on the Channel, I found him on the rear deck, casting an artistic eye into the wake and darkness. Now and then he glanced about but only to hold on to his solitude. There was nothing wary in his manner. If anything, he looked smug and proprietary, as if pleased with the deposits, the excrement, he'd left behind on the continent.

His nondescript outfit - puffer jacket, jeans, paint-dashed trainers - was the same as when I'd seen him boarding, so he'd had no cabin. His child-like frame and smudged features, his lank hair in dark straggles, also singled him out. In appearance, posture, attitude, ambition, everything, he was nothing, beneath contempt.

I watched him from in front of the ferry's Games Room, a poky afterthought adjacent to the cafeteria kitchens. I could hear some movement in the kitchens now. The cabin wake-up call, due at 5.30 a.m., had not yet sounded but they were preparing for the Full English rush.

He turned leeward and a gust fanned up the straggles of his unkempt and scrappy hair and held them a moment about his face, as if in some cartoon sketch depicting horror or electric shock - not a cartoon sketch but a graffiti sketch, of course - while his face in the middle was placid, even introspective, thinking of what he'd done, what he'd achieved, until he saw me standing behind the doors, and straightaway I believe he saw my intentions but refused to give way to fear.

The deck doors were heavily sprung but noiseless.

"Morning!" he called, smiling, insisting on normality with a perfect stranger.

Behind me the doors slammed on their oily springs.

There was no taste of sea air because of the vile black diesel blown back by gusts of tailwind. The *Mont St Michel* thrust on at its maximum of 18 knots.

Oh how those mighty propellers chewed at the dying sea!

"Morning!" I returned.

For a moment, unbidden, the image of his punk motorbike, an old Honda 250 or similar, its panniers crammed with one-man tent and aerosols, hung before me, modest and forlorn on the upper deck, behind the chrome fanfare of bullish touring bikes.

I thought I saw a flex of muscle, a narrowing of the eyes in recognition, and it struck me that he might have seen me from his bike when I slowed under a bridge on the E5.

His phone and wallet bulged under the zips of the puffer jacket.

On the side of a life-boat barrel was a public warning:

An old man who has never played rugby makes an unconvincing low tackle, but the move surprised him and half his torso was over the rail before he fought back. He was too busy kicking and clinging on to shout or scream, and the weight of his head was over already, pointing down at that twenty metre drop, that five storey drop, his straggly hair pointing down past all those cabin windows, all those fresh, blue and white stripes of welded hull dividing deck from deck, pointing past the welded world deck by deck, his eyes pointing down in terror to the grey churn of propeller current. His wriggling ribs beneath the jacket felt like the ribs of a squealing piglet caught at the fair. My shoulder under his skinny thigh gave enough leverage to push the full weight of his torso and his right leg over the edge. His left leg still clung there, as if he were on a spit, longways on the rail, which was a wooden chamfered rail, not metal and therefore not so uncomfortable, perhaps. With both hands I wrenched his ankle - he emitted a terrible squeal! - and levered his left leg all the way over.

He couldn't hang on long and he knew it, knew he didn't have the strength. His chin was chattering with terror but no words came out. I reached over and gripped his jacket tight under both arms.

"I've got you. It's okay."

I nodded to him.

"Password."

Still the chattering terror. The utter bewilderment.

Shifting my grip to his shoulders, I felt him start to slip out of the jacket.

"It's okay. Password."

"Loner!"

The collar was coming clear but the hood pouch snagged round the back of his head, which made him think that would help me drag him back up. I got a good grip on the pouch with my left hand, released my right and set my palm on his slippery forehead and he twisted away as if shy of my touch. I pushed so his neck cricked back and dipped under the pouch and he was gone. There was a mad flailing and spreading out and the beginning of a somersault halfway down so the back of his head hit the water first. I imagine that impact broke his neck and he knew nothing more, never felt the draw of the propellers nor saw their cinema-screen scythes reaching out to him through the green froth.

The whole business had taken but a few seconds.

I looked about, his jacket under my arm. No one at all.

If the whole world had sat there in deckchairs, I could not have cared less.

In the end, there is no choice. When all else has failed you or foiled you, you take up arms against them.

Kloon. Shaft. Moos. Loner. Arus, or sometimes, Anus.

Remember our names. We love this game.

Kloon's disdain is not just for truckers but for whole holiday families, van-drivers and all the rest, including the rare super-rich passing by, touring in Bentley and Aston-Martin convertibles, and the educated bourgeoisie on their way to their gites - there is a triumph in drawing them all down to his level. They cannot avoid him, deny him. And when they see him again, on a bridge or wall two hundred miles later, that second hit - You again! Kloon again! *Yes! Me again! Here before you again and after you've gone again! Miles of smiles! I am permanent, you are passing through. My art is beautiful, I am beautiful, no one can tell me it is not so! I am an artist!*

Remember our names. We love this game.

I do remember your names.

Loner of the deep. A sprat to catch the mackerel.

Here's the place: 5km south-west of Ussel on the A89. *Parc naturel régional de Millevaches en Limousin.*

Some likely ruins and farm buildings but their target has to be the minor suspension bridge: two arcs press the sky, with a single main hawser either side threaded down midpoint, which divides to take the weight of the road through two massive stainless steel unions. The sublime grace of its balance must have brought much joy to its architect on completion. A young architect, one imagines.

Its stanchions offer white virgin flanks of concrete, where Kloon will be the first to cock his leg, but for the last time.

A kilometre or so after the bridge I slowed at the sight of a campfire in a lay-by my side of the road. Not so much a campfire, it turned out, but a gas burner in the back of an open van. There were several people in and around the back of the van, all adults, possibly all male, and I noted a homemade bed structure inside. The van was an old white Ford Transit with UK plates. In its past life it had been a delivery vehicle: *"Purveyors of"* was painted over - not sprayed but hand-painted over with a brush, in white paint - and then below that, covering the flank of the van, were these lines:

> *"They locked up a man who wanted to rule the world.*
> *The fools.*
> *They locked up the wrong man."*

Before checking, I had the idea the lines would come from some troubadour manqué, some Bob Dylan figure, and it turned out they belonged to Leonard Cohen, the pedlar of self-pity to the masses, who died quite recently. The pronouns gave it away. *They did it!* The oppressors who robbed the ne'er-do-wells of what they'd never had in money, property and talent. *They did it! The fools!* The tone is disdainful but resigned, leaving plenty of slack for melancholy singalongs by the campfires of Victimhood. *'They'* - society, or some sect within it, or even History itself - is always to blame for how things have turned out. But as Thatcher said on Woman's Hour, there is no such thing as society. There are families and individuals: that is all.

Everyone is accountable.

It is Kloon's van. This is certain from the group messages and the pin-drop. There has been some curiosity about Loner's silence but it seems he is being quickly forgotten. Some on the group seem a touch relieved not to hear from him.

When I had a chance to look closer, on foot, through the night sights, Cohen's lines blocked out completely whatever the van had once purveyed. The humble work once undertaken by some honest soul to put bread on the table, had now been tarted over with Cohen's religio-profundity, his mobile graffiti.

There would be four, given Loner's absence. Four adults. Not easy for a young, fit soul with some military training, let alone an old ham worrying about his prostate, lumbering through the pine trees - *'Ghoul fourteen to the right of tree six, please! ... Like, Now!'*

Dusk was very late - around nine, another half hour - and the moon was full, so they had to wait, maybe till gone midnight, before they got started. Hence the gas burner. Time for a last supper. And a singalong, perhaps.

No motorbikes in front of or behind the van, which was tipped slightly because the lay-by was not actually an official stop, not an *aire de* anything, but a cleared space of about eight metres breadth at the side of the road, probably a scar left from the original construction of the bridge.

After I shot 'Kloon', 'Moos' went to pieces. Berserk.

She was a pathetic, terrified, sniffling and snivelling, wailing thing, trying to wash the blood and paint off the stanchion with crummy tools from the van, a window wiper and an old blue towel. She was about thirty, with dark, shoulder-length hair, mostly tucked up under a Nike baseball cap with a tick on the peak, and that moronic slogan *Just Do It!* across the brow. She was skinny and floppy but not unattractive, even in this hysterical state.

"All of it."

"I can't!" she wailed. "It's aerosol! It won't come off!"

"Harder."

"I can't! It's stupid! It won't come off! That's the whole point!"

Shaft came up the bank with more water.

They'd tossed a coin for the role - one to clean, one to fetch and carry - but with this caveat: if the cleaning failed, the cleaner would be next. And the cleaning was failing miserably, so Moos would be next. No heroics from Shaft. He never offered to swap places. He was dark skinned but not black, nor identifiably Indian. I had picked up they were in a relationship. So much for that.

I could see from the way he was carrying the bucket that he had a plan: throw the water over me then smash me with the bucket. But it was only a blue plastic pail, a slop bucket from the van, no weight.

Moving the Browning across my knees, I offered the cliché for predictable threats of this nature:

"Don't even think about it."

He set the bucket down.

"What's the matter with you, man?"

Good to hear that fake 'man' making a comeback from the sixties, seventies. Yeah, man. Cool, man. He also spoke with a heavy estuary accent but with some black in it: I suspected it was an affectation, or an affectation grown so familiar it was now part of him.

Arus was still in the van. I had Shaft tie him up in the back and gag him, and outside smash the van headlights with a rock. Then I'd left Shaft in the cab and hurried back to the other side of the bridge to take out Kloon from the opposite stanchion, using the base as a rest. But I was too late: the K and L were both complete and he'd started on the first O. Some defender of the faith I am. Aiming for the centre of the back of his skull with the new night sights, I squeezed the trigger and he dropped as if there had been a power cut, at exactly the same time. That shot and Moos's wailing brought Shaft to the bridge, of course. I wouldn't let either of them touch Kloon.

Now the water from Moos's futile scrubbing was soaking his jeans. He was lying face down in what had been dry earth but had now turned to slimy surface mud. He lay perfectly at peace, with a steady trickle of blood coming out the back of his matted hair, his clotted dark brown hair, and joining another thicker trickle from his face, or what was left of his face, in the mud; the two twisted round a pale stone a few inches from his skull and started down the bank towards the river, thin and tiny and red but perfectly visible, glinting in the moonlight and the bridge lights.

Shaft squatted on his haunches, the blue pail in front of him. He knitted his hands to stop them shaking with fear and tried to adopt a reasonable, non-threatening posture.

"What's up with you, man?" he repeated. "We're just having a bit of fun, for fucksake. No harm done. No one deserves to fuckin' die! That's mad stuff, crazy stuff."

At that Moos set her forehead against the white concrete and wept piteously.

"She needs more water."

"We don't deserve to fuckin' die, man, just cos you

say so. Just cos you don't like what we're doin' an' you got a fuckin' gun. What's goin' down in there?" He pointed at my head. "I mean, *Why*?"

He asked me that. He asked me Why.

"You know," I told him. "You know why."

"No I don't! That's just what I'm fuckin' sayin'!"

From the Costa del Sol to the Basque country, and on through the beautiful French Pyrenees, and then to every port in France, your names are there, on every ruin, every roman aqueduct, on every naked wall or barrier or noise baffle, on every pump hut alone in corn field or vineyard, on each and every bridge and in every underpass and tunnel and on every motorway sign, your names are there.

And you asked me that. *Why.*

Remember our names. We love this game.

You insist on your presence everywhere, in all these places where you do not belong, and that do not belong to you, that you colonise like imperialists, and you ask me *Why*. There is no escape from your faux fame. It is a tyranny. You inspire hatred. Your art is hate-speech. You hate art, mock art, spoof art. The field or vineyard was beautiful before you shat your ten foot name on the pump hut. The physics of the bridge were a wonder before you shat your name on its stanchions. How could Lorraine, Monet or Van Gogh ever paint that field, vineyard, bridge or river, with your name, your art there *first*, your defilement? The beauty of these landscapes, of the Pyrenees mountains and valleys, never belonged to you but you took it, violated it, raped it, ruined all possibility of inspiration to a genuine artist's eye. You are a murderer of art, a denier of art, a destroyer of all the possibilities of art, of the scope of the artist, of the artist himself or herself - the murderer! - and the consequences of your crime permeate the world in eight point two billion different ways, and counting, infinite in number, immeasurable in scope, and the penalty for your crime is Death.

You have no understanding of work, or respect for work, physical work, or any work that demands more abstract thought, no understanding of the work of the labourer, technician, architect. A bricklayer sets the bricks in a perfect vertical; a painter labours to whitewash the wall in the same way they have whitewashed walls in the mountain villages of Andalucia for centuries. They do the work to live, to feed their families. But you have no respect for that. In your unfathomable ignorance and vanity you do not know what skill and effort is involved, what effort of labour, and you do not try to imagine, or perhaps cannot imagine, because all that concerns you is the infantile temptation to aerosol your name on that surface in green or red or blue or black. And then the view has gone. Irreplaceable. The image is destroyed outside, and inside, behind the retina. It has been defiled by your baby-ego-art. The consequences of such a crime, such disrespect for the work and dedication of our labourers, technicians, architects, are infinite and immeasurable, and the penalty for that crime is Death.

What is read cannot be unread: we cannot save ourselves from the ratiocinative process that runs against the will to the thought-waste of *Why* and *For Whom* your defilements exist. Your craving - 'Look at me, mummy!' - is bold enough, but beneath that is the claim to be a voice of counter-culture, a voice of nonconformity, even rebellion - 'You cannot ignore me! I have a voice!' - rendered in the flagrant fonts and colours, which also lay claim to talent, and even courage - *Kloon Shaft Moos Loner Arus*, all painted in places apparently impossible to reach, that demand such courage and skill to be put up there! Hah! You remain talentless cowards and nobodies and frauds. Such straining only defecates your failure to fit in. Your curls and shit-shape defilements violate the beauty of the natural world and whatever beauty our architects have achieved in our landscapes; even to the ugliest, most boring, most functional and prosaic and dilapidated industrial warehouse your names add nothing but screaming vanity.

And you ask me *Why*.

The world will be better off, quieter, infinitely more beautiful, peaceful, without you, all of you.

Sometimes I hear the voiceovers of the documentaries:

'Certain patterns of behaviour prior to the slayings suggest psychopathic tendencies - '

No no no ...

It is the modern weakness to suppose one who kills

is disabled by a severed root to the amygdala or some such, but this takes no account of a mind provoked, taunted, to extremes of anger, hatred, shame, all redoubled by the frustration that such passions can find no expression, except through fighting back - *Fight! Fight! Fight!* - no account of a mind overwhelmed, a mind drowned by such excesses. The goading and provocation continue every time one glances out the train window, or the car window, or the rear-view mirror. The pollution and defilement and contamination of Nature and of human achievement, leaving no surface untouched, nothing unsoiled. How can Eliot write about the moment in the rose-garden - 'and then a cloud passed / And the pool was empty' - when the concrete basin is already fouled by *Kloon Shaft Moos Loner Arus*? *'Remember our names. We love this game.'* How can Yeats write about the wild swans at Coole, with your names all over the jetty and the landing stage? How can Wordsworth write about the beauty of the 'sylvan Wye' with your names on every signpost all the way along the M4? Thus your excrement leaks into everything, and with it the sense of powerlessness and failure that leaks into every aspect of one's life, because *you have won*, and we are the *losers*, impotent against your success.

We cannot co-exist. One must go. One needs must wither.

And afterwards, the repercussions, the involuntary memories, that I must suffer all over again - that image of Loner's face on the Caen-Portsmouth crossing, his hair spread out behind by the tailwind, that cartoon detail, and again his desperate clinging to the rail, the agony of confusion in his eyes when I said it was okay - 'It's okay. I've got you.' - all of these images will return, have already begun to return, to add to the misery and torment. On his phone there were other groups, but they can wait; the chances I will get to them are slim. Of course I know they are slim. Kloon's Whatsapp group had no faces (only their graffiti handles) except *Shaft*, who I thought at first was a mean looking black guy, but the image is actually of the actor from the *Shaft* films back in the seventies (*Shaft, Shaft in Africa, Shaft's Big Score!*), Richard Roundtree. I have never seen those films but know well enough the stink of their shit. More trash.

More excrement. More Americana. Take it away. Blow it away. But Richard Roundtree - perhaps he is a hero of the fellow here, with the blue plastic bucket. Oh yes, that makes exactly the kind of sense involuntary memories and billions of images that torment and destroy the soul make time after time, so from *Shaft* and Richard Roundtree I plummet to TV of that era, to Jack Lord, still playing cops and robbers in *Hawaii Five-0* past sixty - how'd he get that part? - and then reel back to Sir John Mills, playing the nineteen year old Pip in *Great Expectations* - how'd he get that part? - when he was already thirty-eight! Was there no actor in his twenties of sufficient talent to warrant that break? Did David Lean have to give it to his best buddy even though he was *twice as old* as Pip? How hard must the actor's life be? Thus the involuntary memories: connections brought on by images and sounds thrust upon, shoved upon, stamped upon the mind over decades, so that one's consciousness is like that island of plastic in the Atlantic, just a concatenation of trash, and one's subconscious is the sunken islands of plastic at the bottom of every ocean.

One's mind has been graffitified, as has the whole fucking planet.

But Kloon has gone, and the straggly Loner has gone too, and they can do no more damage to the retina, to the peace of mind behind it, and soon this woman, this Moos, and Shaft, they will be gone too. Then the rest will not dare come out at night. They'll stay in with their TV and their video games in their urbanite cells, where they belong, not in Nature, not in the landscapes of Monet, Renoir, Van Gogh, Goya …

Some stevedores wheeled Loner's punk Honda 250 off the ferry at the end of disembarkation, after half a dozen tannoy announcements. Then, one supposes, the *Mont St Michell* had to be searched. I didn't hang around for any of that.

Shaft squatted around five metres away still, with the tatty blue pail, half full, in front of him. From here the rifle would be lethal wherever the bullet went in. His hands were still knitted patiently in front of him.

"Let me reason with you, man," he appealed.

"This is my court. There is no appeal."

"Please. Just let's talk a little here, cos what's going down here is just crazy stuff."

"You talk like your graffiti. You talk graffiti."

"It's just a name on a rock! Come on!"

"But what is read cannot be unread."

Moos slumped to the base of the stanchion, inches from Kloon's trainers. "I hate violence!" she wailed, she whined. "I hate it! Any kind of violence! I can't stand it! Always hated it! Look what you've done!" She pushed up the peak of her baseball cap, opening more of her pale face to the moonlight, the bridge lights. "You killed my friend! Don't you even know that? … You don't know it yet, do you? What you've done? You killed him!"

I looked above her cap, her head, to the defiled stanchion.

"Scrub him off."

"He didn't even finish his name!" she cried. "Poor guy! Killed for painting a couple of letters on a fucking bridge! How about that? That's madness!"

Shaft hung his head. "Look, just …"

But he could find no new way to start. Hah. That sucks, man.

Remember our names. We love this game.

"Who is Arus?" I asked. "Reads 'Anus' most of the time. Why does he call himself Arus, Anus? What's his real name?"

"You're the only arsehole around here, man!" Shaft broke out. "No mistake about that. Look what you've done! Fuckin' killed someone!"

"Answer my question. Who is he? What's his name?"

The Browning is a repeater and loaded with six rounds. I lifted the rifle and without aiming fired a round between them down the bank.

Moos gasped. Shaft flinched.

"Let me tell you! Let me tell you!" Moos wailed.

I rested the rifle across my knees again. "So tell me."

She shook her head and picked at some muddy scraps of grass where the concrete met the earth.

"His name… His real name is Arthur. Arthur Spencer

Harris. I know how fake that may sound but it really is his name. That's partly why he calls himself Arus, because he hates his own name."

"He hates himself," Shaft put in.

I ignored that. "What does Arthur Spencer Harris do?"

She looked bewildered by these questions, these details, with Kloon dead at her feet. "I don't know right now ... like.... like ... he does all kinds of stuff?"

Though she was definitely English, she spoke with that hip American affectation of the rising interrogative, that escape clause, so dated now.

"Specifically."

"I don't know! What's it matter? He's going to die! ... For a while he drove a minicab? What's it matter what he does?" She plucked some more grass and threw it down the bank. "If you're going to kill him anyway. You must be mad as a fucking hatter."

"Did he drive a cab? Or does he drive a cab? Or not?"

"Yeah." She pulled at the muddy grass again, head down. She was calmer for a moment. "For a while. Yeah. He drove a minicab. His dad's old car. All around Yarmouth."

"Great Yarmouth?"

"Yeah. East Anglia. And now he's gonna die, gonna die for a bit of graffiti. Stairway to heaven for a bit of graffiti, knockin' on heaven's door for a bit of fucking graffiti, oh yeah. Fucking amazing! Fucking madness!" She looked at me and a flash of anger crossed her narrow eyes.

"Where the fuck are you coming from, you ugly old prick?"

Nothing came from acting. Only debts came from acting. If one looks even vaguely albino one is cast as albino, which for the industry, in my time, seventies-eighties, meant Ghouls - *The Omega Man* - or a Hit Man - *The Eiger Connection* - or some cranky Bond Villain like Max Zorin in *A View to a Kill*. Of course, I was never anywhere near the latter parts, I was always way too far down the heap for anything but Ghoul 14 in *The Omega Man*, but the point is they represent the acme of an albino's acting career, or an albino lookalike's acting career. And things haven't moved on much because in the 2002 version of *The Time Machine* the mastermind Urban Morlock (Jeremy Irons, to his shame) is typecast as pure albino. Explanations for this kind of prejudice are of no interest. 'The world is what it is;' Salim famously tells us at the start of *A Bend in the River*, 'men who are nothing, who allow themselves to become nothing, have no place in it'.

Some of my money came through promoting minor UK rock bands, and a few not so minor ones, and handling the UK management of one major American star from the seventies/eighties - Barry Manilow - who still tours prestige venues such as The London Palladium today, at 81 years of age. My association with Manilow UK died more than ten years ago but I'll say this: there was more money in a string of summer Manilow dates than in a year's tour of most UK rock bands. The rest of my money I didn't earn. It came from luck. I'm of that generation that owned a freehold in London - just a pokey flat in Fulham, near the bridge - and saw the price of it soar to half a million in a few years. Worth double that now, no doubt, but I sold at half a million, bought big and cheap in Andalucia, and I'll never have to work again.

The bands I promoted - managed is a better word - and toured with, for months on end at the start, were the also-rans of the punk movement in the mid-eighties, the most well-known of which were *DuDChek*, whose lead guitarist actually was a Slovakian emigré, and the notorious *Crucifux*, whose cruel onstage antics sold the tickets, not their awful music. At that time, because the punk movement itself was a rejection of learned musicianship, any bunch of kids could come together and slash out a song which I could pass off as authentic punk, no questions asked - as The Sex Pistols themselves said, 'we can't even think of a word that rhymes'. For those early tours I actually travelled with the bands in my campervan while they shared two old Bedfords I bought from a dying bakery: those were the days, as they say, but they assuredly were not! Of course I was fleecing the bands from the start and as soon as I could afford it, I rented an office back in London, in Dalston - *PunkProms* - and left them on tour. I couldn't stand the noise of their shit music, and pretending otherwise, nodding along, heaving out the speakers and amps etc, added too much strain to life.

The tipping point came when the singer with *DuDChek,* who sang so sharp he'd cut himself, started asking questions and making dry remarks. He'd rumbled me and I knew my touring days were over, thank the lord, and it was time to hide away in an office. But apart from that personal matter, the Dalston move was organizational - or strategic, you might say, to glamourise the unglamourizable - because the secret to making any money out of those minor bands was to keep them on the road all the time. That way they were at a distance from the financial side of touring. They literally didn't have a moment to stop and figure things out, not least because they were having such a good time. Part of what made me convincing to the bands was my brutal honesty about their prospects: I knew the punk scene couldn't last and I told them so; I told them they had better get out there and enjoy the fuck and make as much noise and money as possible while I could still find them bookings. So there was this edge, this haste, this panic almost, about the touring, and the idea carried through to equipment and transport. Even after they'd had a hit and some TV coverage - *Crucifux* made it onto The Old Grey Whistle Test on BBC2, with whispering Bob Harris - and the whole band wanted to upgrade equipment, I told them No No No, not unless they wanted to do it out of their own pockets. Besides, I said, that would be selling out what punk stood for.

But these conversations I kept very short, to an absolute minimum, on the telephone. As I say, the secret was to keep them out there performing night after night, no matter where, so that they were too busy and too exhausted to catch up with the accounting, which was all my business. "Good news, lads! We're fixed for Queen's Hall Leeds all weekend, so wipe your arses double-quick after Birmingham and get 'em over there!" The two old Bedford bakery vans I bought them I let them paint up and kit out as they pleased.

"That's your business. Do what you like. Here's a monkey."

No Leonard Cohen rubbish for them.

That singer from *DuDChek* was a small and nasty eurasian guy called Nat, with a mouth crammed full of yellow teeth. He fell sick up north and came down after me, actually took me by surprise in the Dalston office.

"Where's my fucking money?" he demanded, leaning over the desk, pouring his sickness and exhaustion all over my empty desk. "I'm not leaving till you give me my fucking money!"

It was obvious he was too sick and shrunken with exhaustion to get violent.

I held out my hands: "Listen, Nat. It doesn't work like that. If we had any money, I'd give it to you. Right now. You have my word. But we don't have any money. I'm on the phone here day and night trying to get box office receipts from half a dozen places. Some from months ago. It's coming in, for sure, but it's blood out of a kidney stone. Meanwhile I've got to pay for the diesel, the meals, the equipment, the roadies. You want a list of all the advances you've had? You want to see the bank charges on the fucking overdraft? No one wants that money more than I do. Needs it more than me. I'm the loser here, big time. Believe me."

Actually, I'd just spent all his money at the weekend on a PADI scuba-diving course in Gosport, Hants! First class rail ticket! Plumbing the depths of murky gravel pits just because I fancied the woman in charge! All a total waste because I never took it up and she didn't want to know. Ah, Nat, how different our worlds were then, had you but known. You'd have pitied me.

He had no answers to what I'd said. He didn't know enough. So he got snide.

"All Jews good at showbiz, eh?"

"That may be so, but I'm not Jewish. I'm just a flunked actor with a shabby arts degree who no one wants to employ, trying to make a go of things the best I can, and you're just a guy with nothing at all to recommend him, not even a shabby arts degree, hardly any musical ability, trying to make a go of things while the moment lasts. Simple as that. Let's not pretend otherwise."

That brutal honesty. It worked so well.

He stood back. He looked so tired and sick and unhappy his mouth couldn't close over all those yellow teeth, but the really sad thing was I think he knew deep down he wasn't going to get a shiny sixpence out of me, not ever, but this was such a desperate thought, to be so cheated and forsaken, given all his endeavour on stage, all his hysterics, his screaming and ranting, his histrionics and cruelties, and all the misery on the road, the breakdowns, freezing all night in the back of the bakery vans with the amps and speakers - it was really such a desperate thought that he would never get a shiny sixpence out of me, given the broken state he was already in, that he shied away from it, preferring to believe my procrastinations and bare-faced lies.

Oh, all too human weakness!

That confrontation, and the damage to reputation he was doing with his suspicious talk - not only with *DuDChek* but with other bands they met on tour, who were all on regular money - that suspicious talk of his started some blowback. As it happened, that was when the Manilow gigs began and I quit Dalston and bought my place in Fulham with the punk proceeds. Dumped the bands. Disappeared.

Could I really kill Moos? In cold blood? That was the question she wanted me to keep asking myself.

She was a youngish woman, after all. Might even have been a mother, or pregnant. It was so much easier to shoot Shaft, whose name had already lit a bonfire of tormenting associations, a bonfire of trash, but he had won the toss. So, could I kill Moos? It would be different to Kloon: just being on the other side of the bridge made a difference, and his back was to me, and he knew nothing of what was about to happen. Loner had been a more similar prospect to Moos, though he'd had none of the advantages in life Moos enjoyed, from my point of view.

There was an allure, of course, to having her at my mercy, to hear her whimper and beg, and I felt that sexual tug inside. And her name, which connotes mouse, meekness, weakness, added to that. But that is not my way, the surrender to bestial appetite, sadistic delight, barbaric amorality. Vlad the Impaler using horses to drive the poles up his victims' rectums, before pulling them upright into his screaming forests; Genghiz Khan pouring molten silver into the eyes of his staked captives. Furthermore, I know it is a road to addiction. As with the Taliban leaders addicted to beheading: nothing satisfies that craving for them, the satisfaction of the clean strike with the bejewelled scimitar, and the fallen, gaping head of the infidel, still living, lips moving, and something like a sigh of blood.

Not my way.

"Moos," I began. "Why do you call yourself that?"

I saw her risk a glance at Shaft, with a grimace that created dimples at the corners of her mouth. Cute. I thought this might be some soft secret between them, that her name might be some baby-talk term of endearment. But I was quite wrong. Her eyes came back to me. They were narrow eyes but the moonlight and the lights from the bridge weren't enough to suggest any colour, and most of the time the baseball cap cast them in deep shadow.

"It's an acronym."

I looked at Shaft. He winced at her answer and his head dropped to one side.

I looked back to her: "What for?"

"What's the point in telling you? After all, you're going to kill me, aren't you?" She hoped that by repeating this in one form or another its cruelty, its absurdity, its 'madness', its stupidity, would become apparent to me. And of course the longer she managed to sustain some kind of conversation, the more human she became, the more her character filled out and the more real she would become in my own mind, and the less like Kloon, who was just a figure on the other side of the road with his back to me, with an aerosol can in his hand.

"Okay," I told her. "You can die with your secret intact."

She took a deep breath.

"It means … It means, 'Mother of our sins'."

I admitted no puzzlement. Never do.

"What's the use of an acronym in graffiti?"

"Nothing. No use at all." She too lowered and shook her head. She'd started to mark out figures or letters in the bald mud where she'd plucked out all the grass. "But you think, you hope, that of the thousands who pass by every day, the hundreds of thousands every week, the millions every month, at least one pair of eyes, just one, mind you, might wonder what it means too, and might guess and speculate and from there - " she made a deep, indecipherable mark in the mud with her forefinger, "from there you hope that someone will begin to see it's true. That we spend most of our lives, every single day of our lives, just saving face. It's all we think about. Like you just now. When you couldn't admit you didn't get it."

"Did you put that poem on the van?"

"No!" She looked up, offended. "That's Kloon's shit! Leonard Cohen shit! It's Kloon's van. At least it was. But now he's dead. You shot him. For spraying a bit of paint on a bit of cement."

Shaft was shaking his head.

"Listen to it ..." He looked at me and smiled.

The mood was changing irrecoverably and I felt options slipping away, which caused a rising panic inside. Between them they were out-manoeuvring me, getting the upper hand.

"She's always talking that kind of crap," Shaft added, drawing attention his way. "In bed she told me it meant 'my one and only shag' or 'my one 'onest shag' - oh yeah, apart from Kloon, Arus and god knows who else."

"Oh yeah! Oh yeah! Oh yeah!" Moos mocked. "Cos I like to fuck around I'm a tramp. Shaft's clapped out movie chivalry bullshit."

At this point - about 2 a.m. - a car slipped across the bridge. It left a wake of silence, as if they both realized they'd missed an opportunity, when they hadn't.

So a picture of their lives was emerging and it was not far from what I'd imagined on reading Cohen's lines on the side of the van - the melancholy songs around a campfire in the woods, with the free love thrown in. I had let things become complicated. I had allowed Moos and Shaft to take shape. Had invited that. And that last remark from Moos surely hinted at a prospect, a sexual transaction, a deal - from which I'd come off worse, if I were so stupid as to pursue it. From which I'd come off dead, in fact.

The thought that Shaft, and Moos too, would club me to death with whatever they could lay hands on as soon as I dropped my guard, brought better focus.

"If you're going to kill me," Moos began, trying to draw my focus back to her, and at the same time I saw out the corner of my eye Shaft unknit his hands, "If you're going to kill me," she repeated, "don't shoot me in the face. I can't bear the thought of that. Please. Shoot me - " But she had no chance to follow through with whatever gesture she had in mind. Without taking aim I swung the Browning on my knees and fired into Shaft. I don't know where the bullet went in but he fell back off his haunches and lay sprawled on the bank, quiet, twitching - perhaps I'd nicked his spine. In his left hand he gripped a rock. On my feet now, moving forward, I could see the moony shape of another rock under the water in the blue pail. For her, for Moos. He would have clubbed my skull to pulp, and so would she. I glanced back at her. She was petrified. Shaft began to moan but did not move at all, paralyzed by fear or his injury or both. I stood over him, set the barrel over his forehead and fired.

Without looking at what I'd done I turned back to Moos and signalled to her with the rifle.

"Roll him down the bank."

She scurried over on all fours like an obedient dog.

As she tried to ease him over she kept muttering, teeth chattering, "Oh my god, my god, my god…"

"Under his shoulder. Push."

Grunting and heaving, the baseball cap tipped back sideways on her head, she pushed him past the tipping point and Shaft rolled onto his front, but not in a natural way, in a broken way, with his hips a little too much left behind. And he hadn't rolled down the bank at all.

"Sit and use your feet."

She obeyed, but first she had to take off her flip-flops because her feet slid in them and she had no purchase, but with bare feet she could grip and knead much better and Shaft began to slip down the bank. But he did not roll, as I'd wanted, and his body stopped halfway down at an angle, feet pointing towards the dark water under the bridge, still a few metres away.

Moos sat still with her head between her knees, as if recovering from fainting, and muttered again and again, "You're mad, you're fucking mad … "

"He was going to crack my head open with that stone, then pummel my face in. You would have joined him in some animal frenzy with the stone in the bucket. Who's mad?"

After a heave of her slight shoulders she screamed into the bank:

"But you started it!"

I did not reply.

She lifted her head to look at me. Her narrow eyes brimmed with abject panic, her frown was a fusion of helplessness and incomprehension.

"No," I told her. "You started it."

She hung her head again and jammed her ears between her knees to shut me out. "You're mad! You're fucking mad!" she kept repeating, but now the cry seemed an effort to distract herself, as if she were waiting to be shot too, in the back of the head, and was making it easy for me.

Around the back of the cap there was the same moronic slogan as at the front:

Just Do It!

My common-law wife said that - not *Just Do It!*, but "You're mad! You're mad! You're fucking mad!" - over and over again, but for different reasons, towards the end, and in a very different frame of mind. But actually it was she who was mad, in an everyday way. It took a while for me to notice and then to understand the form of her madness just because it was so commonplace, hidden in plain sight. What I came to realize, after two full years of conjugal living, was that her tone of voice, all the time, whether she was talking about a painting or the washing-up or some news she'd read, no matter what, and her stares and glances too, her manners, her gestures, they all leant in the same direction, subject to the same tropism.

Self-pity.

It struck me as extraordinary at the time, how long it had taken me to condense all those tones, stares, glances, grimaces and gestures into that understanding, and I felt very low on account of that. For example, she would draw attention to herself by her silences but it wasn't sulking, because a sulk is a conscious strategy. Then when I spoke it was if I had disturbed her, or at least taken her away from her thoughts, and there was a tacit blame for that, even though, if I apologised, she would shake her head and say that what she had been thinking about wasn't worth repeating, or offer a harmless lie about shopping, cleaning, projects, money worries. But there was no need to worry about money, not in the normal way. She would worry, though, that she was spending too much of *my* money. That seems reasonable enough, but it wasn't, because she spoke as if she were depending too much of my money *rather than her own*, when actually she had no money at all, and she was dependent totally on my money just to eat and breathe and shit.

"I feel like a whore!" she said, resting her head back on the sofa, with a trickle of helpless laughter.

You are a whore, I silently replied.

"I feel like a parasite!"

You are a parasite, I silently replied.

That sense of dependence depressed her, made her feel undignified, a kept woman, she said, but it also gave her something to long and yearn for, and we all need that. She longed for true independence, surprise surprise, from me, from everyone! Which was ridiculous, because only capital can give you independence, and how was that to be achieved? Certainly not through work - she was too old -

early-fifties - to restart a career of any kind, or do anything but the most menial and poorly paid job, which I would never have asked her to do, or even allowed her to do. I was responsible for all this, of course, she implied. I had brought her to Spain, away from family and connections, cut her off from prospects of any kind. Though accusations like that never crossed her lips, they were always there, but too airy, or rather too spongy, to take shape in words. If they'd ever surfaced I'd have squeezed them dry with a wring of laughter.

"I feel so useless!"

You are useless, I silently replied.

When we had decided, after a cautious few months on-line, that she should fly out, so that we could 'give things a try', and after I'd actually bought her the plane ticket, she told me this:

"You are my last chance of happiness."

I should have heard that sentence clang against the walls, all the way down, to the bottom of her bottomless well of self-pity.

Being good-looking had been her downfall. There had always been too many people interested in her welfare, so she remained spineless, though there was nothing of that in her appearance or demeanour: she carried herself in an upright and dignified way, but not stiffly; she had a fleeting courtesy smile - an air-hostess smile - that had survived wear and tear; and the first time I climbed the stairs behind her, I noticed that the calves of her legs had not skittled, and her ankles had not sagged and thickened: I could have been following a woman in her early thirties rather than her early fifties up the stairs. I thought then: This is someone who looks after herself and knows how important that is to self-respect, and I was grateful, a touch subservient even, because, in terms of Moos's 'sexual marketplace' (coming soon), I knew I was a suitor from a lesser order, from a different stall or pen. My features are acceptable, if a bit narrow and pointed and pinched, but are marred by something that must have happened during infancy which I know nothing about - it is as if the bridge of my nose was thumbed to one side, when the bone was very soft, so my face has no symmetry. There is also the question of my complexion and what's left of my hair: they are respectively so bloodless and blonde people always assume albinism, which was the downfall to my stage career. The stereotype. Ugly or unusual, therefore evil. 'But you are evil,' I can hear Rosaline saying now, in heaven. So I always knew my place with her, in terms of our relative attractiveness. Later in the relationship, she talked openly and with some pride about looking after herself: "No point in letting yourself go and feeling ashamed of your own body. We can all do that. Any fool can do that."

I hadn't done that. Nonetheless I knew the shame she was talking about when we were in company, and I knew well, by then, that she wanted to remind me of it.

But I began by saying she was spineless.

"I paint," she had told me on our very first internet meet.

"Well, I love art," I answered simply. "I mean, I *love* art. All of it." And I do.

"I paint," she repeated, as if I hadn't said anything, "and I must confess to you from the start this ambition has blighted my life, and blighted the lives of people who were very dear to me." Again, amid these words, bashing and clanging down the well walls, was the self-pity, but I was too desperate for this relationship to get started to care. "On more than one occasion," she continued, "being an artist has threatened my very existence. I don't want to destroy anyone else's happiness ever again on account of it. I want to be clear about that with you from the start."

At the time the relationship promised such fulfilment for me. An end, at last, to the single's life: fresh new days of company, sex, a union with someone well-educated, well-spoken, as they say, good-looking, not excessive in any way - 'abstemious' she'd written in the alcohol box - a union that might flourish in my ramshackle Andalucian finca, and she couldn't wait to move down here - "I must have that light!" - and not only because of all that companionship, but also, perhaps most importantly of all, because I really do love art, so we had this god-given advantage. I'm an art fanatic, an art fundamentalist. All of it: music, painting, sculpture, poetry, literature, all except ballet and opera, though I've seldom experimented there. So I looked forward so much to the company of someone like-minded.

She arrived with a case of her clothes. Nothing else at all. Not even a handbag.

She had no equipment. I had to buy her everything. She didn't even know how to put up the easel.

"Damn and blast the thing!" she cried, letting it clatter to the floor. "Cheap rubbish!"

And she wanted to be called Ronnie, not Rosaline, as she had been on-line. Ronnie! How it embarrasses and exasperates to recall that I found the switch alluring at first, her masculinization of such a feminine, Shakespearean name, but here she was, from the very start, showing all the unmanly petulance of the phony artistic temperament. I picked up the easel for her, adjusted the frame, tightened the wing nuts, and set it upright. She put a canvas on the stand, covering her humiliation with a frown of concentration, stood back and ran her fingers through her hair, setting herself up for this great trial.

For weeks all she produced was sunflowers! I couldn't believe it! The most clichéd subject imaginable! And she painted them in such twists and distortions every plant was withering and dying and dripping with pity, even though the subject flower, in a mosaicked earthenware vase I'd bought specially for her, shone bright and full of life.

I was preparing a salad for lunch one day when she came through, very excited.

"Just come look at this!"

She'd taken down a picture of mine and replaced it with her latest effort.

Now, that was a very, very special picture of mine she had taken down, a print that had been hanging there on the wall of my study, now her studio, since I'd moved in. It was one of several prints I had of the 'black paintings' Goya painted directly onto the walls inside his house on the Manzanares, outside Madrid. Like all the black paintings it was unnamed but is now known as *'Riña de Garrotazos'* - roughly, 'Brawl with Cudgels'.

She'd used the very hook where I'd suspended this

print, to suspend her own painting.

On *my* hook - the hook for *'Riña de Garrotazos'* - were four sunflowers pinched in a white IKEA frame, and below, propped against the wall, on the floor, was Goya's dark masterpiece.

"Watch," she said, brimming with enthusiasm, with confidence.

She twisted her painting off the wall, clumsily marking the plaster as she did so, and hung it the other way up. Now the sunflowers drooped down, when a moment ago they had stretched feebly upwards. Pity. Always pity pity pity me. *The quality of mercy is not strained.*

But it is, all the time. Strained and measured. Costed.

"Completely different mood, aspect. Different painting. Just by reversing it. That's going to get them talking."

"Where?"

"Tate. Whitechapel. Saatchi."

I looked at her aghast. "I know, I know," she said, shoulders drooping again, dejected, rejected again. "I know now all your scowls of disapproval and disappointment."

She experimented further with this novel technique, producing paintings that could be hung upside down or at different angles, until, to get her away from this rubbish, I insisted she came with me outdoors to find new subjects. After cruising around, and an inexpensive lunch, she settled on a single-storey ruin, part of which was still used as a shepherd's hut, isolated in a vast rolling field dotted with colinitas and some larger stone heaps. The Andalucian soil was thin and pink and rough and sterile looking, with patches which looked almost white in places, and lesser stones were strewn all over the field, but it had been ploughed or at least spring-tyned and would miraculously bear a crop of winter wheat in a few months' time.

I was surprised to see how quickly she sketched a free-hand outline of the field, filling the whole canvas, that had perspective and likeness. She began on the ruin itself and this too came out with clean lines of jagged walls and sagging window frames that avoided any sentimental aspect. There was a starkness about it that was there in the field too, a desolation despite the part-habitable shepherd's hut, or which the hut extended with its clinging on. I watched her at work, and noticed for the first time how lovely her rather thin, long face was when absorbed like this; her light blue eyes flitting back and forth and her mouth slightly pursed and her cheeks dimpled. She wore the faintest lipstick, that was all, which was a great attraction to me because I can't stand heavily made-up women. So she could draw at least, after all, I thought, looking back and forth at the canvas and the field, the ruin. And without noticing it at the time, I took great comfort in that, because I had begun to wonder if she was utterly talentless and therefore the relationship could not last - was 'blighted', as she had said, because of her deluded belief that her abilities were beyond question. There was no self-doubt in her at all, I had observed; not visibly, anyway. And self-doubt, I had always understood, was the great purifier.

We came back the next day and enjoyed another lunch, and she finished the sketch and opened up the oils.

Things were going very well, and I was about to take myself off on a walk to give her the solitude I thought she might need, when she was beset by wasps. They were the subterranean kind, so we must have erected the easel near their nest. She wasn't stung but was annoyed at the disturbance and at having to move pitch, but we managed a safe transfer to a more distant spot. I hoped she would notice in my helpfulness a new respect for her abilities, but if she did she gave no sign, being too occupied with the paraphernalia. She couldn't manage the extendable legs of the easel (it wasn't 'cheap rubbish' at all) and had to wait patiently with her canvas in hand while I made the thing level.

"I'll leave you to it," I said, when everything was re-arranged.

"Best so," she agreed.

It was too rough underfoot to walk for very long and after twenty minutes I came back for the car.

She said she needed another hour or so, this session.

I was there on the hour for the next two hours before she was ready to pack up.

"I need the toilet," she said. "Desperately."

She sat in the car to be more comfortable while I put everything away, and then we drove back to the restaurant, which was closed, and then quickly home.

I thought her painting was excellent.

Moos had started to rock herself back and forth with her head between her knees. It crossed my mind the attitude was deliberate, even inviting: she may well have been waiting to be shot herself, in the back of the head, as if, with Shaft's death, she now saw her position as quite hopeless, her execution inevitable. But there was now a serious distraction. I had noticed a loose diarrhoea stench. At first I thought it might be from the water below, or even from Moos herself, then I realized it came from Kloon. After death, all sphincters relax: his levellish position face-down had prevented earlier seepage, but now the juices and gases were on their way out, into his clothes and the open air, maybe from the front too, from whatever was left of his face in the mud. Before long the air would be unbreathable. To me, anyway.

Moos muttered something into the grass between her knees. When I didn't respond, she lifted her head and jerked round: for a moment she must have thought I had gone! She was released! Free! But there I was behind her, just the same, on the boulder where I'd been perched before, facing down the river bank where Shaft had come up, and where she had rolled him down again - and where she would go tumbling after, as in the nursery rhyme. All the same. The Browning across my knees, three rounds still in the polished stock. Shaft's blue pail, with its stone beneath the water, was mid-distance between us, where he'd left it, where I'd left it.

She turned all the way around to face me, and reset herself on her haunches with her hands clasped about her knees. She released both hands a moment to refix her cap high on her forehead. I could see more clearly now her small nose and her broad mouth and quite high cheekbones. There must have been some Far East influence in the bloodline. But her skin was very pale, milk white, very celtic, as I like to say about my own complexion; it wasn't only the full moon and the bridge lights lending her that pallor. Whether that was just fear or not, I'll never know.

"It will be light soon," she said. "Then what will you do?"

"Still a couple of hours."

She frowned. "But what will you do?"

I stared back, gave no answer. After a lengthy pause, she asked:

"Are you a nihilist? … You know what that is? A nihilist?"

I nodded. "I'm an educated man," I told her. "Not very well educated. But educated."

"I once thought I was a nihilist, you see," she continued lightly. "I wish you had caught me painting a wall or something when I was a nihilist, because maybe I wouldn't have minded if you'd killed me for something so trivial, so pointless, back then. I'd have thought it was all part of the senselessness and worthlessness and stupidity of things. But now I do mind. A lot."

"You would still have minded. Stop trying to make conversation. It's no use."

"Your mind is made up? You're going to shoot me? In cold blood?"

I nodded.

"So why don't I just take a chance and rush you? You're going to kill me anyway. I suppose that would make it easier, wouldn't it? For both of us."

I raised the rifle and pointed it at her, but didn't take aim.

"Does that mean shut up?"

I gave the same nod, and with a pant of exasperation, lowered the rifle. The truth was the gun was too heavy for me to support freehand, even though it was a modern lightweight thing. Both biceps are now Pop-Eye muscles. Ageing is hideous.

"Look." She stared at the ground, where she started picking at the grass and weeds again, creating a new bald patch. "You can have sex with me if you want. Right here." Then she raised her head and stared straight at me. "You're an old man and not particularly attractive, if I may say so. Not to me, anyway. Bent nose. Wormy lips. Dead white skin. Flaxy hair, what's left of it. But you can have me. Right here. That's a good deal, isn't it? Because I'm - What? Half your age? We're hardly in the same sexual marketplace, are we? You've got to admit that ... What d'you say?"

I left a silence to let her think, then asked her:

"Would you like me to tell you why you must die?"

"Oh, I know why, all right. I know perfectly well. Because I painted a funny name on a wall. Death sentence. Incommutable in any way. And, of course, because you are a complete fucking nutter."

"'Remember our names. We love this game.'"

I could see her immediate recognition from that same fleeting, twitchy smile she'd shared with Shaft, but she wasn't sharing it with me, of course. Secretive dimples. She didn't know what to say.

"And I have remembered your names ... You see, I have nowhere to go any more, nowhere to turn. You are there, everywhere I turn. There is no journey, no walk even, that I can undertake without seeing your defilement - and it torments me, disgusts me, fills me with loathing and hatred every time I see it. You have ruined my life - I mean that. Every word of it. I told you: What is read cannot be unread. It stays behind the retina. Nothing less than the beauty of the world, what is left of it, you have shat upon. All over Spain - " she began to smile again, could not help it!

"Why do you smile?"

"*Miles of smiles*. Kloon used to say that whenever he saw his name."

"In Spain you were in the landscapes of Goya, Bustillo Salomón, Velasquez, in France you were in the landscapes of Lorraine, Monet, Cezanne, Lavieille -

"Oh yeah! Oh yeah! Oh yeah!" she broke out sarcastically, as she had against Shaft, scowling now. "What gives? So once upon a time a bunch of old white dead men, no doubt part of the patriarchal hegemony - "

"Andrée Lavieille was a woman. So was Bustillo Salomón. You see? You know nothing. You've seen nothing, read nothing. I have visited all the landscapes those artists painted that still exist. Every single one. From Andalucia to Brittany. You have ruined all of them. And not only the beauty of many things great artists painted and great architects have designed, but also the beauty of the work of artisans from centuries past - you have seen fit to soil and defile it all with your infantile art. Not only out there, by every road and railtrack - but in *here*!" I tapped my temple hard. I knew my eyes were wide with hatred. "Where it cannot be erased. Where it is Forever!"

All she did was tap her temple too, and shake her head.

Once we had set up stall again at home, I could see the shadows from the ruin were clean and dark in oil, which drew the eye to the undulations of the pink and white soil all around. Still I didn't say anything. Couldn't risk saying too much or too little. Instead, I went to the kitchen and opened the best bottle of local wine I could find and brought her a glass. I went back to get one for myself, and we kissed glasses and smiled. That was all. How early on that was!

When we went back the third day, there, across the tatty whitewashed wall, in letters about five feet high - was something like SKOOB or SLOOS or SHOB, it didn't matter. We didn't bother to get anything out of the car. Neither of us said anything until I put the car back in gear, when I muttered, "Oh well … I'm sorry … Bastards ..."

We drove home and she finished the canvas there as best she could.

She returned to still-lifes for a few months, then we went out again and she painted a bridge over the Genal, which I quite liked, and then she did a portrait of me, which I found deeply unflattering and I said as much, but said as well that I knew the worst image of my face was probably the truest - in common with the great Francis Bacon, I told her, I have always loathed my face. She didn't comment on or correct that remark. Instead she corrected how I'd tied the string behind the frame. "What's that? You need a reef knot. Left over right, right over left. You've been tying granny knots all your life."

By the time she had lived at my finca for about eighteen months, I began to become certain of a truth that had been flickering on and off ever since she arrived: this woman, who had come to share my life in good faith, in my Andalucian paradise, was not an artist at all, as she believed. She was a painter, and quite a skilled painter, but that was all. In the end, at her very best, she would only produce a likeness, a supremely polished form of painting by numbers. She was a journeyman of art. She mistook her forceful assertions and her determination for the irrepressible feeling the real artist cannot escape, that distorts and intensifies the vision. For her assertion and determination would do, not inspiration and imagination. Moreover, there were never any people in her paintings, except the hateful portrait just mentioned, which she hung in my bedroom. She claimed not to be interested in portraiture: that wasn't her focus, she said, but I knew the truth was she had nothing to say, no insight to offer in her characterization of humankind on canvas.

That was why she wanted me to take down Goya's black paintings. I wouldn't and I wouldn't let her either and I had insisted long ago *'Riña de Garrotazos'* went back on its hook. She complained that *Man Mocked by Two Women* was sexist in its depiction of the women as witch-like. I told her I wouldn't stoop to argue with such a crassitude. Similarly I took no notice of her complaint that the black painting prints were too dark and gloomy and that they depressed her. What depresses you, I could have said, is not their darkness but their brilliance. And upstairs on the landing wall that divided our bedrooms I refused to take down a print of Dali's *The Great Masturbator*. It had been part of my life for too long.

You are a singularly worthless person - that is how I began to see her, in our final months, and this idea of her worthlessness, her actual worthlessness, her dispensability, in effect, began to take hold. Why should someone like you, I thought, still be here, when so many others have no chance in life? So many others would have done so much more with the advantages you have had for more than half a century! I had a pretty good idea of her petit-bourgeois biography by then: mediocre boarding school, Art School, and then a series of relationships that kept her financially afloat with her delusions intact right into middle-age. A disgracefully English cadger's life.

The first move I made, in a rather playful way, to amuse myself, was to count up how much money I spent on her food and drink. It had been obvious for some time that her arrival in Andalucia had exacerbated quite a severe drinking problem, so much for the 'abstemious' she had written in the box before our first meet on-line. Indeed, cheap and plentiful booze might have been part of her motivation for coming here. I gave up buying the expensive local wines I enjoyed and brought home cheaper supermarket brands, but it made no difference, they were all the same to her. When I spoke to her about it she just shook her head.

"A bottle of plonk after six. Four or five euros. Dear oh dear."

"Well, I know it's the lush's prerogative to kid herself about how much she guzzles, but it's affecting your work."

"Please leave me alone."

I continued with my private sums and came to a reckoning whose economy actually surprised me. To keep her in the style to which she'd become accustomed cost a humble three to four hundred euros a month. She spent virtually nothing on new clothes, and was careful to clean and iron and look after those with which she'd arrived. A few winter things were all she asked me for. When I left her in town to do some shopping she came back with the supermarket bargains; a keen sense of thrift, husbandry, and guilt, instilled by years of living on the breadline in England, off other people, guided all her shopping. I bought all the wine by unspoken agreement.

Back at the start, those trips to town included coffee or breakfast in favourite cafes, and were enjoyable to me. We looked around for scenes she might paint, but that came to nothing because she was shy of painting in public and refused to work from photographs. And there were too many people, of course. Brush or pencil in hand, she didn't know what to do with so many people.

Trying to hide her self-pity, her blame, her bitterness, her sense of failure, put a strain on her manners. The wan smile, the faraway look, the faint sigh, while she was at some chore, cleaning something or peeling something, were all part of the same continuous utterance: *This is not me. I should not be doing this. I am worth more, so much more, but it is not seen or known. Not by him. Oh God no! I am worthy of far more respect than he can ever give - stuck in the past with his Goya horrors! - for what I am trying to do, for what I have already achieved, with my lightness of touch, in my delicate way, with my Virginia Woolf sensibilities ...*

Actually, Ronnie dear, I felt like pointing out to her, you are worth about minus four hundred euros a month. If you have nothing and earn nothing, you are worth only what you cost other people. As if it were a physical burden of debt, growing month by month, she became oppressed by the weight of it: round-shouldered, slip-shod in her flip-flops. That aged her and the sexual attraction I felt wilted with that change, and as I had never detected in her any attraction towards me - sex had to take place in the deepest darkness, where, no doubt, she could imagine me as someone else - as I had never detected in her any attraction towards me, that is quite a difficult clause for me to repeat, there was a natural and permanent retreat to our respective bedrooms. I had given her that courtesy and luxury from the start, her own en suite. She still found ways, though, of keeping me off the scent.

Moos whipped off her cap, then her t-shirt, and sat there in her bra and jeans. Without the cap, her hair hung flat and straight from a centre parting, so that she looked like a squaw from an old-fashioned comic strip. When I didn't react in any way she reached behind to unclasp her bra but I told her to stop and put her shirt back on.

"You'll bring the mosquitoes up from the water."

She did as she was told.

As she dressed again she tried to assume a casual tone.

"They're already here. I'm being eaten alive."

I thought of Loner at dawn - "Morning!" - insisting all was normal, there was nothing to fear.

She set her cap back high on her head again.

"The Viet Cong used to do that to captured Americans," she began. "They tied them naked to a tree but left one arm free to swipe at the mosquitoes, or any animal that came by. What a terrible way to die, don't you think? I only mention that because I suppose I should be grateful to you for a quick death, shouldn't I? So thanks for that. I'm just wondering if that kind of awry logic appeals to you."

"It's not awe-ry. It's awry."

"God. Thanks again. I'd hate to be killed by some mad peasant who didn't know that."

"And the more you talk the more inclined I am to kill you to shut you up."

"I don't believe you any more. I think you are beginning to see that what you have done here is crazy and stupid and your conscience is beginning to wake up. I know you're angry at us and I accept that I never thought of a bit of graffiti in the way you think about it, never for a moment imagined it could make someone so angry and sad and bitter and all that, but after two people have died tonight, and you are faced with killing a third human being, a youngish woman, in cold blood, a young woman who has parents who love her back in Kent, England, a country you know - perhaps Kent is a county you know too? The hop fields? - and a lickle brother who loves her at uni in Reading, a young woman who is reasonably attractive and could one day fall in love and start a family of her own, a young woman who loves to dance, to read, loves the cinema and good food, a bottle of St Emilion, a female who is real and who is sitting just a few metres away, and who is getting more and more real even as I speak - "

I raised the rifle and took aim at the middle of her

pale forehead, using the tick on her cap to centre my aim.

"Please! … Please don't. I'll shut up, I promise."

"Where is Loner?"

Confusion.

"Loner? Who's Loner?"

"On your group chat."

"Oh. *That* Loner. Right. I'll tell you all about that Loner. Only please put down the rifle."

I was about to do so anyway because again I couldn't convincingly sustain the weight of it. I was getting weaker. I hadn't eaten for about eight hours. I rested the weight on my knees again but with the barrel pointing her way, as it had at Shaft.

"Loner ... So you want to know about Loner. Okay ... So here's Loner. He's a pretty nondescript looking guy, very slight, with straggly hair, who hangs around with us because he has a crush on me. But I'm not interested. Understatement of the century. Again, let's just say we're not in the same sexual marketplace. But I made the mistake of taking pity on him when we first met under a bridge in France somewhere, and ever since he's had this thing about me. To be honest, we don't know how to get rid of him. Shaft treated him really badly, but can do so no more because he's dead. Kloon had a heart of gold and always put up with him, but he's dead now too. And Arus or Anus, who can be a complete arsehole like Shaft, is pretty cruel to him too."

"What does Loner do?"

"Works for the Post Office. Deliveries. He's a little guy all the way. Still lives at home with his parents. Knows everything there is to know about Star Wars movies. That kind of guy."

"And you're his princess."

"Princess Leah. Yeah. That's it exactly. So there's someone else who'll be a bit upset when he hears I've been shot dead in cold blood. He'll never get over it, poor kid."

"He's already dead."

Her eyes, that had been flitting about because she could not bear to look into my face all the time, her eyes stopped still on mine because again there was the same man, the one who'd killed Kloon and Shaft, in front of her.

"I threw him off the ferry."

"*What*? You couldn't do that! He's a young guy!"

"His ribs felt like a wriggling piglet at the fair. I took him by surprise. He would have been drawn into the propellers, if he wasn't already dead. It's a twenty metre drop."

She had nothing to say.

In the game she was playing to stay alive, I had taken her back to square one.

Anyone who can dismiss Goya's black paintings as 'too dark' or 'depressing' has no right even to buy a paintbrush. Anyone who can dismiss the cruelty of humankind caught in the faces of the two women laughing at a man as 'sexist', because they are 'witch-like', has no right to draw the breath that takes her down the stairs, and out of the house, and along the street, and into the shop where she can buy a paintbrush. Everyone knows that artists of any kind must drive out two demons: self-pity and self-importance. But Ronnie had allowed them in and courted them, and they were so rooted there, so comfortable and accustomed to the cosiness of her soul, she didn't even know they were there, guzzling away. They whispered to her that it didn't matter that she'd never had the discipline and humility to study seriously what had been painted before. All the centuries of it. They told her that her English originality entitled her to skip all that.

It fell to me, then, as the last to pay her bills, to drive the devils out, evict the squatters.

But before all that, there was her *'Success'*.

I remember Ronnie saying on-line once - it was part of that early speech about her life as an artist, that had brought her to the threshold of mortality, no less - "By and large, English people - particularly friends and family - don't want you to succeed. They want you to fail, so they can laugh at you. And if you don't laugh too, they'll tell you you're taking yourself too seriously. Because if you do succeed, they will feel like bourgeois mediocrities, and left behind, so they try to hold you back, wreck your confidence."

Just to be absolutely clear - I was not of that party: I respected her for making some money. It was the art I objected to.

From the beginning it was my habit to bring her breakfast on Saturdays. Not very elaborate breakfasts, but I tried to ring the changes now and then. Toast, honey and coffee, quite regularly; tea and figs in September; dried fruit sometimes, and so on. But through the internet she had found a group of expat people who liked to walk at the weekend and she cancelled my Saturday breakfasts to join this group. Some of these, from the English enclave of Coín, were of an artistic temperament, so of course she fell in with a clique. After some visits to their homes, and to various 'private' galleries (meaning, pay and display self-promotion galleries) she brought them round to my finca, in my absence, to see her works in progress and a few completed items. A very special friend, Eileen, whom I hadn't met at that time, told her she could sell her work for her in Marbella, San Pedro and Puerto Banus, and not cheaply either. As a real-estate magnate who owned a string of agencies along the coast, she had access to a portfolio of expat clientele, particularly Russians, who were always looking for original work to fill the walls of their cubic nouveau-riche villas.

So it began. And Rosaline's life changed. Within weeks, she was no longer dependent on me. I spied on what she was doing and silently disapproved, but I had nothing but praise for her commercial nous. She was painting kitsch Andalucian scenes from antiquity - well, most from about eighty years ago, in fact, but also from time immemorial. Her first big sellers were different takes of women washing clothes in the river near El Burgo. There is actually a large tiled frieze in that town which pays tribute to the endless toil of the woman's lot in that era, but in her versions the women were sexualized, with blouses fallen at the shoulder and wet through as they laboured in the stream, and there were pretty infant daughters too with flowers in their hair, looking forward to taking up the same slavery, no doubt.

Kitsch rubbish.

But the money made it serious art. When I disturbed her from those contemplative silences there was no longer the self-deprecating or apologetic remark. There was irritation, impatience, even anger.

Though she was still in my house, and I still drove her about, this leverage became less and less important because her Spanglish friends were only too glad to put her up for a whole weekend or more, and to come and pick her up to go looking for new subjects, or visiting new villas owned by new important contacts -

"Ronnie! Buenos días!"

"Ronnie darling! Guapa! Hop in!"

"There she is! Vamos! Venga! There's someone muy importante I want you to encontrar! Muy guapo too!"

The round-shouldered look disappeared. She wore woven leather sandals with golden buckles; she left my cheap supermarket wines for me to drink. Drinking wasted too much time - there were so many projects to start, to complete. So many commissions.

"I brought you here," I reminded her, when she started treating me with the sexual contempt she had always felt but kept so poorly hidden. "I even paid for the bloody flight. I used to bring you breakfast in bed!"

"And was I not worth it?"

She offered an arch smile but with it a chilling look too, from her pale blue eyes, to deliver this message: Yes, I still desire and feel desirable to others, but it is not you I want, nor did I ever want you.

Two cars passed on the bridge in quick succession. Dawn was still more than an hour away but an anxiety took hold that they might be the first commuters, or holiday-makers up early heading west.

Out of the blue, or at least she thought she was coming out of the blue, Moos asked: "Do you understand the rules of proportionality? In war?"

I was about to tell her to get up, we were moving on, but with no idea what came next. Whatever doubt crossed my face led her to believe her question had thrown me, which pleased her. She then tried to patronize me with a forgiving frown, a downcast look.

I bowled in my own question, which was more to the point.

"What are you worth?"

She raised her head, pushed up her cap, in a dignified, postured manner, and answered the challenge face to face:

"It's a non-question. We cannot measure ourselves in that way."

"But I do measure us in that way. We all do. All the time. We always have done. In one currency or another. There have always been slaves, worth so little or so much, and if there aren't any around we'll stuff people down the mines for a hunk of bread. There have always been ransoms people paid to have sons or daughters returned. Or didn't pay. People marry for money and their pensions are calculated by death rates. It's always about money and greed. Always. Human nature's a shitty thing. So what are you worth?"

"A ransom doesn't tell you what a life is worth. It just tells you what someone is prepared to pay to keep someone else alive."

"So what are you worth to your parents? Your family?"

"They would give everything they have for me. That's not a lot - they're just teachers - but I know they would. But that wouldn't start to measure it. That would only measure someone else's greed. Your greed."

"Would they, though? Give it all. Sell their home?"

She looked down again.

"Go on," I told her. "Say it."

"I want to say, *How dare you? What do you know? You stupid old prick with a stupid gun! What do you know? The price of everything and the value of nothing!*"

"Ah. Good old Oscar…"

I wanted to sit back on my boulder, take up a position of ease, but that wasn't possible.

"Well, let me tell you what I do know, then. So listen. I know I will be caught, probably quite soon, and tried and found guilty and put in prison for the rest of my life. You've seen what I have done. In cold blood I have killed two of your friends - two of your lovers, in fact, but we both know I use that word loosely. That's not the point. I have killed two people here whom you knew intimately, and I killed a third a few days ago, whom you also knew, but had rejected as a sexual partner. From what you say. So make this choice. I am, as all the paperbacks and movies would say - a 'cold-blooded serial killer', a gift to Netflix, pitted against some gritty detective. But suppose, for a moment, in the real world, that the hundreds of thousands you would spend on keeping me alive in prison were in your hands to offer those who have nothing, no opportunities in life. You know there are millions of them, all over the world, even in England. Why not kill me so that someone else can have a chance to survive, to succeed in life? Why not spend the money on them, instead of me? Pick a black kid off the street, pack him off to Eton and give him a future. Why spend it all on me, a cold-blooded killer, guarded day and night in jail? How is it right to pay for me to live at the expense of others dying of starvation and disease, or remaining in hopeless destitution, which in turn inspires more criminality? You know that I am guilty. It is not a question of reasonable doubt. You have seen me kill twice with your own eyes."

She didn't look up for a while. To hear me talk so evenly about being a cold-blooded killer must have been disconcerting.

"Personally," she began, "if I could make that decision, I would make it as you said. I'd let them execute you and use the money to give some other soul a chance, rather than keep you fed and watered in jail someplace. Honestly I would. But - "

"So you're a cold blooded killer too."

" - it's not a personal decision, is it? The law's bound by principles. You can't price the principles. They don't have price-tags."

"I told Shaft - 'This is my court. No appeals.' For me, life now is like being in the middle of a forest fire, all the time, all year round. All the beauty of the world is burning up. Turned to trash, then to ashes. I begin with you because you put yourselves in remote places like this very late at night. Soft targets. But I'm coming for all the trasheteers. I'll pick your rock stars and your rappers off the stage like rubber ducks. And all the rubbish artists pretending piles of bricks or unmade beds are art. Compare a pile of bricks to Kathe Kollwitz's *Mother with her Dead Son.* Compare Tracey Emin's bed with *Le Lit* by Toulouse-Lautrec - "

"I know that painting! The Bed! *Le Lit!* I love it!" she broke in, grabbing at the sense of what I was saying. "And I agree with you about so much modern art. It's just the emperor's new clothes, like they say, but I don't want to kill these people just because I don't like them or their art!"

"But I do."

"And that's why I asked you about proportionality. Even in war - "

"War is just young men having a good time, fucking who they want. It's just hormones. Always has been. Fighting, fighting, fighting."

She was nonplussed.

"*What*?... What are you talking about? The politicians? The war-mongers? The land-grabbers? Powerbrokers? Generals? Admirals? - "

"Take the young men out of it and there's nothing left. Just old men playing board games."

Another car passed on the bridge.

"Get up."

Such anxiety filled her face, arching her dark brows to align with her cap.

"Get up. Time to walk."

Still she didn't rise to her feet.

"The stench here is unbearable. We'll walk across the bridge."

That persuaded her and she got gingerly to her feet. It must have crossed her mind that on the bridge another car might pass and she would hear it and dash into the road, or some such scheme; in any event, on the bridge, on the move, had to be more promising than sitting pinned down by the stanchion. There was the chance of simply making a dash for it - maybe she could zigzag away like a rabbit. Of course she would think that. Bunny rabbit.

I found myself hiding my breathlessness as we came up to mount the road itself and begin the slight ascent at the start of the bridge, single file.

She tried to keep the pace slow, waiting for the sound, then the lights, of that miracle car approaching.

At the centre of the bridge I told her to stop.

She turned, and cast a glance past me back down the bridge, searching for lights in the distance. Naturally there was no corner before the bridge because the approaches to bridges are always straight, and I could see it in her narrowed, distraught eyes that there was no light, nothing at all, for miles.

"Climb up."

"What?"

I took a deep breath. "You heard. Climb."

"No ... I won't. I won't." There was that look of hysteria again and I didn't want that. "Don't do this. Not to me. Not to me too. Please. I'll do anything. I'll say you didn't do it. I'll say you rescued me. From some maniac with a gun, some fucking whackhead."

"This way you have a chance."

"To see what I'm made of? Splattered all over the water? It's like hitting concrete. You know that. You said yourself Loner couldn't have survived."

I glanced across the water, not down.

"Six metres max. That's okay. Survivable. Loner had twenty. Five storeys. Take your chances. Or I'll put a round through your spine point blank, leaving you paraplegic at best. And I'll walk away, leaving you to die in agony on the bridge. Or I'll drag you into the road, where the cars won't stop in time. You saw me plug Shaft point blank. You know I can do it. I'll leave your face, as you requested. Not like Shaft. Not like Kloon, come to that. There's your mercy."

She raised her chin slightly and let her eyes slip over my shoulder a second time. I smiled at this desperate play, this oldest trick in the book, but she carried on. She screamed over my shoulder:

"ARUS! NO!"

I kept staring at her. Nothing happened. At last, she started to cry.

"My life," I told her. "My life I rate at nothing. There's your problem. If he had been there, with a hammer or a jack or that stone from the bucket, I couldn't have cared less. Stop crying. It weakens you. You'll need all your strength in the water."

"You are… just so fucking cruel!"

"And you? What do you care for your friends now? You care nothing for them. Just after an hour or so. Nothing at all. Think about that. Your parents, your kid brother, they may care for a bit, but life goes on and they'll get over it."

"They'll never get over it."

"Depends on the story. Looks to me as if you killed your friends, then jumped when a passer-by gave chase. Case closed."

She whimpered, "Oh my god ..."

"Climb the fence. There's still a chance."

At last she turned and faced the mesh. The gauge was easily wide enough for her toes, and the pain the mesh caused her would surely drive her up faster. It was only a two metre fence.

She slipped off her flip-flops.

She began mounting the wire. As I'd thought, it caused her a lot of pain but she toughed that out and was within grasp of the top. But she stopped. She clung there.

"I can't do it," she moaned, spread out, fingers and toes wrapped into the wire. She could see now the water beneath the bridge, the darkness there. I had lied: it was at least ten metres, but to her that was not what mattered. It was the darkness and fathomlessness of the black water down there, and whatever currents there were, or unknown spikes left over from the construction of the bridge, or tree stumps, or monstrous fish awaiting her frail frame of flesh and bone in the dark cold water down there, that's what she was thinking of. The unknown and all its monsters.

I rested the barrel on her bare flank, where the t-shirt had parted from her jeans, then poked. She didn't move. I let the barrel drift round to rub the vertebrae at the base of her spine, then stroked it up and down her spine, rucking her t-shirt, a lecherous metal finger. She twitched and moved her right foot up again and then her left, so the top cross-member came within reach. The wire was not flush to the metal and must have torn at her as she heaved herself up till her midriff supported her. With a grunt she eased her right leg over and sat astride, despite the edge of the fence, or perhaps it wasn't as nasty as I had supposed.

She still wore her Nike cap. That moronic slogan.

All the mindless trash to deal with, that's pushed out, pushed at you, pushed onto you, to process, deal with, come to terms with, reconcile yourself to, every minute of the day and night.

A car approached at some speed.

I saw the driver - a youngish, grinning fellow with a beard, and next to him his girlfriend, who was leaning over, shoulder to shoulder with him, and I could hear a rap song, not many of the words but the fleeting heavy sound of the rhymes and the bass beating through the car - '*Gonna ride ya till...*' They were utterly absorbed in each other, the music, their world, but still gave me, standing there with my rifle, on the single-file walkway of the bridge, or gave both of us, perhaps, a cheery double-blast of the horn as they sped by - and the doppler of it made Moos twist, made her wrench herself around to follow them, and the girder was too narrow for that so she lost balance and down she went, cracking her elbow on the cross-member and letting out, all the way down, a lacerating scream that will stay with me - like Loner's terrified open, silent, chattering mouth before he dropped - to my death. I heard the water swallow her up.

Her flip-flops I threw after her.

I left a few seconds, listening for any splashing, then crossed the bridge to watch, and eventually, just when I was about to give up, one flip-flop floated by in the moonlight, in the bridge lights, half-submerged, but nothing else, not even the hat.

It is difficult for me to go over what happened to my finca but one of the most lamentable scenes was set up by her, Ronnie, Rosaline. She had invited some of her new-found friends to lunch, which was the kind of event for which I either left the house or stayed upstairs. Passing by the kitchen I saw the table set for five: two places either side and one at the end. There was nothing stealthy or underhand in my taking a look in this way. My leather sandals on the terracotta clacked around the house like castanets, driving her mad, she said. In the middle of the table was a huge earthenware pot, the largest I had, something I'd found abandoned in the kitchen by the previous owners. There were many such things abandoned in the property, and most had proved very useful. Her handbag was on the table too, near the pot, for some reason. I had smelt no cooking but this didn't surprise me because Ronnie only prepared cold snacks or salads. During our early days, I remarked: "One thing I notice about your cooking - nothing's cooked!" That must come from very early on indeed because I remember we both laughed.

There was some fresh but not particularly nervous laughter when her guests arrived. They knew Ronnie well enough by then, and her success had given her such confidence socially. Some of them had been instrumental in that success too, including Eileen, the real-estate magnate.

I was upstairs with my door open and heard the scraping of chairs on the tiles as they took their seats, then there was a warm and friendly, playful call from Ronnie, to me, up the stairs. The tone was new. I had literally never heard it before. She was putting it on for her friends, perhaps, pretending we lived in blissful intimacy. She called again - "Lunch!" - and I called back from my bedroom - "Coming!" - and ventured down. What was she up to? I suspected a trick of some kind. But perhaps, I thought, I should silence my nasty suspicious mind for a moment; perhaps, as a kind surprise, a turnaround, I really had been invited to join them for lunch.

But at the table there were already four guests.

Eileen, and two other women of Ronnie's age or older, all with similarly groomed, brittle hair and crayoned eyebrows, and one younger woman, in her thirties, quite striking, with short dark hair, who looked far too quizzical, with one eyebrow stuck up in arched surprise all the time, as if that made her superior and intelligent. These four were occupying the seats either side of the table, which left the only seat remaining for Ronnie.

No seat for me, after all.

"Come in, come in!" she beckoned, and as I came closer she moved down the right side of the table.

"Hi, everyone!" I offered, with a smile.

"Hi, everyone!" she mocked, in perfect imitation. She raised the lid of the tureen. "And just look how well the man of property has managed things!"

There was nothing inside the tureen but a heap of salt.

"Nothing to eat!" she scoffed. "He's broke! Busted. Bankrupt. Lost the lot!"

I scowled at the joke, the heap of salt, understanding nothing, and the guests frowned at it too; even the youthful intellectual drew down her eyebrow. After Ronnie had let a painfully embarrassing silence pass, she said: "I've booked a table at the Buena Vista. For five, that is." She hitched her handbag over her shoulder and shot me a nod and a hateful glance. "Not six." The others stood quickly and uncertainly, and they all trooped off behind her without a word.

That hateful glance … When I understood more, I saw there was the presumption behind it that as a man I had somehow let her down, I had failed. Failed at what, exactly? Failed to do what? To provide for her? Support her? Wasn't that a bit old-fashioned? But I think it comes from somewhere deeper, the hate and contempt in that glance, and neither of us was entirely to blame for it. When she had first moved in, she had amused herself in the garden, planting this or that, much of which was unsuitable to the climate and died within weeks. She knew nothing about gardening. She called the bougainvillaea that climbed the pergola 'bourgeois villa' in an early, joky attempt - so English! - to belittle what I'd achieved in acquiring this paradisal place. However, those plants that survived her planting and propagated she took great care of, she took a rejuvenating joy in, actually, which came out in her language. She talked of the new shoots coming through as 'babies' or 'little ones'. Oh, so you've not heard about Ruskin's pathetic fallacy, from one hundred and seventy years ago? I might have asked, but I didn't feel that way at the time. This is from our very first days together. Similarly, in a small pond near the house - it had once been a homemade swimming pool, I think - there were fish beneath the weeds, and the smaller ones were 'babies' too. Strange, because Ronnie all but bragged about several abortions she'd had and declared she found the thought of childbirth 'unnatural'. Fair enough, but she seemed to be stuck with maternal feelings nonetheless.

The point is, when I lost my finca I lost any last shred of attraction for her, because she thought I was now broke, could not provide.

Then I discovered, a few weeks after the lunch incident, that she had never wanted sex with me at all, and I had only been acceptable as a partner in the deepest darkness, as part of that role, as provider. One afternoon I came home with the weekly shopping, so my return was not unexpected at all, to hear, from upstairs, the unmistakable sounds of intercourse. The rocking and the moaning, the creaking bed, the muted gasps of pleasure.

I shut the front door softly and set down my crammed bags in the hallway. I hesitated. I stopped a box of eggs falling out.

What?

It couldn't be her!

But … Then, who could it be?

She knew I'd be home soon, so it couldn't be her.

My own instinctual response - Othello's rage! - rushed to the fore unbidden.

Cuckold me! I'll chop her into messes!

Fumbling with anger and humiliation I set up the camera on my phone. I removed my sandals and stole up the stairs two at a time.

The noises were louder, and not just from my coming up the stairs. They were quite uninhibited now. I scowled at this. Again the improbability was overwhelming: she knew

I would return about this time, about two o'clock, in time to prepare lunch with some of the things I'd just bought. It was almost a routine. How could she be so brazen?

But the sounds were hers. I knew them.

Her bedroom door wasn't even closed!

I pushed it gently ajar but did not step inside.

Naked, they were sitting up, clasped in each other's arms. Rosaline's thighs slipped on top of Eileen's, and they were joined by something between and beneath them, so that as one rocked the other moaned. It was Eileen's turn to rock and push, not quite thrust because it was a gentle, tender action. And it was Ronnie's turn to enjoy the pleasure of whatever was trapped between their thighs.

They completely ignored me, standing there, in the shadow, at the slightly open door. It was as if they were on drugs, but I'm sure they weren't. They were so absorbed in this mutual pleasure-giving nothing else mattered, least of all the broke, busted, bankrupt, pale-face cuckold in the shadow of the door. That was certainly the message.

The strange thing was, my jealousy evaporated, and what caused me to retreat as quickly and discreetly as I could was my own arousal. How useless and redundant and distressing was that!

I distracted myself in the kitchen by making my own lunch, with hands so shaky I nearly cut myself, then sat at the kitchen table and searched up on my phone what device it was they were using up there, and found it quickly enough. The look of it was repulsive and made me feel both ignorant and inadequate.

But to return to the lunch incident and the salty joke - what Rosaline said, or assumed, about my circumstances, was not true. I would never have been so foolish as to tell her how much capital I still had in bonds, deposit accounts, investments and the rest. All she knew was that it seemed, at that stage, to her, from her chats with Eileen, that I had lost my finca, and therefore, she believed, I'd lost everything. Disaster. Homelessness! He cannot shelter me! He cannot provide!

When I had first met Eileen, we'd had a friendly conversation about the finca. As someone in the business locally as well as on the coast, she knew of the property, though she'd never been inside. She hadn't known it was up for sale and this surprised her. "Must be losing my touch!" she said, or some such self-deprecating remark. She admired the property politely and asked how much I'd paid for it, if I didn't mind saying. And I didn't mind saying back then because I was proud of the deal I'd struck. I'd negotiated 20% off the asking price, and the place was fully furnished, in rentable condition.

"Oh!" she said, raising her hand to her mouth. "That was a bargain, wasn't it?"

I could see she was secretly alarmed on my account, and that alarmed me too and I changed the subject.

When she had gone I reassured myself by going to my study - Ronnie's 'studio' - and raking out the deeds, the *escrituras*, in the filing cabinet. Everything was in order, everything had been stamped and signed by a notary, and I relaxed again.

The evening after the salty joke, Eileen dropped Ronnie back at home (I had no suspicion, then, of the sexual turn things had taken) and Ronnie asked to look at those same deeds. I fetched them for her and set them out on the writing bureau.

"What's the matter?"

"What's the matter?" she repeated, leafing through the dense Spanish legalese, sprinkled with blue stamps and ribbons and sheathed in handsome cream and embossed folders from the notary. "The matter is, I think you may be an even bigger fool than God made you, or I took you for."

She found a slip of paper in her bag with some names written on it by hand and tried to match them up with the notary stamp and with the *dueño*, the owner, the *vendedor*, the seller.

She took a deep sigh, set her hands either side of the documents, and leant forward.

"Eileen knows this property," she began, and tapped a fingertip near one of the colourful seals. "She knows all the best rural properties coming down the San Pedro road. She'd never heard it was for sale. It's owned by a family in Barcelona who inherited it but cannot agree on what to do with it. It's a very common story, she says - there are too many inheritors and they cannot agree on the price to sell at, or whether to sell it at all, and the property lies vacant, surrounded by dogs, or is rented out for years. She contacted the owners' lawyers in Barcelona. They haven't sold this property - what you call *your* finca, dear oh dear." She hung her head, shook her head, in disbelief. "My god, but you've been so unbelievably stupid. You've been had. Scammed. Thank goodness I have an income of my own now!"

She sat down, a little faint, in the only easy chair available, a tatty, blue-corduroy, youth-hostelish bit of furniture I'd happily paid cash for at a knock-down price when I bought the place. There were items outside too - garden tools, an elderly cultivator, I'd also paid cash for. It was remembering those transactions - paying the cash into the hands of the intermediary, a greasy Swedish guy with swept back hair - that undid me, that forced the scales from my eyes.

She was right. I knew it. I had been cheated. I had been a fool.

The headline 'Artistes Graffeurs Assassinés!' was well syndicated throughout Europe: 'Artistas de Graffiti Asasinadas!'; 'Graffiti-Kunstler Ermordet!' etc, and was quite a sensation in the UK because all the victims were UK citizens. I skipped past the names in my search for Arthur Spencer Harris - Arus - the only one alive, the only one that mattered. He told the story well enough: "a balding, albino guy, late sixties, with a rifle" had made his friend tie him up, and then had taken his friend away. There were further details about my appearance, put into neutral terms to make them printable. Implications of derangement were more plainly made.

He burst into tears when they told him that Moos - Rachel Allsop - was missing, and the others were both dead.

He was taken in for further questioning.

It was heart-breaking losing the finca but I didn't show it and the process was not ruinous, as Ronnie had supposed, or wanted to believe, and there was no pressure on me to move out, apart from shame, of course. The Spanish law favours squatters, 'ocupas', and there were no bailiffs trying to put me out on the street. Eileen spared Ronnie any further embarrassment by shuffling her away to the safety of her apartment, or one of her apartments. I was given no forwarding address. It would not have been difficult to track her down through Eileen's offices but I had no desire to do so. I had already decided my experiment with conjugal living would end on my terms.

But alone again, the spirit began to sink. September. It was getting chilly in the evenings. The finca - not *my* finca any more - is quite high in the sierra and winter is fierce. Minus five I'd seen, in the winter before Rosaline. But we were at the start of autumn, most days were bright. The house underwent that curious autumnal change where at midday it was colder inside than out on the terrace.

I turned to poetry.

'The mercury sank in the mouth of the dying day
What instruments we have agree
The day of his death was a dark cold day.'

Well, anyone who lives alone thinks about suicide from time to time, particularly if they're childless. I took refuge in poetry for a bit, and tried to break out from Yeats, Auden, and Eliot, the poets I knew reasonably well, to others both of the deeper past and the recent past, but in either case I couldn't help myself settling on their more morbid work. I knew Hopkins' *Felix the Farrier* by heart, I read it so often: Seamus Heaney's poems about his father's death, and his own mortality, had taken me there, and I also read some other greats from late last century such as Ted Hughes ('Crow' I kept coming back to, but understood less and less) and poor Sylvia Plath, and Tony Harrison, whose poems about grief moved me to tears, and it was really from there, from my efforts to look for new work, from my failed efforts to distract myself, that the first obsessions took hold, such as uncontrollable impulses to walk and walk and walk in the countryside along the ancient Andalucian *caminos reales*, the rights of way along old livestock tracks, now national walking routes or cycleways; walking and walking and walking through the mountains, appreciating their pine forests, brooks, eagles and vultures, less and less, and then walking some more, as Beckett used to do as a youth, around the Howth peninsula, outside Dublin, to stop himself masturbating. Or cleaning and re-cleaning every surface in the kitchen again and again, even though it wasn't mine any more. All these efforts to expunge the Anger.

Anger at the failure of that supposed 'relationship'.

Anger at the con of our 'sex-life'; the humiliation of being taken for a ride like that. (Unfortunate choice of words, I know.)

Anger at how I had been conned into buying this beautiful finca I could not own. At losing most of my capital in that way, at being made a fool of like that, which reminded me all the time that there was nothing clever about my money, I hadn't acquired it through intelligence and hard work, wit or nous, but only by luck on the London property market, and as Ronnie reminded me ceaselessly, a fool and his money are soon parted.

And anger all the time at the way she had treated me thenceforth. She had always been one for the snide put-down when I did or said something stupid - such petit-bourgeois English baggage to bring to Spain! - but after the calamity of losing the finca her attacks were out in the open and without restraint. There was a streak of vengeance in this, I felt, for those obligations prior to her 'success' and independence - the obligation to have sex with me occasionally ("I feel like a whore!"); the obligation to help with housework and shopping, taking her away from her art ("I am worth more than this, so much more than this!") the obligation to tolerate my silent judgement of her work ("Oh, I know all your scowls of disapproval now!").

During the little time, not even a month, as I remember, that she remained after it became certain the sale of the finca was a scam and there was no remedy, her attacks were relentless. But wait a minute - there had been quite a few levels to the deception, which she would never listen to in my defence: the bona fide agent passing me on to the greasy Swede; then a set up with the phony notary on the coast, complete with silver ponytail and silver Mercedes, who had all the facsimiles of the actual *escrituras*, the deeds, and we went to the Land Registration office and read the registered deed, the *nota simple* together - well, if those hoops had been put in front of her, would she not have jumped? Would not most people? But I could never even begin on my version of events. Her attacks were relentless, as I say, and she even turned to mockery, imitating how I spoke, my occasional pomposity.

"That's a line we should not cross," I told her sternly.

"What?... What line? Do you know, I honestly thought about trying to pay you back for the money you spent on me here? I honestly thought about doing that. Anglo-Saxon fair play. Thank god I'm not half the fool you are!"

And the tiniest things:

"You've burned the toast! How can you be so stupid? Is there nothing in there at all? Nothing you can do right?"

And: "My God. If there's a wrong way of doing it, you'll find it!"

And: "You know, Eileen thought you a terrible chump as soon as she met you. She laughed when she checked with Barcelona. Oldest trick in the book! And you fell right into it! They led you like a *burro*!"

In the end, because I could never even begin to give my side of the story, and never retaliated or threatened her in any way, I simply asked her when she was clearing out. I didn't realise it at the time, but it must have been around then something inside snapped. I'd had enough. My tone of indifference took me by surprise when I asked her that question.

"Very soon, don't worry. I'm not going to be around when the people who really own this beautiful place pay a visit."

It was her habit to keep her passport in her handbag at all times, buried in an inner zip compartment, not so much for security but in case she needed it to answer any random demand of officialdom. A couple of days after she left, such a need must have arisen. She had to call me.

"My passport."

"What about it?"

"Have you got it?"

"Oh dear, oh dear!" - I was ready for her this time - "You don't mean to say you've been such a fool as to lose it, surely?"

"Have you seen it? Or not?"

"I'll call you back."

I left five minutes or so.

"Found it."

"Thank god for that. We'll pick it up."

"Oh no you won't. I don't want you here. In fact, I never want to see you or that ghastly Eileen here ever again. I'll hand it over in town."

I named a place and a time, said I had to go into town anyway, then hung up before she could reply.

My car was nothing special, a mid-range Chrysler I'd bought nearly-new when I'd arrived. I'd been wanting to get rid of it for some time, even though it still had plenty of power and there was nothing wrong with it. I had wanted to replace it with a convertible. Hah! The old dreams ... I parked the wrong side of the El Burgo road, on a slight incline, where I knew I'd find a place during siesta hour. I held the car on the footbrake and left the engine running. People left their engines running all the time for the air-conditioning. It was still too hot in the car in September.

I watched her approach in the wing mirror. As expected, she approached on foot, alone. Eileen herself, even as her protector, wouldn't want to come near me after all she had done. I was wearing wraparound sunglasses and pretended not to notice her approach until she was at the door.

In just a few days her appearance had changed. Transformed. She looked much younger. She looked confident and attractive. She'd been out shopping with Eileen, it seemed, and bought herself a new outfit; perhaps several new outfits. Her sleeveless suit was lilac and quite shiny, with small white buttons, and her woven leather sandals, white and black chequered, were glossy too - all the glossy optimism of a new start. Her face was lightly made up with mauve eye-shadow and pale lipstick, and her hair had lost that brittle look from cheap treatments and was soft and brushed clear of her face. Such an effort to look alluring I'd never seen before. And in one's early fifties. This was not how she'd arrived on my plane ticket.

She had moved on. Left me behind. I was nothing to her now.

Nothing, and men who are nothing … That must not be.

She stopped outside the window and I lowered it a quarter.

"Passport?"

I looked straight ahead in my dark glasses, playing a part. I took her passport from the map pocket, held it up halfway, then put it back in the door.

"Don't worry. Get in."

"No. Just give me my passport … Please."

"In a minute. Get in."

She tried the handle but I'd locked it. She banged the roof in frustration.

"God. What now?"

I said nothing and put the window up. She huffed and puffed but came round to the passenger side.

As soon as she closed the door behind her - she had to close it quickly because the passenger door opened into the traffic - I moved off. Not with a screech of tires but with some spirit, shall we say.

"What're you doing? What's the matter? Where're we going?"

She was fiddling with the seat belt and the seat belt warning noise had come on. She couldn't insert the clasp in the holster.

"Fix your belt," I told her. "Can't stand that noise."

"Nor can I! Bloody thing! Won't go in!"

We were already out of town.

"Stop, for god's sake! Stop and have a look at it! I can't get the damn thing in! Cheap rubbish car!"

She stabbed angrily with the clasp.

"Ease it in. You know it's temperamental."

Still the bleeps came. The noise excited her irritation.

"Just give me my bloody passport!"

"Guardia Civil. Hold the belt in place."

A Guardia Civil 4X4 swept past, ignoring us, intent on lunch or some irrelevant errand.

"You have to stop the bloody car! God! ... Now! … Come on! Pull over and stop! What's the point of this joyride anyway?"

We were ascending into the El Burgo mountains. Glorious pine trees all around. I opened a window.

"Smell the pines!"

"Fuck the pines! And fuck you!"

"Calm down, woman."

"Just give me the bloody passport and I'll get out here and take my chances. Fuck you! Fuckyoufuckyoufuckyou and your stupid fucking games!"

"I wanted to show you that frieze in El Burgo. The tile frieze with the women washing clothes."

"What? *What?... Why*?" She was wild with anger now. Stabbing at the holster again and again. Eyes narrow and flashing in their mauve mascara. Her poise and lovely new appearance were in fatal disarray. "We've both seen that! Whatever are you talking about?"

"It's the inspiration for so much of your kitsch rubbish."

She didn't respond to that.

"Not so fast, for Christ's sake!"

"You have betrayed me. You have betrayed womankind."

We were only driving at 80 km an hour but the rough mountain road bucked the tinny Chrysler, punishing my recklessness. The sign came up for the stopping place I wanted. There was a camera symbol for a *Mirador,* now pock-marked by bored hunters who'd nothing left to hunt. It was a beautiful spot with shady benches crowded round a holm oak, two hundred metres or so after the brow of the hill.

On the brow, I eased up to 90 km an hour.

The mirador came into view. Empty.

"Slow down! Whatever are you *DOING*?"

"If I can't have you," I told her. "No one will."

She was speechless, then panted "Oh Christ!" and tried to pull at the wheel and to dig her nails into my hands, my arms, my face - *"You're mad! You're mad! You're fucking mad!"* - but I had an iron grip on the steering wheel; my Pop-Eye biceps strained beneath my shirt. In the last seconds of her life she let go and heaved at the handbrake.

"Oh, you're thinking well, dear!"

But I had thought of that too, and I'd unclasped the cables from their hooks under the rubber fitting, so the handle whipped up in her hand uselessly as she yanked it again and again.

The reflex to brake was too strong and we skidded the last few metres through a bench and into the tree.

Without the seat belt the airbags were useless and she went halfway through the windscreen, leaving her buttocks high on the dashboard. Her legs splayed so her left shin and her left foot, in its shiny, chequered, optimistic sandal, finished between my knees. The airbags were firm driver's side but I had enough room to move her leg out of the way, and then to lean across and winkle out the cardboard from the belt holster with long-nose pliers, and re-attach the handbrake cables with the same tool. I knew no one in the local *desguace* would take any notice of that, but maybe the car would go through an official inspection from the Guardia Civil.

These details attended to, I squeezed out and left the driver's door ajar.

I was careful not to look at the damage to her head and face but despite that I couldn't help seeing her broken neck: her head was buckled in too tight to her shoulder, parallel with it, parallel to the crunchy edge of the broken windscreen and the wipers. I must keep such images out of the involuntary memory-store. I watched her torso on the bonnet for any movement. Brackets below of strained and twisted metal broke free and struts subsided here and there with the tyre flattening, and busted pipes emitted their steamy noises under the crumpled silver bonnet.

And that was the end of the worthless life of Rosaline, Ronnie, the artist manqué, the bitch who sold kitsch to the rich. She betrayed her art, which was a fatal mistake, and she betrayed me, which was another.

I'd had a Yeats epitaph in mind for some time:

'... Love has pitched his mansion in
The place of excrement;
For nothing can be sole or whole
That has not been rent.'

We'd left the road to avoid hitting a sheep, I told the Guardia Civil. I admitted ruefully that I felt we must have been going too fast but I couldn't recall the exact speed. It all happened *en un abrir y cerrar de ojos* - in the blink of an eye - I told them.

I asked: "Who told you it was a Devon?"

With the Chrysler insurance and a hit on my savings, I was buying a campervan again. The only place to buy rather than rent I knew of was run by a middle-aged couple from the north of England in Churriana, outside Málaga, near the airport. They had tried to persuade me an elderly VW they couldn't shift had a Devon conversion. I knew something about these things from my days on the road in my youth and this conversion had not been done professionally at all. Drawers and doors tipped, tilted, drooped, rattled. Devon were top of the range.

"Looks like a bodge-up to me," I added. "What about your brand new models?"

The question was a put-down. They didn't have any brand new models, and I knew that, because they didn't own a franchise. The newest model they had was a Fiat. I took a look around it but told them I didn't trust Fiat mechanically, or electrically, which didn't leave much to recommend them.

But in the end I bought the most expensive van on the forecourt, a two year-old Ford Transit with Hymer conversion, complete with a fitted awning I didn't want.

We took it for a run, both husband and wife accompanying me in the cabin on the bench seat, wifey in the middle. All I remember about them was their mouths. The only mark of Spain on hubby was a Don Pedro moustache, of the kind you might see on a wine bottle. Wifey's deep, red, tulip smiles were all but flirtatious: she didn't trust her old man to close the deal, so I cut him out and talked to her. The van drove well and had a low mileage. She agreed to the sale at a 5% discount. Hubby shifted uncomfortably and looked at her askance, moustache skewwiff, as if he'd have a few words with her once I'd gone. I shared his anxiety about the sale but was not so demonstrative: even with the 5% discount this would mean living off capital from now. There wouldn't be enough return on investments to cover day to day living.

The countdown had begun.

Having shed all human and material ties, I would soon be on the road once more, a free agent cruising north in what envious men of my generation would called a shag-wagon, fuck-truck, or bang-van. Even as a youngish man on the road with modestly successful rock bands, I had never once persuaded any girl or woman to get in the back of my campervan. The bands naturally had more luck with groupies in their bakery vans, or so they bragged, but for me - No. Never.

In the evening sun, it felt good parking the Hymer on the spacious gravel driveway outside the finca. It weighed much more than the Chrysler and the crunch on the gravel was satisfying. Not the satisfaction of ownership any more, but a new reassurance that this solid, weighty, expensive vehicle signified commitment to a plan, a future, beyond the finca, beyond Rosaline.

Then the pleasure of kitting it out. I packed away my favourite books, mainly poetry and plays but some Kafka and Chekhov short stories too, and art biographies, cook books, which all fitted neatly in the overhead cupboards. I de-framed my prints, rolled them up, bound them with rubber bands and stowed them aloft the other side. Whatever I needed to complete my new home I stole from the property: blankets and duvet from the bedroom, all the kitchenware I needed, tools for breakdowns, and some bigger tools from the outhouse that might come in useful - bolt-cutters, chisels, a club hammer and so on.

In a couple of hours I was sitting at the unblemished Formica foldaway table, in a fully furnished, practically equipped and very tidy rear cabin, with a bottle of local red wine, a potato salad (to test the cooker) and a jar of black olives from Aragon. A delightful early last supper.

And that very evening I set out the plans for my wonderful tour northward. It was a tour of the imagination, of beauty, of hope, history and erudition. Back then it had also been a tour that would end in a single, well planned assassination, and in my own suicide. I am well aware how cheap it is to slot in that last phrase. It was easy and comforting not to think beyond the assassination. There would be a good end, and my own neat death - far too sweet, I know, I know. But that was the endgame way back then, incredibly naive, even adolescent, as it seems now.

I would take the most leisurely, the most scenically beautiful, yet the most economical route up through Spain and France; a route conceived around the landscape and seascape paintings of the last two centuries that I knew and loved best. At first I was far too ambitious and thought of going south for Guillermo Gómez Gil, to the vistas of Málaga and Cádiz, but realized, after another glass or two, and consulting my laptop, that would be a complete waste of time. There was nothing left there. Instead, I planned to head directly west to Elche for Carlos de Haes and up through Asturias for Sorolla's haystacks and more, then on through the Pyrenees and up to Arles and Saint Rémy, for Van Gogh's *Wheat Fields with Mountains*, and *Rain*, from his voluntary stay in the Saint Rémy asylum - How did he miss out the bars on the windows? - and then on to Renoir's landscapes at Wargemont and up to Essoyes for more Renoir, Monet and Sisley's *View of Marly-le-Roi*, and his suspension bridge at Villeneuve-la-Garenne.

So that trip, including the Caen crossing, began in a very different place psychologically to where I ended up at the suspension bridge on the A89, 5 km south-west of Ussel, hunting down graffiti artists, the murderers of all imagination, beauty, hope, history and erudition.

To illustrate that difference: two of the inspirational paintings back in the Hymer that evening, with the red wine and Aragon olives, had been Renoir's '*A Box at the Theatre*' 1880 and *'La Loge'* of 1874. These took my imagination to a quite similar box - Box FF, actually - at The London Palladium, a venue which had opened not so long after, in 1910.

The London Palladium was where Barry Manilow was performing at the end of September.

Dates, stretches of time, attempts to fasten time and make sense of stretches of time, become important with only a few months separating one from seventy years of age. How much more important, then, as I fondly imagined, pencil in hand, planning the route, when one has only a few weeks left to live. One keeps trying to locate oneself, drag oneself back up onto the rails of time-lines, after being washed off by emotional tides and surges, and now, being effectively homeless, and alone again, the question of what to do with my remaining time had become something more than a dispiriting mindgame. Living alone, I have always understood, is not good for the sense of proportion. Slippage of that kind was one of the reasons - how it embarrasses me now to think of the other reasons, the other fantasies! - that I had trawled the dating sites two years before.

After the finca fiasco, a turn my mind had taken from which I could find no way back, led to a sickly, clammy sense of guilt and shame that clung to my late youth and all of my middle-aged years. How could I have poured so much of my own life, my finite time, my precious days, months and years - for more than three decades! - into managing the Barry Manilow schedule in the U.K, and with such assiduous dedication. Poured my life down that particular drain. There are no question marks because these were not questions, not even rhetorical questions. They were sighs of despair. Towards the end I was so successful many of Manilow's European dates came my way too, and an agent reached out from *Headline Entertainment* on behalf of Cliff Richard, another octogenarian still performing today, but I turned him down, thank the lord.

Here I was, someone who had, for most of his working lifetime, shamelessly poisoned the nation's cultural drinking water. I remember avoiding or glossing over this part of my life with Rosaline.

"Barry Manilow?" she laughed. "You're kidding me!"

"You remember him?"

"Of course I remember him! A total drip! A sentimental balladeer who couldn't even admit he was gay! More Americana! And you promoted him? My God!"

"Well, I wouldn't say - "

"Do me a favour," she said, quite seriously, turning to me. She was at the sink washing up and she had a carving knife in her hand, which she pointed at me, in all earnestness - "If we are ever in company, of any kind - in the supermarket, in a bar, in a lift somewhere - you never mention this. All right? Not in English, not in Spanish. That you promoted this guy. This man. This drip. Barry Manilow."

Of course I hadn't 'promoted' him, but that was not a distinction she was interested in, and deep down I saw her point, understood her shame and embarrassment, that I had been part of the machine, as it were, the trash machine. That I too had been a 'trasheteer', to use her own neologism. I did not identify with her stance completely because I harboured doubts about her own abilities, and suspicions she might turn out a hypocrite, and in the end my suspicions were vindicated, but at that stage of what we must call our 'relationship', I kept my opinions to myself and didn't defend the past at all.

Taking up a dish towel, I said: "Our modern world offers many ways of keeping body and soul together, you know."

"But are they all worth it?" she snapped back, stopping again, turning to me with another knife in her hand. She was serious about this. "Better to let them drift apart than sink so low, in my view."

All very well for her to say, from her privileged background; but again, at that stage, for the sake of harmony and building trust, I kept my mouth shut.

So the journey I was planning in the back of the Hymer, and the schedule I was following to get there, had nothing to do with graffiti artists. They did not become targets until I set out on that journey, until I saw their motifs on the pumphouses of every wheatfield, their signatures on every bridge, and panic took over, the forest caught alight. The original destination, that September evening, had been The London Palladium, where Manilow was playing for three consecutive nights at the end of the month, 25th-27th Sept. Each performance was sold out. Some of those fans would be going twice or even three times, so the total number to make the venture worthwhile in London might not have been more than five thousand fans; yet just that number could entice Manilow, at the age of 81, with his entourage, to keep pouring his poison into the veins of the nation's capital, and then Newcastle, Birmingham, Cardiff and so on.

I had bought both seats in Box FF for two nights at a total cost of £360, £90 per ticket. The view is restricted with little depth to the stage but I knew first-hand there would be plenty of room for Manilow's piano at the front and a good sightline. The rest would depend on ground-based reconnaissance from the box itself, on the first of the two nights.

In the end I tried to resell the Box tickets on eBay but found they'd blocked all that years ago. I wrote them off as a dead loss. Out of date and out of pocket.

He was staying at The Savoy, where we had always managed the bookings for the London gigs, and this gave some advantage, because part of the groundwork of my old job had entailed visiting hotels to double-check on arrangements immediately before his arrival (down to toilet details: I could entrust that servile task to no one else) and though there was not much call to see all was well at somewhere like The Savoy, in provincial towns and lesser venues - the Utilita Cardiff, for example, where he stayed at The ParkGate, and the Utilita Newcastle where he settled for The County, because it was close to the Arena, a preliminary visit was essential. Those places changed year by year, usually for the worse. Even season by season.

I knew where the car pool was at The Savoy. There were only half a dozen luxury cars and sightlines to access and egress of the carpool were not difficult. To my surprise, the driver for the Range Rover models was the same old lackey - he must have been in his mid-seventies now himself - that I'd known when it was part of my brief to arrange chauffeured transport for Manilow and entourage. The driver had been demoted from the Rolls, but Manilow never wanted that anyway. He'd asked for it the first time he stayed there, in 1983, but after that he didn't want the fuss of it, the head-turning car with the S8 VOY number plate attracted too much attention wherever he went. Now that he was in his eighties, he opted for one of the modest Range Rovers, in two-tone bridegroom grey livery. Much easier to climb in and out of. I saw his car come out with this card propped in the windscreen - *Barry Manilow Only.* I now had the details I needed: the car, the number plate, the driver by sight, and this lucky bonus - *Barry Manilow Only*.

He would exit via the stage door on Great Marlborough Street, unless, by some sleight of hand, he exited through the entrance of The Palladium on Argyll Street. As that had been pedestrianised, I ruled it out.

The stage door of The Palladium, behind the 'Wall of Fame' facade, sketched with the ghosts of entertainers past (Bob Hope, Bing Crosby, Danny Kaye - more Americana) is down a broad passage from Great Marlborough Street lined with bins, security railings and a PortaKabin for the Palladium porter. This is only visible when the facade is opened during the day for rubbish collection or the delivery of catering supplies, stage equipment etc. Normally you can see nothing because only a poky door within the 'Wall of Fame' serves human traffic.

There had been a sudden turn in the weather.

Midnight on the second of the three Manilow dates was cold, overcast and miserable, with a chilly north-easter too. Nonetheless, sixty or so elderly fans, women outnumbering men by 20-1, stood in a loose group spilling onto the road, left of the 'Wall of Fame'. They were all five to ten years my senior. I picked out just three men, presumably husbands or partners, all bald and hatless and looking down-in-the-mouth, cold, bitter, impatient. This was not a difficult fan-group, with no pushy parents escorting unruly children, and no ardent or hysterical fans. They also observed some decorum in keeping well back from the stage door. Being so old they could not be a threatening group in any way, no matter how provoked. Trouble-free fans. There might be some commotion if any broke away and strayed down Ramillies Street to be beset by muggers, but they were safe enough in a sizable herd of this kind.

The old driver from the Savoy arrived half an hour early and parked his Range Rover tight to the kerb opposite the door in the 'Wall of Fame', so when the door opened Manilow would have a direct line to the rear door of the vehicle. No doubt the host staff at The Palladium would be quick to organise a safe corridor. I found it difficult to imagine Manilow would want to dally signing autographs or having selfies taken in this weather. There was plenty of that kind of thing after his recent performances at Westgate, Las Vegas, but here, in the narrow and busy confines of grubby Great Marlborough Street, with the north-easter whipping up, the whole business would be too fraught with security concerns and physical discomfort.

After locking up his polished, bride-groom grey Range Rover, the driver stepped up and knocked on the centre of the door. He adjusted his Savoy cap and waited, stamping his feet on damp leaves, and shooting contemptuous glances at the Manilow fan herd, and wary, disdainful, suspicious glances down the street at the stream of pedestrians heading for bars and restaurants after their own shows had finished. He hitched his trousers and dusted his uniform with some pride and swagger, impatient to be off the street.

I was in that crowd he looked at downstream. We didn't warrant his disdain and suspicion. Around me there might have been a few low-life chancers, but most of the more ragged among us would surely be settling down in doorways hereabouts for another freezing, godforsaken night under the stars.

I was wearing a broad-brimmed black hat and the anonymous puffer jacket I had taken from Loner that fateful dawn on the *Mont St Michel*. The hat - for the security cameras - was a touch extreme, but no outfit could attract attention in these streets at this time of night. Here and now, the only attraction was tattooed flesh: despite the cold there were bare midriffs, cleavages, thighs, sixpacks and some half-naked chests under waistcoats. The general public no longer exists: they have become part of everyone's audience. Bobbing amidst such vanity and self-consciousness, my hat would not stand out.

The old driver was taking such care not to catch his polished toe-caps on the door frame, I had time to pull abreast and help him through, with a firm and friendly shove between the shoulder-blades. He tripped onto the fellow who'd opened the door, knocking both of them to the ground. I stepped through and heeled the door shut behind me. The porter had fallen with the full weight of the driver on top of him. Only his long grey mullet and tight Palladium cap saved him from cracking his head open on the greasy granite setts leading down to the stage door proper. The old driver's Savoy cap had come off in the fall and had rolled down a fair way. He too had rolled over. He lay on his back, still half on top of the doorman, with his arms flailing in front of him like the legs of an overturned beetle: he was trying to defend himself against the carving knife that I now waved for silence, with a finger to my lips. He made no cry for help but kept up this frantic, instinctive, helpless waving.

With the knife I signalled them both to their feet.

"Jacket."

The driver hesitated, understood, then slipped out of the Savoy blazer he'd worn with pride for quarter of a century and handed it over. I let it fall to the granite setts.

I nodded to the Portakabin and in they went.

Inside was a cosy scene. A kettle was heating up on an elderly gas ring and on the table places were set for two persons. An empty teapot of plain white design, tea bags suspended, stood waiting to be filled. A mean-size, one-person-size, cheap metropolitan cake was already divided. There was not much room for the three of us in the Portakabin and their closeness brought my decision to a head. The old driver had cast off his bravado with his blazer. It was the porter who looked more likely to try something.

The porter's mullet suggested a shiftiness to me, and a lifetime of pursing his lips in know-all scepticism had left him with no mouth at all, just a tight slot, and his lips were pursed now too, and his chin held high, and his short sniffs were telling me in no uncertain terms that I would never get away with this. I told him to sit down and rest his hands on his thighs. We were so close together the carving knife was an immediate threat to one and all. With a grunt of disapproval to save face, the porter did as he was told. From Loner's puffer jacket I took a roll of surgical plaster and gave it to the old driver. When he hesitated I nodded and smiled at him as if he were an idiot. The first piece I had already cut and when it came off he dropped the roll.

"Leave it."

I held the point of the carving knife close to his mouth, drew a ring, then nodded again.

He came round to apply the tape to the porter's face. I held the point of the carving knife under the porter's chin and he tipped his head to receive the tape over his lipless mouth. Despite the baleful look he gave the old driver at this betrayal - they had been about to share tea and cake! - the driver fastened the tape tight over his mouth, a professional job, and with no further instruction from me he came back, picked up the roll from the floor, and began wrapping the tape around the porter, fastening him tight to his chair. After a few rounds I saw his intention: he was trying to use up the tape and leave too little for me to bind him as well, or at least cause some problems. I let him have his way and after five or six rounds he slowed, realizing I must have a second roll.

When he looked up at the end of the tape I smiled and cut it for him six inches from the roll, leaving him his own gag.

"Then put your chair back to back."

A lifetime's subservience came into play.

There was a noise, a grunt from the porter now, and an accompanying thrust in his chair, as he cursed the driver. My character assessment had been astute.

The old driver's eyes were soggy and bloodhound and brimful with anxiety as he applied his bandage over his mouth and smoothed it tight with fluttering, pianist's fingers. He immediately started to breathe heavily through his nose and that concerned me, but he managed the exertions with the chair well enough and took his seat.

At this point the kettle began to boil. I should have dealt with it at the start.

"Leave it."

Its screaming whistle added to the dramatic tension and stress, affecting both of them, I sensed, which I took as an advantage.

The tongue of my second roll of surgical plaster was already undone.

"Hold that tight."

Even after I had done a few rounds, binding the pair of them back to back, the driver still held his end tight. I thought of his glances of haughty contempt and wariness outside the Wall of Fame towards the fans and the street crowd, of him hitching his trousers, dusting down his uniform. Where was all that swagger now?

Only when I had finished binding them to their chairs, and had bound their heads together too around their sweaty foreheads, did I attend to the kettle.

As its noise shrivelled, the faint, tinkling, distant sentiments of the concert surfaced in the silence. The song - I think it was *Mandy*, but it could have been anything: *Copacabana, Can't Smile Without You, Looks Like We Made It* - seemed to swell too as the whistle died.

With the Portakabin door closed behind me, I took in the surroundings more thoroughly: the smart blue rubbish skips that lined the left wall; the row of neatly arranged chrome safety railings opposite, beyond the PortaKabin, that shone beneath two strings of makeshift fairground lights running down to the stage door proper, which was lit up all around the architrave like a dressing room mirror. On a reel on the wall before the skips was a roll of hosepipe, presumably for keeping things washed down so the stars and stagehands didn't suffer any foulness as they stepped up briskly to the Wall of Fame doorway, into the drab reality of Great Marlborough Street, and the night-bus home or the limousine to the hotel.

I picked up the driver's jacket, wiped the handle of the carving knife on its lining then tossed the knife into a bin. I would never have used it. The thought revolted me. There's the difference between using a rifle and using a bayonet. My broad brimmed, Stetson-style hat, I frisbeed into a further bin. The jacket was a good fit, and once I had donned the handsome purple cap I felt a moment's complacency - until I remembered the Range Rover key. But I was in luck. It was in the jacket pocket. I was spared going back inside the PortaKabin and delving into the driver's trousers.

The chrome safety railings were of an expensive design that locked together with single ball-and-socket joints halfway up the frames. They were easily assembled into a gangway up the slope from the stage door proper to the door onto Great Marlborough Street. The frames were also quite high, offering protection to just below shoulder-height.

There was only the nervous wait remaining.

Who would come out first? What routine were staffers used to with the porter? What fuss might arise on account of the porter's absence?

I checked how to release the door - a Yale latch and two drawbolts - to make sure that if I had to abandon the project there would be no delay. The door opened with a twist of the latch and I slipped out, leaving it off the latch, to familiarise myself with the Range Rover. Its push-button start arrangement gave me some trouble but once I understood the order - footbrake, Start button, handbrake - there were no further challenges. Lights, air conditioning, automatic. Everything automatic.

Just as I locked and left the car, a question was hurled at me from behind, heavy as a brick, from one of the three down-in-the-mouth husbands in the fan herd. I had already stepped back over the high wooden skirt of the doorway when it hit me.

"Oi you! ... When's Mandy comin' out? ... Fuckin' freezin' 'ere!"

Without turning round to face the husband, I called back - "It ain't over till the fat lady sings!" - and laughed loudly to seal up the exchange. I closed the door on the latch and drew the bolts before there could be any further unpleasantness.

Back down the slope at the stage door proper I could hear, much more loudly now, the choral refrain of *'Copacabana'*. This time it was definitely that song. Manilow was closing with his biggest hits, saving the best till last. This rendition of '*Copacabana'* seemed to have a built-in encore because it repeated interminably, and interwoven with the orchestral rock sound were the croons of the adoring fans, not so loud because they were very old and bound by a different decorum to a rock-concert audience. I remembered my conversation with Rosaline - "That drip!" she had called Manilow. "Couldn't even admit he was gay!" Complete contempt. "More Americana!" Loathing. And I remembered the shame I had felt during our conversation, the shame of one exposed for his part in an escalating treachery against my own country, for three whole decades, betraying my country to American culture, a villainous treachery that made me nothing less than another trasheteer, a dilettante, an art low-life, an art bottom-feeder, who could never hold his head up to the world and declare he had earned an honest living all his life, making this or doing that, like a carpenter or a plumber or a welder, a lawyer, a doctor or teacher, oh no, one who had cast in his lot with the American dogs of taste and sentimentality, one who had spread the American disease, assisted in the arrangements to bring low-brow, dumbass American culture in the form of the mindless puppet Manilow to Glasgow, to Cardiff, to Newcastle, to Leeds - and to this top-of-the-range, historic venue, built in 1910, to The London Palladium, no less, where it all began for Manilow UK a lifetime later in 1983. The shame rushed up through me again from head to toe, molten and inexorable.

My life, my life, my life. What had I done with my life?

I thought of the two murderers in Truman Capote's *In Cold Blood*. Not Perry Smith. Dick someone. I couldn't remember his name but I remembered very well what he had said:

Someone must pay ...

At last, the show was over. The cheers were finally

subsiding, there were no more encores. The *Copacabana* was empty, *Mandy* was dead, the concert was finished, and Manilow was finished. He would already be off-stage. He would need the toilet, perhaps, but then he would be down here directly. I knew he did not change out of his show-outfit because there had been shots in *The London Standard* of him signing autographs and having selfies taken with fans last night in Great Marlborough Street, when it had been much warmer.

Such a spectacle to put in the capital's newspaper!

The stage door proper had no handle outside. It could be opened only from within and presumably there were some bolts fashioned in 1910 about that arrangement too.

There was nothing I could do but wait and see how things turned out, but I didn't waste the remaining minutes getting nervous about that. Instead, I came up with some ham theatre of my own. When the door opened at the foot of the slope, I would remain at the Portakabin, with the door open, in mid-conversation with the porter inside. As the party ascended between the chrome railings, I would shut down the conversation and close the PortaKabin door - "Night, Les! Thanks for the tea and cake! Delicious as always! Goodnight, goodnight!" - and move to the street door, which I would open wide, ready for the exit of whoever came up first. Hopefully, Manilow himself. If it were Manilow, I would be out onto the street in a trice to open up the rear door of the Range Rover. If it were not Manilow, I would just have to keep the door wide and my face averted, allowing only attentive glances to slip down the chromium rails ...

I heard heavy bolts drawn on the stage door below and opened up the Portakabin.

What had happened in there threw me completely. I lost my place in my own script. The old driver's head lay dipped, chin on chest, and he was unconscious, and the weight of his head pulled the porter's head back so he faced the ceiling, eyes wide, aghast.

I could say nothing, do nothing, but call - "Goodnight, Les!"- and slam shut the Portakabin door.

My skills then hit an even greater challenge, and again they were not up to it.

To turn and see, at last, the octogenarian star in the flesh, in a close-fitting, humped, silvery green jacket, a carapace that shone with glass or jewels as if glistening wet, set over a collarless vest of the same material and design, to see him under the strings of fairground lights, his stiff auburn hair twisted and buffoned into designer scruffiness, to see him moving up the chrome railings head humbly lowered, careful never to let go with both hands, was no less shocking than what I'd glimpsed in the PortaKabin: his slinking, upward, writhing movement was like something pulsing to emerge from pupa form, writhing from its sheath in the earth, or even from beneath the surface of a pond, using strings of weed glistening with silvery air bubbles to bring its new wet form to the surface. The head, leaning down and forward, seemed as yet too heavy for the frail frame, whose humped green carapace behind might unfold into clammy wings at any moment. The glistening green garments did not move with him, they kinked and folded and crumpled with his ascent between the railings. When he stopped, his slimy green boots, which came up to his knees, coalesced into one piece, like a tail or flipper or sting.

With both hands still clasped on the last railings of the slope, he slowly raised his head, and stared up at me coldly, directly. The others ascending - some in stage dress, some not, but all dejected and depressed beneath a common burden - bunched up behind him. The baggy eyes of the octogenarian shone under phony blue contacts, shone at me, on me, in particular. He responded to my own rude, dumb stare.

"Pleased to see me? … Or what?"

Immediately behind Manilow was a short and jowly Palladium host in blue serge and cap, on whose neck I could see the turquoise tattoo of a long and vicious dagger.

"Where is he? My driver?"

And this was the object of female desire and adoration.

For this, the fan herd awaited in Great Marlborough Street, in the chilly north-easter.

Good god! All my singleton years!

"Taken ill, sir," I said. But it was too servile. Try as I might, I couldn't bring myself onto a stage or set: this was raw, real life and my skills were not up to it. "I'll see you back to The Savoy tonight, sir. No worries."

Again: hollow, inept.

But the mention of the hotel must have triggered some overwhelming desire for rest and comfort, because, after looking down again a moment, exposing to me how his hair had been whipped up in a floss, a net, about his speckled pate, he set himself in motion again, clinging to one rail then the other, and passing over the wooden skirt of the doorway without incident in his long green boots. By which time I had opened the rear door of the Range Rover.

"No fans, tonight," he said, looking back to his pudgy Palladium host with the tattooed dagger. "Too cold. I'm too cold."

The Palladium host nodded respectfully and ducked out the way. As relieved as I was, no doubt.

I closed Manilow's door, cutting off his thankyou, and nipped into the driver's seat, and we were away, slipping past the disconsolate fans. One of the husbands - the one who had shouted earlier, no doubt - shook his fist at me as we passed, shouting, "And fuck you, Jack!"

The Hymer was in a Q-park facility in Poland Street. I had checked a few underground car parks and had chosen this one because it was the deepest: at the very bottom, four floors down, there was no internet signal at all. Manilow relaxed and shut his eyes, but I remembered an interview detail where he said he survived on four hours sleep a day, so I didn't trust the idea he was cat-napping. I read this eyes-shut, head-back pose as a signal he didn't want to talk.

Until we dived into the darkness of the car park in Poland Street, he didn't open his eyes again.

"What's this? What's this? ... We here already?"

The Savoy is only a couple of miles from Argyll Street so the mistake was understandable.

"Sir!"

The servility was no more convincing than before and he picked up on that. In the rear-view mirror I saw him reach into his green jacket for his phone, and then lean forward, so he was hidden behind my driver's seat.

We were two floors down with two to go.

The Range Rover tyres squealed on the corners as if we were in a movie.

This car park had an appalling record for break-ins, for filth and lift break-downs, for unreliable CCTV, and I knew the Hymer would be a prime target, particularly with its left hand drive and foreign plates. In the multiple bad reviews of the car park, there was repeated mention of the uselessness of surveillance here. I had also noticed the stench in the place, particularly the stench of urine around the lifts, and could well believe other rumours in the reviews that people actually lived down here, in the bowels of this car park, leading a permanently nocturnal troglodyte or Morlock existence. The break-ins were all about stealing property, not cars themselves, and I had been scrupulously careful to leave nothing in view and all blinds up on the windows so thieves could see there was nothing to take. Of course, they might break in just to see if there was any food in the fridge, or just to foul the toilet, or have a kip on the foam bed. I had taken a chance leaving the Hymer down here, but it was deliberate because the last thing I wanted was a highly secure and well guarded place with fully functioning CCTV and officious guards on patrol.

"This is not my car park!"

We had descended to the fourth level now.

And there they were, two predatory figures stalking the Hymer, both with hoodies so large and loose they may as well have been balaclavas. From behind, their thin legs and scrappy buttocks showed through baggy jeans. One carried something like a carpenter's bag, big enough to contain a crow-bar and assorted tools.

With horn blasting I screamed down the aisle and they scattered for the ramp.

"This is not my car park!"

There was no point in replying. I left him in the back fiddling with his mobile while I opened up the Hymer and retrieved the Browning. It was assembled and loaded.

Strangely, Manilow didn't seem much surprised when I opened his rear door and gestured with the rifle for him to dismount. It was as if this had all happened before, or was something he'd had to rehearse for back in America, surrounded by gunslingers wherever he went. No doubt there were regular checks and drills he had to do for insurance purposes.

'Armed Kidnap: The Long Game. Staying in Play. What to do. What not to do. Ex-marine heads up Team.'

"Listen," he said, climbing down into the intestinal winds of the fourth level. "I'm an old man. More than eighty years old. Please - " he held his hands together in the prayer symbol. "Please. No violence. I have no money with me, you must understand that. But I can get some fast. Plenty."

"Phone."

He handed it over without complaint.

Rule One: Golden Rule - Comply. Do as They Say, until you see The Advantage. It will come! Believe!

"Into the van."

He sighed and turned towards the Hymer. I slid the side door back for him and he climbed in. I don't know if he was now putting it on, but his movements were suddenly those of a very old man. *The Copacabana, Mandy, Could it be Magic?, If I Love Again*, all gone now.

"You can make yourself some coffee," I told him. "Crackers and cheese. Toilet's at the back."

"Thank you." With a smile that was more a wince, he nodded and settled at the foldaway table. He sat on the thin foam rubber seat that doubled as half a mattress once the table was lowered. He set his empty hands on the formica. "Thank you," he repeated.

Rule Two: Stay Calm and Polite. Show You are Human, even if He or She is Not. No Anger. No Outrage. Remain Likeable, prepared to Listen. Relatable. But Dignified. Stay Admirable in this Extremity. The Advantage Will Come! Believe!

I slid the door back and locked it, then stooped to wedge his mobile under the rear wheel.

Before getting into the cabin I shed the Savoy jacket and cap on the bench seat.

With the Hymer out of its space, I left the engine running and took the Savoy jacket and cap with me to the Range Rover. After parking the Range Rover in the Hymer's space, and rolling over the phone again for good measure, I wiped down the handles and controls with the jacket, locked the car and kept the key. It was only at this point, locking the car, stowing away the key, that I realized how stupid I had been not to bring any gloves. I consoled myself with the promise that I would be doubly cautious because of that oversight. And I kept that promise: looking over the car before departure, I saw the cardboard *Barry Manilow Only* sign still wedged behind the windscreen passenger side. I opened the door and tucked it under the seat.

I left his phone in the bay under the Range-Rover. Whether the data was still retrievable or not didn't matter to me.

There was more than an hour to run before the prepayment for the Hymer expired and we glided out onto Poland Street, only hesitating for the barrier to read the number plate.

By chance I offered Manilow a quick scenic trip: we followed the river past The Savoy, which must have confused him, then east past the Tower of London, north past The Barbican Centre and onto the A10.

It was just a six mile journey from the Thames to Tottenham Marshes, the southernmost section of the Lee Valley Conservation area, with its chain of thirteen reservoirs. London's drinking water. Past midnight the roads were quiet and we were there in about a quarter of an hour.

The car park was deserted.

When the engine died, I sat in silence for a moment in the cabin with my eyes shut, thinking about the 'Lee Valley Camp & Caravan Park' further on, the more natural stop. But there were bound to be other vehicles. Even gypsies, trailer park families. Bound to be a bad mix.

But what was I *doing*?

What was I doing? With Manilow in the back now?

I could hear him in the back, moving about in the dark, or in the half-light from the toilet, whose light was automatic. I could hear him opening and closing cupboards, feeling for something resembling a weapon, finding nothing. Or maybe he was just looking for food. There were both cheese and crackers, as promised. And plastic cutlery.

His noises made me remember the sad and moving

poem Seamus Heaney had written about the child who was discovered living in a chicken-coop, back in 1956. *Bye-Child*. There was another he had written in similar vein about a desperate mother drowning her newborn on the sea shore, but I couldn't remember the name of it. The images, yes, but not the title. Real art. For once the involuntary memory served a purpose: a reminder about what I was really doing here, dealing with here, and how I had promised myself, at sixty-nine years old, to dedicate my remaining time to pushing back against the tide of trash and Americana no matter how futile it might seem, just as an environmentalist must lobby against oil giants and multinationals and governments despite the Goliathian odds, because there is nowhere else to go to save ourselves. In my case, the tide of cultural rubbish had thrust itself all the way up to the Nobel Prizes, and left its grubby tide-mark when the American Bob Dylan, Robert Zimmerman, venerated pop-culture icon, supposed poet, was lifted onto the same platform as Seamus Heaney, Doris Lessing, William Golding, Samuel Beckett, and his own great countrymen, T. S. Eliot, Ernest Hemingway, Saul Bellow, and a host of other genuinely brilliant men and women who one way or another changed the way we see the world and ourselves, and could have changed it so much more, and for the better, if not for the leaden counterweight of popular culture. For the sake of Heaney's legacy alone, Manilow and all he stood for had to be taken out of our future.

The interior lights came on automatically when I slid the door back. He was sitting at the foldaway table again, with both hands open on the formica surface, just as he had been when I left him in the underground car park.

There was an awkward pause, then he tried to smile, but the result was a twist to his aged lips that fixed one tanned cheek high in a sardonic grimace, and drew the other tight into a flat panel.

He sighed again and rolled open his empty hands on the table.

"What do you want, old man?... Eh?... I mean, what the fuck do you really want?"

I stooped, not under the irony that he should call me an old man, but because I needed to stoop in order to climb up into the compartment with the Browning over my shoulder. I slid the door shut behind me. As it clicked home I was acutely conscious for a moment of shutting out the natural darkness, of shutting out the watery noises of Tottenham Marshes and the nocturnal world out there with all its terrors and wonders. I had been outside for a moment only but I had definitely heard - and nearly just ignored! - the steady rush of water escaping Stonebridge Lock. Certainly I'd heard an owl. An owl! Six miles from central London!

In the cosy, softly lit compartment of the Hymer, I took the seat opposite and stowed the rifle to my left, into the corner of the bench seat, and then I sighed, as if to say, 'The difficult part is now over, friend.'

The rifle was just an encumbrance. We both knew I had the strength to overpower my kidnap victim easily.

Naturally his green and silvery outfit lost its sheen under the Hymer's lozenge lights. I reached up behind me and adjusted the dimmer to brighten the lights, but still the spangles could not reflect. They had been taken out the jeweller's shop glare of The Palladium and the stage door and rendered dull by the 12 volt glow inside the Hymer. There was something orange in the lozenge lights too.

The incongruity of his figure at the table made me smile and he mistook this. He leant forward, raising his trimmed and whiskery eyebrows, still powdery with stage make-up. It was the first time I had really appreciated the Hymer's interior lights: in my heart, I thanked them. I thought a face lift or face-lifts were still discernible though: that tightness of the cheeks over the cheekbones, the skin giving way to clusters of new unnatural wrinkles around the eyes, and, where visible between the crisp curls of auburn hair, fine copper fissures along the hairline too.

"Hey."

He wanted to draw my attention away from my rude inspection. He had something to say. To ask, it turned out.

"Are you a fan?"

I couldn't help but extend my smile.

"Are you a fan? … Really? Because you don't have to do this. I can personally make sure you get top - "

"I am not a fan," I told him, speaking up for myself

at last.

He sat back, shut his eyes. “Thank god for that.”

“What? What’s that?”

I remembered strange posts on his Facebook fan-site of middle-aged American mothers in his embrace, and the freely expressed jealousy of rival fans, internationally, from mothers all over the world, who’d never shared that embrace. I remembered all of their devotion and adoration. That madness. That female madness. Some actually lived out their lives with Manilow included as a member of their own families, in their own homes. Even if the husband were still around, going out to work early, before the family had breakfast - there he is, look at him, stopping to stare at snapshots of Barry Manilow, his rival, from *“Hello!”* magazine, magnetized on the fridge, when he goes to get some milk; and here he is glancing at framed photos of Manilow on the kitchen wall, hung there by his wife - ‘My wife, my wife,’ he says to himself, ‘I have no wife.’ He shakes his head. ‘No wife. No life.’ And when he’s gone to work, she asks her family at breakfast: What would Barry think of this weather? Such wives ask themselves things like that out loud in the morning, and ask their daughters, their sons, and each other. What would Barry think of this or that on the news? I wonder what Barry’s doing right now, they ask themselves. Do you think he’d like what I cooked for you this morning?

Aw, Mum! Please! Cut it out!

All day. Every day.

Now the real Barry Manilow sat back with his eyes shut as he had in the Range Rover after the concert, in my Hymer. There was some connection there in mood, sentiment.

“I loathe them,” he told me, eyes shut. “Despise them. Hate them.”

“What? Your fans?”

“All of them. The women and the men. But the men are just … innocent. Stupid.”

That dismissal made me think of the impatient husband in the fan herd - “When’s Mandy comin’ out?... Fuckin’ freezin’ out ’ere!” - and how we had swept away into the night without Mandy signing a single autograph, or posing for a single selfie. Too cold, he'd said. I'm too cold. "And fuck you, Jack!" from the impatient husband.

Maybe this is what I hadn't seen after the concert, what I had mistaken for post-performance fatigue. I hadn't seen this overwhelming relief within him. The 'performance', in this other sense, was over for another night. The trial of affectation had stretched him to his outer limits once more but those limits remained unbreached.

I told him frankly, "Your attitude interests me."

He didn't answer. I was about to pursue the matter in some other way, when, still without opening his eyes, he asked:

"Are you going to kill me?"

His tone was even. It was matter-of-fact. Whatever the answer, it would not draw his excitement, his tone implied.

"I think you will die tonight," I answered, in kind. "Yes. I am sure you will die tonight. Quite early this morning. Before dawn. But I do not plan to kill you myself. I shall be here for you, shall we say."

Now he opened his eyes again but did not lean forward at all. His head still rested on the back of his seat, which was higher than mine because it abutted the fridge and cupboard units between the table and the toilet-cum-shower at the back of the van.

"Shall we say," he repeated, but muttering the phrase. "So would you mind telling me why you want me to die? Would you be so kind as to explain? I mean… God…. What the *fuck*! You think you can just - "

"No!" I shut that down. "I do not intend to tell you why. Ever. If you don't know why you must die, if you cannot understand, you need to read *The Penal Colony* by Franz Kafka. That is all."

"Oh sure."

"I will lend you a copy, maybe. But first you must tell me what you meant when you said you despised and loathed your own fans, because that doesn't sound credible, and I'm interested in the truth about that."

He leant forward, braced his elbows on the table,

steadied himself.

"Doesn't sound credible," he repeated. These muttered repetitions: it was as if he had been drinking. He even wagged his scruffy head in mockery of me when he repeated that. There were plenty of heavy scents about him, but not one of them was booze. They were the mixed up perfumes and hormones of the lucky few to whom he'd granted selfie access while still in The Palladium.

"Well," he went on, as if nothing could matter less, "you better believe it, friend. I loathe them for what they are - old, misshapen, mixed up - and I loathe them for what they're doing to me. To *me*. And that's a fact."

"What are they doing to you?"

"Getting too fucking close, for starters. Ignoring protocol. Ignoring my fucking personal space. Clinging and pushing and shoving their disgusting boob-flesh and belly fat and buttocksacks against me."

"Even now? When you're eighty? That bothers you?"

He nodded. "Even now. Tonight. And I'm eighty-one, but we'll let that pass."

I couldn't help but smile again.

"I'm sure most men - "

"But I am not most men. Hence where we are now."

It seemed to me his attitude, which I put down simply to his homosexuality, to an outmoded, exalted, highfalutin, Noel Coward, Somerset Maugham smoking-jacket, Royal Ascot jockeying-for-status in a need for acceptance form of homosexuality, about how repugnant he found the proximity of his female fans, was rather harsh. Merciless. After all, it was these fans, women outnumbering men by twenty to one, who had given him everything he had, his millionairedom, his luxury home, his exotic sports cars, and who had maybe sacrificed a great deal themselves to come and see him at The London Palladium or the Utilita Arena in Newcastle or Cardiff. And I had read whining complaints from women who had longed to see him in Leeds and Glasgow but who simply could not afford it. Others wrote back to say they hadn't missed much because the concerts were largely spoiled - for some, completely ruined - by women talking all through the songs, or muttering or drooling the lines, or drunkenly singing along, even dancing on their seats and in the aisles. Mothers and daughters, sometimes, dancing together, on their seats.

"These fans have given you everything you have. You must respect that."

To which he offered that lopsided smile, turned an open palm again, and I had to wait for his answer.

"It's all a trap, man." His tone was patronizing. He gave a long sigh. You know nothing about this crazy business, he seemed to say, with his sigh.

"This is what people like you don't understand," he continued. "A trap. You know why I'm still on the road? I'm eighty-one years old and still on the road. You wanna know why?"

I shrugged. The clichéd show-biz answers - that he still loved performing, that it was in his blood, like an addiction, that he owed it to the fans and so long as they still wanted to see him he would keep on coming out here - were obviously all wrong and not worth mentioning.

"Tax and tour cycle." He patted the table with his beringed fingers. Silver and gold only. No jewels. "TTC. Tax 'n' tour cycle. There's the trap. The tax for the year I'm touring now must be paid next year, but I won't have enough to pay the bill because the tour costs are so heavy and they have to be paid up front. No tour manager will wait till the tour's done to get paid. No way. So they cancel each other out. The tour receipts are more or less spoken for to pay the loans, and the interest on those loans, don't forget, for the tour costs up front. So where's the money to pay the tax? Album sales, and what's left over from ticket sales after the tour loans are paid off. I can only keep going by touring. So it's a trap, as I said. I wanted to quit years ago."

"No shit."

"No shit. And where's the money in album sales now, when it's all streamed for nothing?"

I left a pause before pursuing this. It didn't convince me, but the down-to-earth reasoning, his complete lack of pretentiousness or self-importance, was as unexpected as it was admirable. I couldn't help warming to him. "So that's what makes you despise the fans - that bitterness, because you can't stop?"

He shook his head. "No no no … You don't get it. I can't be bothered to explain any more. Fuck it." He stared hard at me, challenging me, those blue contacts suddenly fierce, angry, in their wrinkly pits, despite the dullness of the lozenge lights.

"You go ahead and kill me, then. Go on. Now. Shoot me. I've had enough. Go ahead and shoot me. Do it."

It was my turn to sigh. But I also knew I couldn't hesitate in the face of such a challenge.

I lifted the rifle out the corner, flicked off the safety catch, and, easing the barrel across, called his bluff:

"Don't grab it," I advised. "Don't grab because my hand's on the trigger. You'll just grab at being maimed, disfigured, paraplegic. Not death. Don't grab at death. I promise it will go off."

He nodded, staying with it.

"... So lift the barrel gently and put it into your mouth ... Your skull's not tough enough to stop messing up my cabin, but anyhow … "

He pushed the barrel aside, despite my warning.

"I'm not ready… Not yet."

I left the rifle where it was but took my hand from the trigger. "Tell me, then."

"What?"

"Why you hate them."

He shook his head again, very bored by the question, but then asked, in all seriousness:

"Do you understand the concept of sublimated desire?"

"I think so."

"Then maybe you can get this after all." He took a breath. "Sophomore at Yale does a lot on sublimation - "

"Wait a minute … Yale? … You went to Yale university?" I was astonished, yet not incredulous, given the impression he'd already made.

He offered a half-smile. "Sure. I was reading psychology. Real psychology. Not pop psychology like they do these days. Then I saw Simon and Garfunkel come out of Queens and Columbia, New York City, and make their fortune by their mid-twenties, so I quit. Biggest mistake of my life."

"But you made your fortune too."

"Yeah. But at what cost? After *Mandy*, my first big hit, I tried to give it all up and go back to college but they wouldn't let me in. My tutor said, 'You made your choice. Live with it.' She was actually quite insulting. Said I looked ridiculous. My hair and everything. 'Little boy blue' she said. She laughed at me."

"You were always faking it, then. In a different way. From the very start."

He nodded. "I read the market. I saw the gap, understood the psychology, saw the kind of male star that was needed to fill the gap, and composed for that gap. Just like The Monkeys were designed to follow The Beatles. But I don't want to talk about all that now. Too painful. Back to these women, these fans. They're all mixed up, right?"

"Must be, I suppose."

"Sure. Don't think I'm insulted by that." He waved his lcft hand freely over the rifle barrel. "Most are middle-aged, some older, some much older, some ancient. But we'll leave those out. The ancient ones." He looked down, interrupting himself. "Christ. Do you have any idea how many want me to come to their funerals? Who'd have thought that was going to be part of the job? Part of *Mandy*? And they think I *should* come. Oh yes. That I *owe* it to them. That I've got nothing better to do. But the middle-aged ones …" He dry-washed his face, but then he was suddenly angry again. "Oh Christ. Oh fuck! What the fuck am I doing here? Explaining this to you. You! You're just another fuckwit with a gun! Trigger-happy Joe!"

"You were saying - "

"You're nothing better than a fucking terrorist, you know that? This is what they do. Get hold of a lump of mechanical violence and dictate. I don't like your songs so you must die. Pow! Pow! Why don't you go kill Kim Jong Un? Do something useful? Stop him trussing his people up till their spines pop out. Why not him? For his torture, his Gulags, his murders, all his crimes? Why me? For a bunch of crappy songs?"

I left a pause, patted the stock of the Browning,

pulled him back. "The middle-aged ones. You were saying."

He sighed again, but continued.

"Yeah, well, the middle-aged ones … They still have some hormones, see. But they don't want sex with their husbands any more - if they're still around. That's a given. They haven't wanted that for years. Okay. Natural. Common knowledge. Most would like sex with another man, maybe, but, either there is no one around fits the bill, or they just can't stand the physical side of it any more, or it's too complicated, too risky financially, even though desire's there waiting. Like I said, all mixed up … So instead, that desire is sublimated into this adoration - if that's the right word, in my case - See? You can't insult me about this. See that?"

"I wasn't trying to insult you."

"Whatever. That desire is sublimated into desire for a form that is unattainable, into desire that cannot be consummated, and is therefore safe, and - big bonus - " he tapped the table with his beringed fingers again - "the open expression of sexual desire is now in an acceptable form, acceptable to everyone around, that is, not just those husbands that are left, about one in twenty, like you saw, but everybody, acceptable to society, is what I mean. So everyone's happy. The women are empowered, enabled. They enjoy their desire without the obligation of consummating it with anyone. Like religious women's fetishistic desires for Christ on the cross, you know?" He had started to freewheel but now he stopped and frowned down at the Formica as he had before, and his tone became angrier, but not with me now. More embittered. "But it gets worse than that, because for these women the desire is intensified by perversion - don't get me wrong. Nothing sado-masochistic where I'm concerned. Maybe for Jesus, but not me. I just mean a perversion of the maternal instinct, nothing more than that." He looked at me seriously, wanting to convince me on this particular point. "They see me not just as sexually neutral, and totally unthreatening - I will never tear down their illusions, I will only serenade them and inflame them with my virginal songs - my appeal is also the appeal of an adoring boy or teenager, who can be hugged and cuddled, whose hand can be held. Their desires are so mixed up and unclean, so dishonest. It's such pretence, such make-believe. That's what disgusts me. The sublimated desire. They express their sexual milk, as it were, all over the little boy, the baby. These are unfulfilled people, women with undeveloped personalities. But as you said, financially I cannot walk away from them, and you're right, I can't, so that makes me hate them even more."

The insight he had into his own condition, and the prestige of his education, had struck me deeply and I warmed to him more and respected him more than I could ever have thought possible. The event had turned out to be a revelation. To me, that is. And what I was about to do to him now seemed sacrificial, as if he had to be slain to propitiate the Venus-Devil that had got inside his fans, his cult. And that made him their victim. There would be no exorcism, as was necessary, to rip out the Venus-Devil. Of course not. Impossible. It would remain intact, thriving within the cult, perhaps leading to new forms of hysteria and necrophilic idolatry once the idol was slain.

The case was hopeless but that was no excuse for letting this go on, condoning the status quo. To back off was to cop out.

"Take off your clothes."

He was still a moment, then he dipped and shook his head, scowling, cringing with revulsion at the very suggestion.

"Your fans must see you for what you are. It's the only way forward. The world must see you for what you are. Take off all your clothes."

"So that's my chance of survival? Outside? Naked? Hypothermia? Freezing to death?"

"It could be worse," I told him, touching the rifle.

"That's so undignified. You are so undignified. You are a fucking crazy whackhead and you are so fucking undignified too. You are worse than my worst fans. I hate you for this."

"Of course," I said. "Of course that's how you feel. How you see it. But it has to be this way. Undignified. To destroy the delusion you perpetuate - and so dishonestly, by your own admission. The delusion that there is any dignity, honesty, honour or talent in being Barry Manilow."

"Don't do this. This is inhuman. Please don't be such an asshole."

"I'll leave you to get undressed." I stood and picked up the rifle. "There's your dignity. You'll find that book I mentioned in the overhead cupboards. Kafka short stories. *The Penal Colony*. Leave your clothes folded on the table." I nodded to the travel clock set high in the partition dividing the living compartment from the driver's cabin, a luxury I was grateful for at that moment.

"I'll return at one-thirty," I said, leaning back to dim the lights.

"Listen," he said. A final plea, but he kept his desperation rational. "You've got this all wrong. You think they'll put me naked in the paper? Semi-naked? On the news? That's ridiculous. That's just stupid. They won't do that. Not even a sketch or likeness will appear. They'll put up my old photos from forty years ago. That's how the world works, my friend. The world you don't fucking understand, you dumbass."

I left with the rifle under my arm and locked the door behind me. The lights went out again, but he had the half-light from the toilet as before; he could read in there too, but I didn't believe he'd bother.

Without returning to the driver's cabin, I spent about ten minutes walking round the Hymer, first close by, then in larger circles, the rifle at my side, on guard, as it were …

Well, well. From Yale to Las Vegas to The London Palladium to Stonebridge Lock, Tottenham Marshes. Again, I could hear the sound of running water from the lock. No owl this time. Some broken traffic on Watermead Way, but not enough to smother the sound of the water running away in the dark. There was a light, distant chugging which could have been from a barge on the navigation channel, but was more likely a generator somewhere on the industrial estate the other side of Lockwood Reservoir.

Quarter of an hour passed and I was bored and cold.

I unlocked the Hymer warily, expecting some surprise attack, but he was there at the table as before, but naked, his clothes neatly folded in front of him. To my surprise, his nakedness was not offensive; his physique was not depressing in any way. He certainly did not look as if he were on the threshold of mortality. And now he stared at me with calm defiance. His torso reminded me of those Picasso male nudes from before the first world war. Not undignified at all. I had expected the denuded Lear - *unaccommodated man is no more but such a poor, bare, fork'd animal* - a figure unhoused, in terminal decline. But Manilow, sitting there so calmly, had kept something else about being a man, even a very old man, something strong and defiant and dignified in extremis.

At this moment I had a minor epiphany: I appreciated the show outfit he wore for what it was, now he was without it. He had folded it with very deliberate neatness on the Formica table in front of him, the bejewelled green carapace, as if inviting my appreciation and understanding of what it really was. All show outfits are fanciful, of course, but his was in a different class. It had a personal symbolism for him that I now understood, and that he was now presenting to me, folded up on the table. The outfit was a shell made from the excrescence of pure falsity, and he only wore it to work. It was his confession, lying there, hiding in plain sight.

Rain. It had been getting cold and breezy and I should have expected it, but again I was surprised. The interactions with Manilow had distracted me, made me unalert.

Quite light rain, but steady.

After removing his clothes I left him again and locked the Hymer. I set the clothes on the slippery, sloping bonnet in the rain, let another couple of minutes pass, then returned to the compartment.

I nodded for him to get up and leave.

As he stood he made a cup with both hands over his genitals, robbing himself of support, so his movement was crooked and awkward as he came to the door.

And then it happened. He had fooled me. He sprang onto me and I fell back and cracked my skull on the ground, just as the doorman had done at The Palladium, but not so hard, because the weight of Manilow was nothing, like a child. But a child with murderous intent, because he sank his teeth into my neck, trying to bite and tear at the arteries there.

Rule Four: On Attack, Bite Deep and Tear Hard at the Base of the Neck!

But he didn't have the strength in his jaws to see it through and I rolled on top of him. He made a jab with his knee which was meant for by testicles but missed and then I lashed out, catching the side of his head, and stood up with the rifle.

"Turn over."

Whimpering, defeated, he turned over, onto all fours. His hair was already laddered by the rain across his mottled pate.

"You can hear water," I told him. "Listen. Listen to it. Crawl towards it till I say. Then stand and walk towards it."

With a weary groan he crawled a few yards to the edge of the tarmac and onto the grass verge, then stopped. He tried to wipe his right hand on the grass.

"Stand and walk now. Towards the water."

Before standing, he kept trying to wipe his right hand on the grass. Dogshit.

"Fuck you!" he cried, standing up. "This is disgusting!" he cried. "HELP!" he shouted.

"Keep walking."

"You have no human dignity! Remember that!" he shouted. "No human dignity! And you understand nothing about this world!"

That was the last image I had of him, walking away, shouting, stooping to the grass to try to wipe the dogshit from his hands, then a few more steps before crying out, "*Oh God*!" as he trod in more dogshit and tried to wipe it from his feet.

"Towards the water. I put your clothes by the water. You can wash yourself there too."

I watched him walk a little further, then picked up his clothes from where they'd fallen off the bonnet, put them on the passenger seat in the cabin to dry them out, and drove away, heading for the old North Circular road.

I read about it all eighty miles away, over morning coffee in the back of the Hymer, in Margate, in *The Dreamland Car Park* off Margate Sands.

The papers were stacked on the formica table. I sat Manilow's side of the table because from there, out the side window, I had a view past the buildings to the sea. Manilow's clothes, still very damp, occupied the seat the other side, where I had sat opposite just nine hours previously. I hadn't decided what to do with his clothes, though I had some ideas.

'After the event
He wept. He promised "a new start".
I made no comment. What should I resent?'

'On Margate Sands.
I can connect
Nothing with nothing.'

I wanted to read that his body had been found at first light in Stonebridge Lock -

"Manilow overboard!"

"Manilow Kidnapped and Drowned!"

"Manilow Murdered!"

"Manilow Slain by Mad Killer!"

- to read that someone, filling up Stonebridge Lock at dawn, keen to set off up the River Lea's navigable canal in order to establish, perhaps, how far he or she could venture on a day trip, saw, after a brief blockage, Manilow's body belched through the sluice gate, and rolled over and over in a grotesque spiralling motion in the froth and scum of London's drinking water, and I wanted that symbolism reported in a wholly new and vivid -

But this is not what was reported.

There was a picture of Barry Manilow, indeed, but he was smiling warmly, wrapped in a thick blanket, wedged between a young husband and wife and their two girls, a five year-old and a seven year old, in the cramped cabin of a narrowboat. Manilow had heard their generator, seen the lights through the curtain, and knocked on the window. His hosts had been playing a game of late night rummy, sharing sandwiches and a bottle of wine, and their girls were asleep in the forrard compartment. They didn't hesitate to give Manilow a blanket and let him into their cabin. They offered him a glass of wine and something to eat but he declined. In their late twenties, they were far too young to remember Manilow. He asked them to check the internet. He tried to do it himself but his fingers were too cold to operate the mother's phone.

The young family had a naked star from the eighties in their narrowboat.

That picture, that story, was all over the front pages of the tabloids.

The focus was on the happy ending and on Manilow's heroic survival. The photograph shone with smiles, goodwill, relief, gratitude, companionship, humanity. Some broadsheets also printed a smaller picture of Manilow as a young star, inset later in the text so the contrast was not tasteless. The family had been about to begin a week's holiday navigating the canal up to the source of the river in the Chilterns, some twenty-eight miles away. Manilow not only paid for the whole round trip, he also bought them a fortnight's holiday in Disneyland, Florida. On a sadder note, every paper reported, he also said he was quitting his tour, and the country, and that he would never return to England.

There was some solace for me in that but the context, the backstory, my background story, did not lead in any report. Everyone could be sure there had been serious foul play because the driver and the doorman had already been discovered hours earlier, as soon as The Savoy raised the alarm that neither Manilow nor their driver had returned. The driver had been hospitalised, but the porter gave a description that surprised me with its lack of detail. Height, weight and age were right, as previously given by Arus, but he expanded on Arus's description only to say my face "looked weird, fake … like Andy Warhol … " I'd worn the black hat low over my eyes, so they were in shadow, and this came out in the police identikit, which included the hat, and which was just ridiculous, like something from a spaghetti western.

Manilow himself offered no further clues. He didn't

even mention that the van was left-hand drive, but since Americans drive on the right too, that may have passed him by. He also described the Hymer vaguely, as "a kind of U-Haul, or a VW camper", he wasn't sure, and he hadn't noticed the Spanish plates, or didn't mention them anyway. His description of his kidnapper confirmed the porter's estimates of the basics but he added virtually nothing about my face or clothes. "He was just a nondescript guy, a regular Joe, an ordinary kind of guy," was all he offered. Hypothermia may have affected a more detailed recall, the police said.

The stack of discarded papers grew on the Formica table, and my understanding stacked up too, paper by paper.

Barry Manilow had outsmarted me.

He knew what I wanted - I had declared openly what I wanted - and he had denied me any hint of that reward. Instead of his degradation and exposure, his loathing of his fans, and of his whole career - the hideous lie of his popular art - we had a heart-warming story of heroic survival, maybe material for another song, and the kidnapper was cast in the shadows, along with his motives, of which no mention whatever was made. From the police, not even a speculation. Perhaps this was because Manilow had so downplayed everything, shrugged off his kidnapper as "a crazy fan who wanted to run away with me, but I took a chance and escaped in the dark, while he was asleep." He concluded that I was, "Just a harmless guy who'd fallen off the rails a bit … " No mention of the rifle. Nothing in the least incriminating.

My purposes remained unknown, ignored, denied, despised - by him - and he carried on as if nothing had happened, no exposure, so the status quo had just rolled over me, crushed me.

'... just a regular Joe, an ordinary kind of guy ...'

I was nothing.

Now, in the car park at Margate Sands, very slowly, I let my head down to rest on the pillow of stacked newspapers, and closed my eyes, and allowed the disappointment to overwhelm me, to derail me … just a harmless guy ... just a regular Joe … ordinary guy …

The Dreamland Car Park has space for four hundred cars but in late September, at noon, I had the place almost to myself. The amusement park, with its Big Dipper and assorted lesser attractions, was closed behind me. Beyond the car park, from Manilow's side of the table, visible between a couple of hotels, or what looked like hotels, lay the beach, where the summer dog ban had just expired, and several pensioners were out there already, standing still as Lowry figures, leads in hand, waiting for their dogs - some hefty dogs, big-eater dogs, far stronger than their masters - waiting for their dogs to shit on the beach.

It was difficult to shrug off the melancholy of the place: English seaside towns, gulls crying over Salvation Army cornets, or worse, electric organs, xylophones, such clichés demand the melancholy mood.

Why had I come to Margate?

I closed my eyes, shook my head. *Why* had I come to Margate?

What was I doing?

These seaside towns ...

I knew why I had come to Margate. I had come to Margate for the Art.

There is the Turner Contemporary Gallery near the front, and another private gallery in town, but neither was my destination, though I did intend to visit the Turner if time allowed. The gallery I wanted was in Victoria Road. This was the space known as TKE (Tracey Karima Emin) Studios, opened in 2023, a charitable investment by Dame Tracey Emin.

The portrait artist, Alan Hawkins, started out earning his living as a carpet fitter. As a young man he was babysitting for a friend whose partner was connected in the art world. She saw some drawings he had done to idle away babysitting time, and she recognized his gifts and helped him secure a place at art school. Now he is established and exhibited, with celebrity clients to his name such as Chris

Eubanks and Princess Diana. Alan Hawkins has declared openly that Emin can neither draw nor paint. She simply cannot draw. She simply cannot paint. That is, she cannot make the pencil lines on the paper create a likeness to the object or figure before her, nor the strokes of a brush. That basic skill, from which an artist can extemporise and distort, is not in evidence in anything she has ever done. Insider powers secured a commission for her to recreate the doors of The National Portrait Gallery: every drawing in every panel shows the same rough and ready daubs and scratches at portraiture. Not one panel shows that she can draw a likeness of the human face.

To express his disgust at the commercial standing the marketplace has given Emin's 'work', for the profit of those investing, Alan Hawkins painted her naked, defecating on a Rembrandt self-portrait, with her Installation Art, *My Bed,* as background. Writing in the London Evening Standard, the late Brian Sewell dismissed Tracey Emin as utterly talentless and wrote off her installation art, her painting, sketches and sculptures as worthless rubbish.

The financiers of the art world will not allow any scratching at the varnish of their pretences, not only to protect their investments, but of equal importance, by Moos's reasoning, Rachel Allsop's reasoning, because of the Loss of Face to their own self-portraits. And Moos was absolutely right: it is the most powerful force in the world, more powerful than money itself, than the £2.5 million they paid for *My Bed*, and it always has been. Loss of Face. The 'artists' never engage in debate for fear of loss of face, but in addition, being far less articulate, knowledgeable and intelligent than critics such as Brian Sewell, as the 'creatives' they are far more vulnerable to exposure of their posturing when trying to defend themselves. Meanwhile, their financial manipulators don't have to answer in any way for the commodities in which they trade. A piece of art has no balance sheets, no accountancy firm obliged to present a set of accounts by law, no shareholders to answer to.

And yet, for all their provocation, the trasheteer millionaires and profiteers of the Art Market are mere background noise to the pitch of anger that soars through me in screaming crescendo: the reason I had to stop Tracey Emin pursuing her artistic career any further, to stop the sliding, imperceptible progress of the slagheap her art adds to, the Aberfan her art is part of, was completely different.

With a presumptuousness, an effrontery, a greed to secure her reputation that defies belief, Emin insisted - such is her power over gallery curators - that her 'work' should be exhibited in the same space as the painting of a major artist of the last century, Francis Bacon. Her reasoning was, she said, that her work had a similar sense of 'movement'. With this sleight of hand she literally put herself in the same room as an artist of genuine originality and stature, whose reputation - for works such as *Three Studies for Figures at the Base of a Crucifixion*, for his devastating self-portraits, for his portraits of his lovers, his *Study after Velázquez's Portrait of Pope Innocent X* - for art such as this, his reputation as one of the foremost talents of the last century is ungainsayable. By insisting her scratches, daubs and stabs, paint spills and dribbles go in the same room, Emin has committed an act of such gross self-aggrandisement, she has told such a bare-faced lie, it cannot go unchallenged, unjudged, unpunished. Would she ever have dared ask Francis Bacon, as he lay dying in Madrid, if she could share his exhibition space? And what would he have said to her?

Trasheteering at this level, to gain Face and save Face, has but one sentence.

Emin was scheduled to open an exhibition, a 'celebration of the work of five young female artists and sculptors', at her TSK Studio on Monday 30th Sept. The opening was at 11.30 a.m. Taking no chances, I found a place to park the Hymer some way up Victoria Road at 8.30 a.m. The height of the cab gave excellent visibility of all traffic arriving, even when cars had parked in front of me and traffic filled the street.

I had prepared a brief note which I printed inside a greetings card. I used the envelope but wrote nothing on the outside except her name and title. *To: Dame Tracey Emin.*

The message read:

A certain show outfit, not unconnected with recent unpleasantness at The London Palladium and Tottenham Marshes, has come into my possession, and I was just wondering - Would it be of use to you iconoclastically?

We could discuss at The Coffee Shed, on The Parade, at 5.30 tomorrow afternoon, or Wednesday, whichever suits.

Once you are seated on your own with a coffee and a pastry, I will bring the outfit to you.

Quite something, I promise.

The problem was how to get the envelope into her hands without being seen. I had no idea how to do this, and had decided I would just wait the event out from the van and see what opportunities arose. If none, I would drive away and rethink.

Some years ago, Tracey Emin decorated five Fiat 500 cars for sale at auction, all proceeds going to charity. The first sold for £42,000 but what the rest fetched I have no idea. At the inaugural auction she expressed a fondness for the cars: she thought they were sweet and called them her 'mouse cars'. It didn't surprise me, then, that the millionairess arrived in nothing ostentatious - a modern Mini-convertible. She was with a young woman friend with a bulging headscarf and they were slightly late so they left the car locked but with its roof down. There was now a growing queue in Victoria Road for the gallery opening. I waited nearly an hour. The queue shrank but the road was never quite deserted.

And then it began to rain, just as it had for Manilow. The exact same drizzle. The remainder of the queue bunched inside the building.

The rain would demand the closing of the car roof. I slipped out immediately, crossed the road some fifty yards up from the convertible, and as I passed, dropped the envelope onto the driver's seat, whose blue leather was already beaded with drizzle. I didn't dare look behind. Only when I reached the end of Victoria Road did I glance back: no one at all apart from two young Indian men in colourful Achkans, on the way to a wedding perhaps, squabbling, almost fighting, over a broken umbrella. I turned up the other side of the road towards the Hymer.

Just when I unlocked, the young woman from the passenger seat dashed out, without an umbrella, and without a headscarf now, and I froze in the rain at the cab door. Her hair was a high and mighty unnatural frizz. I saw her stuff my envelope into her back pocket before climbing in to close and secure the roof. Once the windows were up, she locked the Mini and hurried back, chased by quite heavy rain now.

Of course there was a risk here, and the risk multiplied now that a third person was involved. But my hunch was that this passenger would never open something that was obviously a card of some kind - presumably from a fan - that was addressed to her famous friend and dropped onto her driver's seat. Secondly, I had absolute confidence that the lure of Barry Manilow's stage outfit from his last UK performance at The London Palladium would have an artistic potential for Emin she could not resist, and that she would pursue the arrangements for the rendezvous without informing the police. Not in the first instance, anyway.

There would be no second instance.

The tide was in, the pensioners gone.

The Coffee Shed - at the end of The Parade there is also *The Wine Shed*, presumably owned by the same restaurateur - faces a pedestrian precinct with back to back benches. To the sea, most overlook a broad swathe of new concrete steps that descends directly to the water's edge, built with sea-defences in mind, and the sheltered bay of the Harbour Arm, with its colourful dinghies and toy motor craft. From the benches facing more or less into town, the view of *The Coffee Shed* and its alfresco tables is uninterrupted.

Emin is quite a tall figure and in the bulk of her blue duffle coat she looked as if she was carrying some weight. Nimbly enough, though, for someone turned sixty. Recent health problems, about which she had been very brave and open, complicated her gait only slightly if at all, but she looked weary and depressed as she settled at one of the outside tables.

Evidently the waitress did not recognize her because there was nothing exchanged between them apart from the order.

I couldn't waste time on further observation or trying to guard my approach.

Manilow's outfit, still a little damp because there had been no proper opportunity to dry it inside or outside the Hymer, was by my side in a Tesco carrier bag. Apart from the tall green boots. The boots I planned to withhold.

She was typing a message on her phone as I approached and didn't look up when I drew out the seat opposite and set down the Tesco bag. You're cool, I thought, absently. Not an expression I often use, but right then it felt right. She finished the message, slipped her phone into her handbag, then looked up.

Her face was heavily lined and her skin had that sagging grey hue of poor health, but it was still obvious she had been an attractive woman in her youth. One respected her defiant lack of make-up. In fact, her forthright honesty about many things over her career - her looks, desires, depressions, addictions, drunkenness, and so on - which her audience found so refreshing after the self-serving exclusivity of the British art closed-shop, within which everyone seemed to come from Haberdasher Aske and the Courtauld, like Brian Sewell - this honesty, still there but not so fierce any more in her brown eyes, could not go unadmired, not face to face, no matter what one's opinion of her art. And it made her look strong, despite the betrayal of her health.

The waitress delivered her order: mint tea (a bag in a tea-cup) and a Danish. I shook my head to the expectant waitress without looking up at her. When she had gone inside Emin said, stirring her tea:

"No like dark specs."

I was wearing my reactor-light glasses.

"No like bald coots. Who the fuck are you?"

There was that voice, that estuary accent, and that disrespect, which had had such appeal in her youth, the favoured accent and attitude of her generation. It was a real estuary accent in her case, because though she was born in Croydon this is where she had been brought up: Margate Sands, at the estuary of the Thames, where she had come back to do good work, even great work, perhaps, accidentally or otherwise, in providing shelter for others' art out here at her own expense.

"It doesn't matter who I am," I answered, "because I am here on behalf of someone else. A fan, shall we say. I'm just a go-between. I will not explain further so don't ask. Let's just get on with this."

She frowned and cocked her head quizzically a moment, then undid her curiosity in circles, stirring her tea.

"As you wish."

I reached down and took from the shopping bag Manilow's green embroidered jacket. Dampness darkened it in some places, particularly around the neck and under the arms, as if the sweat of his last encores remained there, but on the main body of the garment the broad daylight of The Parade served the glistening effect well.

Still looking deep into my glasses, she smiled a lips-sealed, one-sided smile, and reached across the table to feel the cloth. There was something professional in this immediate need to touch the material itself.

"Barry Manilow."

"I can guarantee authenticity, if required."

"Nah. I can believe it. I checked the pictures ... Wow."

Still feeling the cloth, she began: "So how the fuck did you - "

"Someone tried to kidnap him, maybe drown him, murder him. You may assume I don't know a lot about that or I wouldn't be here on said Parade, as it were."

She nodded and sat back again.

"Well, I know where you got it, anyway," she declared

dismissively, and with absolute confidence. Perhaps it was the front of confidence she had always put on to punch self-doubt out the ring.

I said nothing and she sipped her mint tea. She didn't touch the Danish.

"Boy George." She nodded to herself. "Gorgeous George. And his weirdo friends. That's how you got it. Coz he hates Manilow for feigning het for his fans! Hah!" Her sealed smile broadened triumphantly, warmly.

At this I took a sharp intake of breath through flared nostrils, another expression I seldom use, but here it expressed both defeat and impatience, to flatter her that I felt panicked she'd rumbled the whole business so quickly.

"We need to move on," I told her. "In this bag is Manilow's underwear, his trousers and his socks from his last performance at The London Palladium. Fact. As you will know, he has now quit the tour and left the country, and he'll never come back. So this is it. All that's left of him in the UK. I could not bring his boots because they are too big for a single bag and carrying two bags of this stuff would look ridiculous." The impression I wanted to push now was that this quirky, dangerous assignment was not at all to my taste, that I found it undignified, and the quicker we could get the business over the better. The performance I turned in here was far better, far more fluent and spontaneous, than the one I'd offered Manilow as a Savoy chauffeur.

She started to laugh.

I remained poker-faced. Another flare of the nostrils. "If you want the boots I can get them from my van. If not, well, I'll return them."

"How much?"

I shook my head. "There is no charge. These are gifts from a fan of yours. A big fan. A major fan. Shall we say, my client certainly does not need any money in return."

She replied to my shake of the head with a curt nod and a narrow-eyed, sceptical, searching look. Everyone needs or wants more money, she seemed to be thinking, and almost saying; I had the impression she might be having second thoughts. She took another sip of her tea, and turned in the chair to look at me sideways. "Shall we say …" she repeated. I thought of Manilow himself repeating that phrase of mine. Then, unexpectedly, she smiled again but more openly this time, which exposed too much of her dull teeth under her short upper lip.

"Gorgeous George," she said again. "Well well." She was almost coy. "I could tell from the note."

"Do you want the boots, or not?"

"How tall are they?"

I stood up, assuming the lead now.

"Taken together they are like a mermaid's tail. Do you want them or not?"

"Hah!" she laughed again. Manilow as a mermaid lit up her face.

"You can pay my fucking bill, then take me to 'em," she said, enjoying treating me like a nobody now, a go-between, a lackey for her friend.

I replaced the jacket carefully, obediently, in the Tesco bag and without a word went to pay for her coffee and her untouched Danish, taking the bag with me.

When I came back she was standing, ready to go. She left the Danish.

"That's for the waitress," she said. "Coz a mean fucker like you wouldn't give her a tip, I know." She looked directly into my glasses again. "Tell George that whatever I do with this, it's for him, because I love him."

For purposes that will become clear I'd practised my parallel parking with the Hymer until I could draw the van up exactly on the limit lines, forward or reverse. In the last slot I'd chosen there was nothing on the other side of the sliding door but the car park fence protecting the fairground rides, and some wind-strewn litter. Cans, plastic bottles, tissues and the inevitable condom.

"This place has gone to seed," she quipped. "Margate used to be so sexy."

I unlocked and slid back the door, then stood aside, head down, the footman, her gentleman's lackey, to allow her to step up first into the Hymer.

Manilow's boots were on the table, pointing our way, at the open door, each with its calf folded to one side. Together they looked like some winged lizard about to leap for the light of the exit. The scene was all the more dramatic because I had closed and locked down the window blinds so the only light was from the doorway and the automatic interior lozenge lights. I now turned the dimmer to full power.

"Wow," she said, in genuine awe, climbing up, approaching the boots. She set her bag on the floor, respectfully leaving the boots their uncluttered space on my table. "Heels … "

I stepped up too and stood next to her, gently toeing her bag back to the step as I did so.

She was absorbed, feeling the soft green leather of each calf fold. "Wow," she said again. "Yeah... Them's boots all right …"

"Oh! There was something else," I said. "A bracelet or watch. It's in the cab."

I left her side. She had stooped to admire the zig-zag stitching on the boots close up and didn't notice me slip her bag out with me.

Once on the tarmac, head low again, I opened my driver's door first, then gently slid the side door closed, as if, in keeping with pulling down all the interior blinds and turning up the lights and parking next to the fence, I were discreetly ensuring her privacy over our transaction. Even as I did so, before the latch went home, I realized I hadn't checked the rear doors: I couldn't remember if I'd locked them or not from the outside, with the key. Once we were on the move it wouldn't matter, and as soon as the latch went home I pressed the lock on my armrest and slipped back into the cab. I heard her shout and try the door, then bang and kick the door, but in a moment we were already at the car park exit. After a short service road seaward we were on the A28 for Canterbury, the quickest route out of town.

There was now fierce shouting and banging which wasted time she should have spent on trying to free the blinds and show her face at the window, but that wouldn't have been much good as dusk was upon us now. She must have tried the rear doors and found them locked.

Canterbury was not the destination at all. As soon as I could, I headed south east for Ramsgate and the A2 to Dover.

The noises did not subside and they were disturbing. Shouts. Screams. Crashes. She started breaking up the van. I heard her smashing what must have been a drawer, or the sides of a drawer, against the driver's partition, and when that failed she was using that weapon against the windows. Even when none of this worked, she did not let up. There were sounds of more doors and drawers being pulled out, twisted off and smashed to pieces, followed by more attacks on the partition and the windows. I had unleashed a fury inside her. It didn't seem natural, commensurate. Completely opposite to Manilow' s response. It made me think that all her life she must have felt trapped somehow. She was intent on completely destroying the Hymer, trashing it from inside.

But she was also sixty-one years old and in poor health, and after forty minutes or so she tired. I'd no idea what she'd left herself by way of furniture and comfort back there. No doubt the table had been pulled off its mounting so there would be nothing to lie down on. She could sit the rest of the journey out on the foam rubber seats, perhaps, but that was all. Our destination was *St Margaret's at Cliffe*, just outside Dover, but it was still too early to visit, so we slipped past Dover and took the M20 towards Kent Downs and doubled back at about eight o'clock.

All quiet at *St Margaret's at Cliffe* and no traffic at all on the Bay Hill to Granville Road, which broke up into a lovers' lane track. By day there are always people at the Dover Patrol Memorial, including motorhome folk, but it is forbidden to park up by the Memorial overnight and there was no other vehicle there.

Not a soul.

Nonetheless, I reduced the lights to sidelights only.

My options were either to cut the chain securing the lych gate, or cut the spiked metal chain surrounding the Memorial's vehicular path. Both gave onto the grass tops of the cliffs. In the end I was more confident my bolt cutters would deal with the lych gate chain than the low fence around the Memorial.

As soon as I stopped the Hymer the banging and shouting began again but we were some distance now from any habitation and I took my time with the cutters, working under sidelights. The chain parted easily. I pulled the gate wide.

Then I had to risk headlights to rumble through onto the grass and gently to the cliff edge for my expert parallel parking. Not quite, though: I reversed the Hymer at an acute angle, so the van was side-on to the cliff with the sliding door facing the abyss, leaving the rear wheel no more than half a metre from the edge, sealing off that end.

When I had finished the tricky parking there was silence. I turned off the engine and the lights and sat there enjoying a moment's relief and satisfaction. A complex plan, successfully executed. The updraft of the coastal wind gently rocked the van, but not in a disturbing way. I was more worried about the damage she must have done in the back. Water leaks. Gas leaks. It had been quite a journey.

With typical and admirable frankness, her latest 'work' - a series of ten lithographs, a record of her feelings throughout her recent illness - had been entitled, *A Journey towards Death*. Which now confronted one of us, or both of us, here, at the Dover Patrol Memorial.

I hoped there would be time to talk this through with her, so that she could see the significance of where she would die. The Dover Memorial, its design and construction paid for by public subscription, honours the sacrifice of some two thousand navy personnel and seafarers who lost their lives defending this stretch of coast during the first world war. Two other similar monuments were erected after the Great War, in Calais and New York. The memorial is a piece of art. Seventy-five feet high, seven storeys high, hewn from granite. It is something purposeful, honourable, built to withstand centuries of coastal winds and rains, a sculpture set there to defy all cynicism about the human spirit, and to show how art can remind us of our courage, our honour, our deeply-felt sense of right and wrong, and the creative power, not the tyrannical power, of our solidarity. It was already more than a century old and as good as new.

If she showed signs of artistic honesty equivalent to her personal honesty, signs of repentance, we might, in good faith, visit the church where the names of the two thousand are listed. There I could run my finger down to my grandfather. He had been a rake and a wastrel in his time, but in his forties he had harnessed himself to the endeavour of the Dover Patrol with his own vessel, not much more than a small gin-palace, but relatively fast, and useful therefore in getting emergency supplies out to others, and, on more than one occasion, getting the wounded back to shore. Easy enough to mock amateur heroics today, but with some personal connection of that kind it might be possible to make Emin understand the pettiness and triviality and dishonesty of offering a tent, stitched with the names of those you have fucked, to the world as Art. In the name of my grandfather, I would call her to account. If sculpture can be plain and simple, like a tent, here is sculpture, in this seven storey granite memorial, that is not pretty but it is aesthetic - it provokes feeling, excites awe, defies cynicism, on a monumental scale.

And I shall unroll all my prints and show her: Look, Here is Real Art, in Goya's black paintings, in his depiction of the two women laughing at the man, in that meanness of the human spirit, of the cruelty in the onlooker's eyes, and Here is Real Art in *The Arnolfini Portrait* by Jan van Eyck, 1434, and in his *Portrait of a Man*, and in Picasso's *Harlequin Portraits* of 1905, and, god bless the mark, in Francis Bacon's portraits - Francis Bacon! In whose company you have chosen to place yourself! Without his permission! Would you also place yourself with Jan van Eyck?

I heard her use the toilet. She should be spared any indignity. While she was in there I busied myself going through her bag for her phone and switching it off, then assembled the Browning under the interior lights of the cab. I switched off the cab lights too and depended on my phone torch. Outside, the light was adequate but made me nervous so near the cliff edge - such a puny glow against the abyss! And the gusts, the *rachas*! I pushed my driver's door back so it clicked open. Each end of the van was now blocked: the rear of the van as good as abutted the cliff edge, the driver's door behind me sealed this end. I felt behind for the sliding door lock on the armrest.

To my surprise, the sliding door opened as soon as I unlocked it and she dragged it right back, fully open. The updraft from the cliff caught the inside of the van and the whole vehicle rocked with its force. I felt the armrest rub the small of my back.

For a moment I wondered if she was going to make things easy for me, but there was no further movement. The lozenge lights from inside showed her enough: the cliff edge, tufts of grass and clover, clusters of trefoils, and the abyss.

"Oh Christ. Oh fuck."

The Hymer motorhome weighs just shy of three tonnes. I had left a margin of about one metre where I stood, at the driver's door, which narrowed in a long triangle to the far end of the sliding door, to just that half metre at the rear wheel. I had to wonder if it was safe, particularly in these coastal winds; if the rocking motion might not cause subsidence. The cliffs were only chalk. Compacted plankton skeletons, that was all.

"Oh Christ," she said again, but more softly. "Mad fuck." She stepped back from the doorway, back into the van, out of sight, muttering to herself, "Stuck with a mad fuck … "

"Save your soul!" I shouted to the wind.

She did not answer. I waited but she said nothing more.

I thought of the bits and pieces of drawers and doors she would have to hand as weapons. Protruding screws and staples. She wouldn't need much.

A minute must have passed in silence except for the noise of the gusts, those chilly, frightening updrafts.

It was becoming clear that she wasn't going to jump.

I hadn't anticipated a waiting game of this kind, where she had the clear advantage. I thought of firing a round from the Browning but knew that wouldn't do any good. A curious excitement took hold, though. There was a sense of combat here that had not existed in any of the other slayings, or attempted slayings. Emin was up to the challenge of this. She was going to play me at my own game. She knew I couldn't hang on here indefinitely. From my very limited understanding of chess I remembered the basic strategy of answering a threat with a counter-threat rather than retreating.

These thoughts were scattered by Emin's next move: she threw a broken drawer out the doorway, over the cliff. Then a cushion. Then the table top. Then some of my books. I couldn't see which ones, but all were precious to me - my books of poetry, short stories, art biographies, maps, cook books.

She stopped.

Silence again, but for the wind; and in lulls of the wind, the sea on the rocks three hundred feet below.

Then my prints! Unrolled. Unfurled. Van Eyck! Goya! Sorolla! Bacon! Torn up and scrunched up and tossed to the winds!

When the last was thrown away she called out:

"And That Is All!"

The feeling of being outsmarted returned. First Manilow, now Emin. I had no idea what she meant.

"So Come And Look!"

Her head appeared, loose haired and wild. An ageing understudy for a Macbeth witch. She stared at me, then her eyes slipped down to the rifle at my side, but showed no fear.

"I'm done here."

She said that so gently the wind took her words.

There was something like a shrug of her shoulders. She was no longer in the blue duffle coat. The heat of her destruction must have made her uncomfortable. She wore a baggy fisherman's smock over her loose trousers.

"I'm done here," she repeated more loudly. "I'm finished."

It came to me from nowhere that she wanted me to say out loud the title of her last 'work': *A Journey towards Death.* I did not say it.

She stepped down onto the lower step of the doorway. Defiance.

"Come and look!" she said again, but with less theatricality, and she came down the final step, and then she was out onto the skinny ribbon of grass I had left her at the end of the sliding door, no more than fifty centimetres between her and a crumbly ledge of plankton skeletons. She gripped the sliding door handle with her right hand. I saw her grip, white-knuckle hard when the updraft rocked the van again. Courage. Defiance. I had to admire it.

Another half-step forward and I had a clear side view into the Hymer living compartment. I took a snapshot in my mind's eye and looked back at her. She was smiling.

What kind of smile was that? Mocking? Leering? The smile of the women in Goya's black painting, laughing at the man? Some said he was masturbating.

But no. Now she was tearing up, crying. Or was that just the cold?

The interior of my camper van, my top of the range motorhome, was completely ruined. She'd been thrashing around in the back to escape some lifelong torment but I had never imagined anything like this. Apart from the lozenge lights - and some of these were obscured by torn ceiling fabric - everything had been pulled apart and smashed and twisted out of shape. I had seen, on the floor, where the table should have been, the interior clock which she had somehow prised out from the partition wall and thrown to the floor with such force its glass was smashed on the linoleum.

But beyond that, between the bulwarks, were Manilow's clothes and boots, neatly arranged, amid the chaos. The boots stood proud with their calves folded down either side again, like wings. Their pointed toes were tucked together, as if ready to dive out of the van into the abyss. All around the interior, mad, white chipboard shapes, like fierce whitecaps carrying a ship's wreckage, were scattered everywhere, strewn about on any remaining surface, some with twisted hinges or drawer rails still attached. The fridge door hung wide and loose, a smashed jaw.

But Manilow's clothes, his boots, were reverently arranged, were on display, were prominent, dominant, central.

"You have destroyed my home!" I screamed. I don't know where these words came from, but they were said in outrage. I had expected to leave this scene, if I survived it, with a comfortable motorhome, and she had scotched that fantasy. In fact, she had made me homeless again. No finca, no campervan. It was the thought of the practical problems that she had now created for my life that must have forced out that anguish.

"No," she said, in gentle denial. "No. I have not."

Silence followed her denial.

Oh God, I thought, understanding at last. Oh hell. Oh God no. She was impenetrable.

"It is called: *'The Death of Barry Manilow'*."

When she said that, I glanced again at the neatly folded green outfit that lay between the seat bulwarks, and those tall green boots about to take flight from the van, into the abyss.

The immeasurable, unsustainable weight of her delusion was upon me, three metric tonnes of it, pulling a split-haired metal cable on a rasping pulley right across my brain, which lifted the rifle by counterweight to the height of her midriff. There was no longer any point in prefatory remarks about The Dover Memorial, not with this unutterably trivial person, nor of demanding why she had insisted on sharing gallery space with Francis Bacon, no point in demanding if she would have dared to do that - move in with him! - while he was alive, back in 1992, if she would have dared to ask the dying artist if he had any objection - no matter how fine! - to her sharing his artistic space and reputation.

The immortal part of him. All that's left is bestial. And it was.

I had no words for her. There was a kind of grunt from me as I shunted forward with the rifle, casually aimed at her midriff.

But, before any god you choose, I will swear, for a moment, at that moment, I understood her, and admired her, understood her point of view, understood her 'art', though for me that would be forever a misnomer: I had a fleeting apprehension that for her, art could exist in a combination of actual events, whose coincidence defined or symbolized for a few moments in real time something momentous and evocative, and that the fleeting nature of it didn't matter to her, the absence of any creativity didn't matter, only that passing image mattered, of the empty, broken-up, luxury motorhome and the green outfit, boots neatly folded, facing the abyss, pointing into the abyss, into the coldness and darkness, the feeble interior lights aglow against the terrible coldness and darkness, a life's feeble, twinkling, paltry stardom, against the darkness, the hollowed shell of homely comfort, mobile, transitory, always on the move to escape, to outface death, but only getting closer to the cliff edge, all the success and achievement of a life added up to, against cold, stark, oblivion, beyond the sliding door, only that fleeting image of reality and truth mattered to her, in real time and space, about to finish, extinguish, go out forever.

The horror. The horror.

It was there, then, in that image.

In response to my shunt forward, she had backed up, eyes still full of tears but not crying aloud, into her acute triangle of scrappy grass and trefoils, still clinging to the sliding door handle. A stone fell, we both heard it go, heard it smash on a rock somewhere on the way down, then her left foot slipped into the new hollow, there was a fragment of a moment when her grip on the doorway took her weight, whitened further, then she pulled herself back up onto the step and into the safety of the van. She disappeared from view. I stood waiting, with my rifle. I do not know what for. Perhaps half a minute passed. The wind was gathering pace and made new howling and whistling noises, played new mad tunes on the holes, cracks and edges of the ruined interior.

I wanted somehow to tell her, before one of us died here, that I both understood and respected her now, but no words would come, and still I waited.

Eventually, I called out. "*Listen to me! Tracey Emin, listen to me!*"

But there was no response. Only fresh howls and ricochets of wind through the van.

Through the van!

I stepped forward, rifle raised, ready for ambush, until I had a complete view of the interior.

The rear door was open!

Without bothering to close the sliding door I got back into the cab, started the engine and flicked the lights on full beam. No sign. I swung the van away from the cliff in a slow arc, all the way round to point back along the cliff edge, full beam. No sign. The land was flat and barren for hundreds of metres. Just a bold concrete bench facing seaward in the dark. Nowhere to hide. Though I had been waiting like a fool, there had not been enough time for her to escape, not in her frail state of health.

I could think of only one thing. She must have gone over of her own free will, but not on my terms. Of course not. To save face. Her defiance and courage had continued, had prevailed. And they had been real tears, after all, not just eyes watering in the cold wind. Or perhaps she had been intent on fleeing, but, confused and with no light to help her, stumbling in the dark, with only the wind to guide her, she had missed her footing and fallen.

Either way, it was all over, and I had to leave.

After the gate I stopped and left her bag, intact, quite near the Memorial itself but close to the cliff edge, nestled deep in a clump of weeds, to assist enquiries.

Cheltenham was still a couple of hours away at least but I was determined to get there before breakfast, or brunch, it would be, and to move on apace. Once on the outskirts I forgot about eating and searched for an industrial estate or retail park where I could find some replacement bits and pieces: a new camping table, an air mattress, some storage boxes or similar. The toilet and shower still worked and she had left the gas system intact, but the fridge door would no longer close. A portable fridge or ice box would have to sit on the floor, in the way all the time. I cursed Emin out loud for all this inconvenience and expense. I would also have to buy a few tools to tidy up what remained of the doors and shelves. She'd left no working drawers at all. Smashed every single one.

Once I'd found Cheltenham Retail Park and bought all I needed from B&Q, I headed for the drive-through McDonald's and ate brunch in the cab while listening to the news.

Nothing yet.

From there I tracked down the bleakest, loneliest and cheapest caravan site I could find: a field of pasture on a bankrupt farm twenty miles or so north of Gloucester, with no commercial attractions at all. Virtually deserted. I parked in a corner next to a fence, as I had done in Margate, and for the first time pulled out the on-board awning. I set the camping table and chair under it, facing into the van, to give a semblance of normality while I got on with repairs.

There was actually much less I could do about fixing the interior than I had imagined. Some bits and pieces that I thought could be repaired had to be unscrewed and thrown away. Similarly some of the tools I'd bought proved useless, redundant. Things were too far gone. So the interior became just a series of holes and blanks of various sizes, all of which were damned, condemned, in darkness, hollowness, starkness. It was like living in a dovecote where all the doves had died. The gangway was now blocked by a camping fridge. I cursed Emin every time I had to step over it to get to the toilet. The only real success in my purchases was the foldaway camping table: it fitted snugly between the bulwarks, rising just a couple of inches higher than it should. The remaining foam rubber seat and a couple of bright olive cushions I'd bought completed the only place where I could sit and read and eat and think and plan. Driver's cabin was still best for sleep.

During the evening I began writing my speech for the Booker Prize winning novelist, Bernadine Evaristo, who at that time was also the President of The Royal Society of Literature. She was at Hay-on-Wye on a 'creative retreat', a freebie for accepting an invitation for the 2025 Hay-on-Wye Literary Festival in late May, where she would give a keynote address. This is the festival Bill Clinton called "Woodstock for the mind". The Chair of the Royal Society of Literature, Daljit Nagra, was on the same retreat, on the same terms.

It took me all the following day and the day after to finish the speech, which came in at more than two thousand five hundred words. That was far too long for the attention span of the people at the Festival, but it was never my intention that she would deliver it there. That was eight months away and no one would take any notice even if I found a way of blackmailing her to do it. It had taken me precious days to write, revise and rewrite, and I felt it was as concise now as I could make it. Three whole days, in fact, at the overgrown campsite, labouring away in the back of the Hymer and giving myself backache on the crummy cushions from B&Q.

Not so much from Evaristo's internet footprint as from Daljit Nagra's, I was able to trace their hideaway. I spied Nagra unloading shopping at a pair of 'glamping safari tents' called "*By the Wye...*", inverted commas included. They were two newish, broad, permanent wooden structures overlooking the river. The only canvas aspect was the roof. Stained poles supported their verandas on hefty joists. From Negra's Instagram the wooden theme continued inside, with the double bed jokily made into a four-poster with bent but sturdy looking branches, and a cloth bound canopy of leafy design. What must have been an en suite lay behind a tongue & groove wooden cabinet in the corner.

"Cheers!" said Daljit in one of his selfies, sitting on his double bed, glass of red in hand. "Not bad. Gratis for a couple of weeks! Gonna get some serious work done!" Serious work, but not digging roads. And the wine was probably blackcurrant because I believe he's tee-total.

Cheers, Daljit, I replied aloud. I will be right with you.

But first, my boat. My Viking drakkar.

The Wye is not really a navigable river, not in the commercial sense. A thousand years ago they used it for transporting iron rods for the construction of King Ethelred's ships, that kind of thing, but the boats they used must have been flat-bottomed barges or similar. Today, at its deepest, it's only about three metres, and it's too narrow, and with far too many natural stoney shallows, for even the lightest sail-boats. So punts or rowing boats with light outboards are the only usable craft.

Walks down the old towpaths at the riverside gave a measure of the rental fleets. Their vessels all bore sign-painted or stencilled trade-names: *Black Mountain Expeditions; Wye HireCraft; WyeCanoeWhenYouCanKayak.com*, and so on. The *HireCraft* kayaks looked the most likely to fit inside the Hymer, but nothing available seemed quite right for the impression I wanted to make. They were all too heavy. They were robustly built for renting out year after year, not for what I had in mind.

In the end, I went online and found a rigid double Kayak fit for purpose. It cost just shy of £500 and I had to drive into Hereford to buy it.

On the journey I caught a news bite on the radio:

'Missing artist, Dame Tracey Emin ...'

The report covered her absence from the ongoing exhibition in Margate from last Wednesday, at her TKE Studios, nothing else of substance. From the phrasing it was clear the full story had broken earlier and I'd missed it. A spokesperson from the gallery - I matched her with the woman with big hair in the Mini - was reassuring, and seized the opportunity for some repetitive panegyric: Tracey was very much her own unique woman and she was very strong; Tracey had resources to do what she pleased; Tracey was only too capable of looking after herself; artists had to be by themselves sometimes and we should respect that .... There was something about her tone that suggested she was in on something, as Emin's co-conspirator, as it were, or she was trying to appear closer to the star than she really was, and prolonging her moment in the limelight. She went on to cite a precedent when Emin had skipped an interview and taken herself off on holiday to the Bahamas instead. A media snub.

Her agent, Jay Jopling, sounded more anxious, and called for Dame Tracey to get in touch as soon as she felt ready.

Early days.

As soon as I saw the kayak in the store I knew it was the right thing. To be honest, I fell in love with it. I had been worried the seating bays would not be big enough but they were more than adequate for my purposes. A pale beige model was the cheapest, discounted 10% because shop-soiled. At 3.5 metres it would sit up in the back of the Hymer at an angle, but it would fit. Suddenly it didn't matter that so many of the interior fittings, which might have blocked this plan, were no longer there. The kayak was around 30 kgs - just about liftable - but impossible for me to manoeuvre once lifted, so I used the store assistants to get it over to the van but dismissed them before opening the doors, and kept exchanges to a minimum. I lifted the bow inside, slid it in from there and propped it up crosswise.

What I had in mind, but as yet had only loose ideas about how to manage, was something along Manilow lines. There had to be connections, no matter how watery and slippery. I had entangled myself in loose ends. Following Manilow's subterfuge, I felt a need to put in place the connections myself which would straighten everything out, draw the lines tight between the graffiti slayings and Barry Manilow and bring about meaning, purpose, and, at last, investigation and publicity. It was time to wind things up, or rather to stop them unravelling so much. Now I wanted to meet my very own D.I. Know-All, my hardback toughie detective, in the flesh, face to face, my once-bitten-twice-shy whisky-driven Gorbals Scot, or my beery sleazy smokey Scouse, or my sly and sexy Cockney, or my arch and artful Taff, and have it out with him or her, once and for all, raincoats off.

From the dates on Daljit's Instagram posts they were already in their second week of the retreat.

It was the President's habit to take her coffee onto the veranda at about 8.00 a.m. She would either sit down on the steps, clasping the cup on her knees with both hands for warmth, or she would stand leaning on the veranda railing, staring upstream, as if awaiting some imaginary steamer of inspiration. The three times I saw her at this hour she wore loose fitting, modest clothes. Nothing colourful.

The regularity of her habits and appearance suggested self-discipline. From all I had read about her, it would be true to character: self-disciplined, not prone to excesses of any kind, no self-indulgence, and neither pompous nor pretentious in any way. Thoroughly likable, in fact. She never ate anything with her coffee. I watched her from the woodland on the opposite bank. Even though the Wye is a good forty metres wide at this point, I hooked into the woodland and used binoculars. She might have spotted me on the towpath the first time but anyone on my side of the river would stop to look across here because the glamping cabins were so new and of such striking design. Hay-on-Wye itself is a couple of kilometres downstream. Further upstream from the cabins, another two kilometres, on their side of a sharp bend, is a tourist attraction called *The Warren*: a place to stop and stare, with river beaches from their bank. At this time of year only the hardiest use it. The advantage to me was that at this bend the road passed fairly close to the opposite bank and I had found a way down through the trees, brambles and bushes to the water.

On the Wednesday of their second week, at dawn, I parked at the very edge of the roadside, along from the posts forbidding such parking. I opened up the back, had a last look around, then dragged the kayak out to the tipping point. Before levering it any further, I lay a blanket down on the tarmac. I knew I could just about lift it off the road but that was all, so I drew the stern down onto the blanket, then lifted the bow up on the painter, swung it out the van and dragged the kayak across the blanket into the roadside foliage. Once the hull was resting on the dewy undergrowth it was easy to slide it the twenty metres or so to the bank.

The denser foliage there was deceptive. I tested it with my brand new yellow paddle and discovered the solid looking thatch curling in at the bank gave way. The bank was only firm a yard in from the water's edge. This creeper material I turned to my advantage because a couple of yards back it made an ideal hiding place for the kayak. It was so easy to cover it up I squashed a packet of tissues into a tree hole to mark the spot.

There had been two deaths already in the Wye in 2024. One had been a tragic suicide: a middle-aged man suffering from depression had left home one morning in February and was only discovered months later, a couple of miles downstream from where his wife said he had gone for a walk. His body was discovered under flood debris by a police dog. The other death was a misadventure. An unfortunate youth, only nineteen years old, had drowned at the bridge. With a friend he'd come down from the towpath at the bridge to the water's edge. According to the friend, he had missed his footing on the muddy bank. The water is very fast there, where the arches narrow the waterway. The coroner reported that there was alcohol and evidence of cocaine in his blood but the cause of death was definitely drowning. These deaths are of interest because there is a common denominator not mentioned at either inquest, perhaps because it goes without saying. Even at the height of summer the river water, coming down from the Welsh mountains, is cold - maybe sixteen degrees maximum. Now we are in October the water temperature will not be more than twelve degrees. Unless one's body is accustomed to temperatures that low the shock to the system of being immersed, and fully clothed too, would be too much for most hearts, and given the speed and currents of the water most victims would die of seizure or drowning in a few minutes.

When the morning turned out clear on Thursday, with only three days of their retreat left, I parked at the official car park for The Warren and made my way along the roadside by foot, all equipment in a haversack slung over one shoulder. I had no difficulty remembering the spot where I had slipped through and hidden the kayak. No need for the tissues, but I retrieved them for any tears later.

The tools I bought for repairs to the Hymer had come in useful for modifications. I'd screwed a cupboard hinge onto the left side of the deck and attached a bracket strong enough to support a clamp for my mobile. Because the hinge locked on itself when open the mobile clamp was steadied by its own weight when upright, making a secure fixing looking forrard. In the haversack was the Browning in its separate parts, a paperback copy of Evaristo's Booker prize winning novel *Girl, Woman, Other*, and, on top of my speech, nestled in a bag in the hollow of a new hat, were two fresh croissants, both for madam President.

Once in the water, the bow of the kayak buoyed up and I felt the tug of the river. I didn't dare put the haversack in the front seat cavity, though that was what I'd planned and the obvious thing to do. Instead, I slung it over my shoulder again. The rear seat, my seat, was still on terra firma. I didn't believe I was strong enough to push off with the paddle from there and shunted the kayak further into the river, but had to correct that immediately because the bow twisted downstream and I hadn't the leverage on the bank to hold it straight.

Conclusion: a man approaching seventy years of age had to get aboard on dry land first, and then see what his feeble strength could accomplish from there.

Once settled in the rear seat well, still with the haversack over my shoulder, I tried to push off with the paddle, but its sharp yellow blade sank into the foliage and offered no purchase at all. At this point I had another of those crises and screwed my eyes tight shut in overwhelming anguish -

What was I doing?

What was I doing?

Still with eyes tight shut, and ignoring the blackflies that tried to nest in my ear, my nose, or drink from my eyes, flies that had been a torment in every shadow of my towpath walks, and that had wrecked the peace of my early morning espionage in the woodland, still with eyes tight shut, sitting stiff in the rear of the new kayak, I invoked my Hatred of Daljit Nagra to give me strength, recalling the effrontery of his patronizing response to his Fellows' protests against his policies - "*Please Resist and Desist!*" - and that collective insult of describing his Fellows as being all of "the same tribe"; and when he'd said they had to give up judging greatness by the criteria of T.S.Eliot and George Eliot, and that he wanted the Royal Society of Literature to be "for everyone", meaning he wanted it to be for those like him, someone who wrote amusing poems about grocers in immigrant communities, not *Prufrock and Other Observations, The Waste Land* or *Four Quartets*; or someone else like him who wrote novels called *The Hate You Give* or *My Mate Shofiq* or *Hello Mum,* not *Middlemarch, Silas Marner* and *The Mill on the Floss*.

But brought together in one lump, all that hate didn't float the boat. It anchored it.

Then I thought of *Richard Booth's Bookshop*, that magnificent achievement in Hay-on-Wye, the legacy of an extraordinary man, with storey after storey of hallowed wooden shelves dedicated to real literature, and without further doubt I shunted my weight forward in the kayak and the vessel responded willingly beneath me. With the next shunt it slid at least a foot forward into the water. My weight held the kayak at a steady right angle to the bank and the clear, cold water rushed over the bow, covering the painter's chrome eye at the end there and christening and blessing my boat, my enterprise and ingenuity, my whole endeavour.

And when I thrust my virgin yellow paddle into the bank this time the river took us eagerly, and we were on our way downstream.

What is it that creates such a sudden sense of calm and well-being when drifting downstream, so close to the water, in the patchy sunlight?

Is it just detachment from worldly anxieties left on the bank? The horrid black flies that nest in one's concentration?

No.

No it is not.

Before the final of the Van Cliburn piano competition, the seventeen year old Korean Yunchan Lim, who won the competition in 2022, the youngest winner ever, spent time between practice sessions walking in the surrounding parks: he felt the great composers, whose music he was about to play, took their inspiration from nature, or were at least influenced by nature in some indefinable way. It was not a belief he tried to explain any further. To do so would be to abstract and theorise about something that was ineffable, just as the flight of a bird or the song of a bird while he was walking might strike him as wonderful or beautiful, without his feeling any need to explain what was wonderful or beautiful about it. He sensed a connection between nature and the music of Rachmaninov and Liszt that influenced how he played their music. Similarly, when an urbanite is struck by a landscape or waterscape, paintings of places he has never seen before, he is struck because those images resonate with images in the mind already there, images in the subconscious that are part of our ancestry, just as we have ancestral feelings about the dark, a fear of certain sounds, such as a growl or sniff or footstep behind or below, or feelings of awe before a vast and terrible black mountain, or a sense of tranquility before the openness and space of a lake-filled valley.

And this river, this river to me now, away from the insect life of the bank and the restlessness of my plans, and thoughts of the progress I have made so far, nagging and distracting thoughts about what to do with Manilow's outfit and his boots that are still there, in the back of the Hymer, and the involuntary memories that flow from there - Stonebridge Lock, the young family on holiday, their Disneyland gift from Manilow, Manilow quitting his tour; the drive out to Margate and the appointment at *The Coffee Shed* with Dame Tracey Emin, and the trip to The Dover Memorial - this river to me now, with its quick ripples and wavelets, its magnificent breadth, brings to mind the lines from Wordsworth I have prepared for the President: *Lines Composed a Few Miles above Tintern Abbey, On Revisiting the Banks of the Wye during a Tour. July 13, 1798*:

.... that blessed mood,
In which the burthen of the mystery,
In which the heavy and the weary weight
Of all this unintelligible world,
Is lightened:—that serene and blessed mood,
In which the affections gently lead us on,—
Until, the breath of this corporeal frame
And even the motion of our human blood
Almost suspended, we are laid asleep
In body, and become a living soul:
While with an eye made quiet by the power
Of harmony, and the deep power of joy,
We see into the life of things.
If this
Be but a vain belief, yet, oh! how oft—
In darkness and amid the many shapes
Of joyless daylight; when the fretful stir
Unprofitable, and the fever of the world,
Have hung upon the beatings of my heart—
How oft, in spirit, have I turned to thee,
O sylvan Wye! thou wanderer thro' the woods,
How often has my spirit turned to thee!

I have to persuade them this is something they have missed, this transcendence nature offers into the sublime, away from "the fretful stir unprofitable" and towards the inexplicable mystery, the "seeing into the life of things", which lies beyond the scope of their frustrated, angry, bitter themes. Why have so many artists, since the 18th century, and some much before then, why have so many talented people painted this scene: Hatton, Hearnes, Samuel Baker, Thomas Girtin and David Cox, and the great but eclipsed Richard Wilson, who painted Hay-on-Wye about twenty years before Wordsworth's Tour:

Ruskin wrote that 'with Richard Wilson the history of sincere landscape art founded on a meditative love of nature begins in England'.

The ripples, wavelets and currents gently led the affections on towards the sense of the sublime in this beautiful place. I was early and spent some pleasant minutes tacking as far as I could from bank to bank, never too close to the stony shallows. The truth was, I had no appetite for what had to be done, for more roles, charades, chicanery and death, and yet this beautiful place did nothing but compound purpose and resolve.

The glamping lodges came into view on the starboard bank, and before them the short landing with steps to the water, made in the same style as the lodges themselves, with stout timber posts and joists treated with deep ochre preservative. I checked the time: 07.52. Enough time to moor the kayak at the landing and prepare myself physically and mentally.

Once moored, such preparations included taking from the haversack - still perfectly dry - the croissants, and the hat in which they'd nestled. Unfolded, the hat was broad rimmed and similar in style to the one I had worn for entering the stage door of The Palladium, but this hat was a dark green Tilley Endurable, the expensive Canadian brand meant for sailing and the great outdoors. It is the kind of hat popular with bourgeois elderly men self-conscious about their baldness and their age but still concerned about their attractiveness, for whom the Tilley is a symbol of a carefree challenge to one and all.

Thus the hat was a stage prop: I had to dress my way into the role I had chosen here, which had pretences of eccentricity and erudition, and an irrepressible tendency to show off in a mock-theatrical way. The Tilley's new greenness and white seams also brought out the whiteness of my hair rather than hid my phony albinism, and this too is what I wanted - to have it both ways - because if I pretended to be albino now, I not only made the connection with Arthur Spencer Harris's description of me, I offered an identity that could be cast off as soon as I cast off the empty kayak after the event, just with some hair dye and an Andalucian tan. *The Albino Alibi* might serve as a title for some professional crime writer someday, for his or her fictional account of all I've achieved and its consequences.

Bring on that day.

My reactor-light glasses completed the effect.

08.02.

When I heard her door open I climbed with nervous tread up the new wooden steps to the landing.

"Morning, Madame la Présidente!" I hailed, hail-fellow-well-met indeed, reaching for the newel at the top of the steps, my face turning up to her all a-wrinkle with warm smiles beneath my new hat and my darkened glasses.

She was dressed in a white collarless blouse beneath a rugged jumper, and some loose fitting jeans. With a light coat over the top, this would be the perfect outfit for the kayak. Her wild hair needed a ribbon or clasp but that was all.

She came to the veranda railing, leant there and scowled down, coffee in hand. Her head retracted. She was bemused, but not hostile. Not yet.

"And who the fuck are you?" she said, and laughed. How white and clean her teeth looked in that strong jaw.

I bowed for a moment. "Allow me to introduce myself, Madame la Présidente - "

"Cut that. Fucksake."

"Very well, very well …" but I still swept another humble bow, "I hail from the basement of Richard Booth's Bookshop, from the Humour, Westerns, Science Fiction and Horror sections, and I have come to escort you to a surprise coffee morning held in *your* honour - " I risked one more small bow - "at which we have a collection of *your* titles for *you* to sign, to sell and make yourself a handsome profit. A very handsome profit, given the crowds already assembled!"

"Sorry but I can't talk to people in dark glasses. Bête noire. Can you take them off? Please?"

"Can't oblige, I'm afraid. Medical condition."

"Oh, I see … Of course. Sorry."

"No problem." I smiled. "Used to all that. Hence the basement in the Horror section rather than classics upstairs - we ghouls love the dark, you know!"

She frowned, let that pass. "Book signing? No one said."

"No need to be so sceptical." I couldn't help a touch of reproach because to my mind she was being so ungracious. "The queues extend all the way downstairs from First Floor Literature, Poetry, Classics and Plays and spill into Lion Street. I am your gondolier for the day, as it were, and in my trusty kayak - " I gestured to the landing - "we can be there in about eight minutes. Hordes of fans await you at Hay-on-Wye quay to escort you to the bookshop. It is the perfect morning for one to be out on the water, is it not?

Don't you think? And - " I held up the bag of croissants - "I have here a delightful pair of croissants fresh from the Hay Bakers this very morning! Both are for you to consume on your *bon voyage*!"

I had caught the tone exactly by the end, and phrases such as 'trusty kayak' and 'delightful pair' kept up the air of hail-fellow-well-met innocence; in England these days, 'delightful pair' could only be collocated with legs, breasts or 'tits'; and 'to consume' rather than to eat, with the French to finish, would surely convince her I worked in a bookshop. My moment of reproach would be glanced over, I was sure.

She started to shake her head, but smiled at the same time. "I am very busy today!" she declared. "Very busy indeed! I don't want to lose my thread, do I?"

A horrible echo came back to me in her voice. It was similar, that estuary accent, to the voice of the late Dame Tracey Emin.

I over-shrugged my shoulders, and then shrugged them again but kept them hunched in abject apology, and smiled back at her, and held the smile fast.

Sunglasses, hat, smile, everything was trained, concentrated on this pivotal moment of deception.

"They told me it would be okay." I shook my head, hung my head. "I am so sorry to have disturbed your concentration."

I turned back to the landing. I had time for two steps.

"Wait."

I looked back, but did not turn back.

"Who's they?"

Then I did turn and retrace my steps, and with gusto.

"The Festival! The organisers! Rache Allsop! Art Harris! They said it would be a lovely surprise for you. So we arranged everything at Dicky Booth's. You do know Richard Booth's Bookshop, I take it?"

She shook her head.

"Oh! You *must* come then! You simply must come, Madame la Présidente! It's the biggest bookshop in Herefordshire and Richard Booth was the man who started the whole secondhand and antiquarian book trade here. He was the one! Amazing guy! A micronationalist, you know?

Declared himself King of Hay-on-Wye! The whole Festival started with Richard Booth, OBE!"

She seemed to be weighing things up now.

I put my hands together as if in prayer, the bag of croissants dangling below, and crumpled my face in what I imagined was a humorous exaggeration of Uriah Heep humility.

"Pretty please?"

"How long will all this take?"

"I promise you'll be back here by eleven. By car. Kayak's not much fun rowing upstream, and I ain't that fast neither! Back by eleven I promise I promise I promise. Please please *please* come! Pretty Please? … There are so many fans waiting to see you and share the surprise."

She closed her eyes for a moment. "So … we go by boat?"

"Kayak! It will be beautiful! Just ten minutes down the river. What could be finer on a morn like this? You'll be queen of the Wye, arriving in style! You'll hear them all clapping and cheering when we come into sight, just as we used to at the boat race!"

By this time, I must admit, I was beginning to stifle an irritation inside that she should be so incredibly unsporting.

"Okay," she said at last. "I'll get a coat. And I need the toilet."

"Not big topes, one hopes!"

"What?"

"Nothing!"

I too needed the toilet but there was no time to ask and I was confident I could hold on. I had drunk very little the night before and only half a cup of tea in the Hymer this morning.

When she returned she was in a new, blue puffer jacket, zipped up to the throat. A top-of-the range version of the tatty garment poor Loner had worn before meeting his own watery oblivion.

She didn't have a handbag but she was carrying her coffee in one of those capped thermos beakers.

"Can't start the day without it. Coffee addict."

"Great idea!" I said. "The kayak has cup holders too!

High lux!"

People who say they are 'coffee addicts' invariably own at least one cat.

"You have a cat, perchance?"

"Not here. Why?"

"Oh, I just thought you might have. No matter. Love cats, me."

"Best not bring my phone, right?"

"Absolutely right! No purse, no phone, no need," I said, turning back towards the landing. "Rache and Art took care of everything. No point in risking anything getting wet, though I personally guarantee dry passage!"

More innocence of English innuendo.

I had already started down the landing steps with the bag of croissants.

"I'm going to hold her steady while you get into the front seat," I told her over my shoulder; and as I crouched on the last step, I added: "Then I'll slide her forrard and get in myself ..."

"Beige!" she said, and laughed. "Any colour but beige!"

Oh! … Oh God!

Oh why had I gone cut-price, shop-soiled - such a false economy! How it bit me now.

She leant down and installed her coffee in the cup holder. "First things first," she said, and she laughed, but not nervously at all; she was warming to the whole surprise at last. The grip of her fancy baseball boots, not trainers, cut low and tight, served her well as she got aboard. I handed her the bag of croissants and she looked inside.

"Noice!"

She was definitely warming up now, but I hoped there wouldn't be too many more words like that.

"The buttery best, I promise!"

And suddenly there she was: the President of the Royal Society of Literature of the United Kingdom, in the front of my kayak, with coffee and croissants to boot.

I untied and eased the kayak along until my seat came parallel with the step. Keeping hold of the landing post, I slipped in next to the haversack, which I then placed between my legs. I had stowed my shiny yellow paddle at the edge of the steps and now I slid it into the water until I could take it by the central handle. That manoeuvre splashed her a little, and the croissant bag, and I saw her shiver and suspected she winced, though I could no longer see her face.

So much for my guarantee, I thought she would say, but she didn't, to her credit.

As soon as I let go we were into the current. No need to push off.

With the paddle dipped in portside I guided us gently into the quicker water mid-stream.

Only two kilometres separated us from the town. We were already out of earshot of the glamping lodges.

After about one third of the voyage, on the starboard side, there was a narrow inlet where a stream met the river. This was my target and I had to be careful not to miss it. One chance only.

"It *is* beautiful!" she declared, really quite elated now. "You were right!"

"So glad you're enjoying it," I replied. "Don't forget your croissants! And your coffee!"

"Yeah!" she called back, and laughed. "High lux indeed!"

For the next few minutes we maintained human silence and enjoyed the sounds of the wavelets against the kayak hull, the birdsong, the sightings of moorhens, and even a grebe in the deeper, darker, slower water to portside. When the inlet came into view, I dipped the paddle to starboard and steered us gently towards it. The change in direction was very slow and she didn't seem to notice what was going on until the kayak started passing through the long stringy weed ten metres or so from the bank.

"Oi! … Is that the right noise? *Oi*?"

"It'll do, ma'm!"

"We're getting too close to the side bit. The bank thingy."

"It's okay. Don't worry."

"What're we doing?"

The inlet might once have had a sluice arrangement or been a sewage outlet. At its entrance were two stone plinths to support a weighty apparatus long since gone but whose sockets were still sunk into the inner faces, with long beards of rust under their iron mouths. The plinths rose to four feet above the waterline, making it impossible to get out here, unless you forced your way against the current of the incoming stream to find a place where the bank was climbable. Each plinth had an ancient rusted mooring ring on the outside face.

"What're we doing?" she repeated, trying to twist around.

I didn't answer.

She was still eating the croissants. "We can't get out here, can we? Or do a couple of toughies like you bring a rope ladder?" She laughed when she asked that, to show she intended no offence.

How civil.

I had already moored the kayak to the ring on the right hand plinth. The bow was pushed out a couple of feet from the second plinth by the current joining the Wye. In seconds I had the Browning assembled.

I poked her gently in the back.

"Oi!"

She laughed again, still eating, still understanding nothing.

"Watch who you're sticking your oar into!"

"Exactly," I began, but faltered. Her laughter and good humour undid me. Shattered my resolve. "You need," I told her, through locked jaws, "to turn around in your seat to face me, but no sudden movements or you'll take a bullet through your kidneys."

She jerked about, making the kayak lurch, and caught sight of the barrel.

"What the fuck."

Neither question nor exclamation.

"Turn around carefully to face me. Any wild movement and that will be the end of you. You'll collapse over the side, spewing your lifeblood into the freezing river. Do as I say."

She was already turning about carefully while I spoke.

Good. Obedience.

"Ohgod,"shesaid,breathily."WhatthefuckhaveIdone … what the fuck have I done." Again, neither questions nor exclamations.

"In order to keep a finger on the trigger all the time, I'm doing everything single-handed. That makes every move very slow and dangerous, given the movements of this boat, so just stay still."

From the haversack I retrieved my speech, rolled in a polythene envelope, and leant forward with it in my left hand. After a moment's uncertainty, she leant forward in turn and took it from me. She looked quite pale now, but also a little ridiculous, sitting there in the kayak the wrong way round, with a flake of pastry on the collar of her blue jacket, in front of my gleaming rifle. The sun had come out fully and had a good run before the next clouds.

"You are going to read a speech and I am going to record it. You have a few moments to prepare while I set up the camera."

The bracket for the camera was a spring fit. Left-handedly, I had to force my mobile between its jaws and then wriggle the camera into the position I had marked on the side of my phone.

She had already removed my speech and trapped the polythene envelope under her thigh.

She was still pale, or even paler, perhaps, and she was shaking her head in disbelief as she read the first page. "What the hell? ... What's this shit?"

"It's not shit," I replied testily. "It took two days and nights to write and it's not shit."

"It's still shit. Pompous, opinionated shit. Rationalised prejudice."

"Keep reading to the end. I don't want you to start until you know how it ends."

"What if I refuse?"

The camera was fixed now and I had both hands free. I lifted the Browning and took a loose aim at her chest.

"Then it ends for you here."

She frowned, more perplexed than afraid. "What's the matter with you, old man? … I mean, can't we talk? You on something?"

"Read on. You will find out soon enough what is the matter with me."

I set down the faithful, all-powerful Browning.

As she read, she silently moved her lips; she frowned; she shook her head again incredulously; once or twice there was an incipient smile that accompanied that shake of the head. I was unsure whether I liked that or not.

"It is a long speech," I admitted. "More than two thousand words. Take your time. Get it right. Take note of the instructions in brackets for emphasis, and the directions for gestures."

While she read, I listened to the stream water lapping the bow, pushing the kayak out until the current of the Wye had its way and pushed it back.

When she had finished - I think she skip-read some parts - she looked up.

"This is all so scary," she said sincerely. "But somchow, you are not. You are not scary at all. You're just a flophead. An old fart in a green hat."

"I am going to recite some poetry to you now. I know it by heart. It is from Wordsworth's *Lines Composed a Few Miles above Tintern Abbey, On Revisiting the Banks of the Wye during a Tour. July 13, 1798.*"

"Please don't."

"Relax and enjoy."

"You've got the wrong girl, old man. Billy Wordsyworthy's just another dead whitey from the patriarchal hegemony - "

"NO!"

Such talk incensed me so!

"Shut it! You stupid *bitch*!" I shouted at her, beyond all patience, losing control. "And *listen*... Now you've disturbed me and I must recompose myself."

She said no more. My loss of control had been real enough but I gained from that: I wanted her to have the impression my balance was as unstable as my boat.

After a couple of deep breaths, pre-performance breaths, I recited:

".... that blessed mood,

She laughed briefly but I carried on, louder, overriding her laughter.

In which the burthen of the mystery,
In which the heavy and the weary weight
Of all this unintelligible world,
Is lightened:—that serene and blessed mood,
In which the affections gently lead us on,—
Until, the breath of this corporeal frame
And even the motion of our human blood
Almost suspended, we are laid asleep
In body, and become a living soul:
While with an eye made quiet by the power
Of harmony, and the deep power of joy,
We see into the life of things."

"Bravo."

"That was not the end. Just one stanza. There's one more."

She sighed. "Ah well. If you must."

"If this
Be but a vain belief, yet, oh! how oft—
In darkness and amid the many shapes
Of joyless daylight; when the fretful stir
Unprofitable, and the fever of the world,
Have hung upon the beatings of my heart—
How oft, in spirit, have I turned to thee,
O sylvan Wye! thou wanderer thro' the woods,
How often has my spirit turned to thee!"

"Now," I began. "What do you think that is all about?"

"Pantheism. God in Nature. God is Nature. A clapped out, stupid, out-of-date belief. But I'm beginning to see where you're coming from. In your fancy green hat.

Which doesn't hide your albino hair, by the bye."

"You'll be good enough to leave my affliction out of this. Before you read, take a moment to think on 'that blessed mood'."

I started the camera.

"Your turn."

She too took a deep breath. She closed her eyes. When she opened them again she looked directly into my dark glasses.

"This'll never work, you know. Won't achieve anything at *la société*."

"My ambitions are somewhat larger."

"Somewhat larger. Oh really. How sweet. How cool."

"Let's get it over with."

She looked down at the pages, pouted, shrugged and began.

"Salutations! Thanks to sponsors, etcetera.

"Hullo all. Everyone. And I mean Everyone. Inclusion! Great to be here today at this most famous, world famous, world class, literary festival. My speech for you today has a theme, and it comes from something Daljit Nagra, Chair of The Royal Society of Literature said last year:

"He said: 'We can't just judge everything by the criteria of T.S.Eliot and George Eliot any more.'

"I say to you here, today, everybody, no exceptions, I hate Daljit for saying that because it's bullshit.

"We can and we must continue to judge the literature of our nation by the criteria of T.S.Eliot and George Eliot, and others of their distinction, because they constitute an elite. Daljit and many like him, and many of you here at this Festival, no doubt, confuse elites with elitism. Elitism is a pipe-dream. Elitism says we should be governed by those with the most talent and education, and maybe the most money too. But it turns out those with talent and education don't want to govern anybody - they find the rest of us so boring - and that some of the richest might want to extend the power they already have over us - tiresome tyrants

and megalomaniacs that they are, whose psychoses repeat throughout history, whose baggage we all end up carrying, the shameful stuff on the carousel no one goes near, even if it's hiding one's own bag - "

She stopped. "I like that bit. Well done."

"It embarrasses me now, hearing you say it aloud. But too late to edit. That was always a risk."

"Don't be so hard on yourself. At least you tried."

"Carry on."

"There's so fucking much of it! Get to the fucking point!" She flapped the pages. "YouTube? For the great debate?"

"That's my business. Get on with it."

She flapped the pages more violently but gave in.

"Listen everyone - I declare to you, as President of the Royal Society of Literature, that Elites are Good! Elites are Natural! They are meritocracy's great gift to us. Becoming a Fellow of the Royal Society is recognition that you are an elite artist. Maybe Mary Ann Evans set a standard no one else can ever reach, but what she achieved can still be compared to what you have achieved, so that criterion must remain ... I call witnesses for the Prosecution! Summon The Summoner himself, and The Miller, The Pardoner, The Wife of Bath, The Franklin and The Host. Call Dorothea Brooke and The Very Reverend Edward Casaubon. Call Doctor Lydgate and Doctor Faustus. Call Macbeth, King Lear, Hamlet, Claudio and Isabella, Iago, Othello, Caesar and the best of the rest. Call Pip and Mr Pumblechook. Call the blessèd Joe Gargery, and call Estella. Call David Copperfield and Uriah Heep ... Literature is not history, everyone! Literature is a city. It is alive. It is peopled."

She stopped. "I can't read any more of this, to be honest. Edit that out, if you like, or don't like. I don't care. Pompous, opinionated, white-establishment crap, like I said."

"You can and you will read it! All of it!" I touched the rifle as I repeated that. "It is a small price to pay."

"Christ!" She exhaled, inhaled, panted her frustration. "Pay for what, exactly? Just what have I done to deserve all this shit from you?"

"You have to pay for the damage you have done. And - worse - the damage others have done in your name. You had no third-party insurance. You have to pay for all of it."

"What's that mean? Last bit."

"Those plump, white, literary ladies who gave you the prizes, acclaimed your merits."

"Oh yeah. Them."

"Continue the speech."

"So it's a hate speech."

"Exactly."

"Illegal."

I nodded. "I don't care any more. That should be obvious to you by now."

She leant forward. "Look," she said, and it was clear she was in earnest, and found this difficult. "I can't work it all out, see it whole, and I'm sorry if I've got it wrong, but is this something to do with you being what you are? Some medical thing? Or the prejudice you have suffered?"

"It has nothing whatever to do with that. You must stop seeing everything in black and white."

She shut her eyes a moment, but then clenched the script, and I was worried she would chuck it overboard. Then she started reading it again in an angry, impatient tone, unintentionally lending it exactly the fire it needed.

"They will remain because they are more real - point to three faces in the crowd - "

"No! Point to faces in the crowd! Start again, from *They will remain ...* "

She stabbed at me, with violence, all three times: *"They will remain because they are more real than you, or you, or you! More real than anyone you will meet at this festival. The artist has shown their inner life as well as what they say and do so we know them inside out, as in the portraits of the old masters. They are more real to us than real people because in life we only know what people say and do, not what they really think and feel."*

She stopped again.

"I'm going to steam on, don't fret." She had lost her place and seemed befuddled. "I just need a moment. Then

I'll get it over with. All of it. I swear."

"Take as long as you need."

"This sublime gift Mary Ann Evans had - to see into people's souls, to inhabit her characters and at the same time show them from outside, and to command language to match such invention - this gift is very rare, but over generations artists like her have peopled a city. No, not just Michael Henchard and Emma Woodhouse and Leopold Bloom, but also people such as Rufus Scott, Ida Scott, Ahmad Abd al-Jawad and Saleh Omar. These are the living creations of an elite group of artists, and to recognize such excellence we have The Royal Society of Literature. Other countries have other honours and prizes, and we have The Royal Society of Literature. So my Chair at The Royal Society, Daljit Nagra, is quite wrong to try to set aside "the criteria of George Eliot and T.S.Eliot" because in doing so he sets aside a standard of art.

"Shame on you, Daljit! You have brought the Society into disrepute with this glib and facile remark! I wonder if you have even read Middlemarch! I dare not ask. Similarly, the poetry of T.S.Eliot. Why would you want to set aside, or 'go beyond', The Waste Land? Or Four Quartets? Eliot's verse has such music you can hardly read it without being able to recite it by heart. Who doesn't know the opening lines of The Lovesong of J Alfred Prufrock by heart? Who, indeed, Daljit? Step down into the audience and see who knows them!

"If the gifts of George Eliot and T.S.Eliot cast giant shadows that make aspirant authors and poets feel small or inadequate, worthless or hopeless, that is as it should be. When the portrait artist Alan Hawkins came down to London to see the Rembrandt exhibition, he felt in such awe of Rembrandt he went back home never wanting to paint again.

"If all your literary gifts enable you to do is write monologues or angry rants like this one, that is not good enough for the Royal Society of Literature. When asked about the disadvantages of being young, poor, black and homosexual in the 1950s, James Baldwin replied, What disadvantages? They were advantages.

"And for my part, as President, on my watch, I

confess that the Council of The Royal Society of Literature has done great wrong in its election of Fellows for 2024. The Constitution provides that for a fellow to be elected he or she must have published at least two substantial works of 'outstanding literary merit'.

"Above all, it must be a judgement made **entirely** *on the merit of the work.*

"It would not do if that judgement were prejudiced by the race, age, religion, gender, sexual orientation or class of the author.

"And yet, Councillors, last year, in 2024, we judged entirely by race, age, religion, gender, class and sexual orientation, and not by the merit of the work at all! Of the forty new Fellows, thirty-three are women. 82%. Of the seven men selected, five are British African or Middle-Eastern. Of the two white males, one is young, and one is middle-aged.

"Can it be, Councillors, that in England and Wales, home to fifty-nine million people, where eighty-two per cent are white and eighteen per cent are BAME, that only one white man, among twenty-four million white men, has managed to write at least two works of outstanding literary merit by middle-age, whereas five times as many men of BAME origin, among only five million BAME men - some very young indeed, only half the age of the solitary white man! - have achieved exactly that already? I think not, Ladies and Gentlemen!

"Finally, as President, I have one more thing to say. I have never been afraid of biting the hand that feeds me, that hand generally being extended by the patriarchal hegemony I so much despise.

"I will conclude with this avowal. There are Hay-on-Wye Festivals now all over the world, from Peru to Barcelona. They are a segment of the multi-million dollar LFI group of literary festivals, consultancies, creative writing programmes, agencies, competitions and so on, whose profits, taken together, exceed any publishing empire in the world. But I declare before you today, so everyone can see this publicly, that I want no part in it any more. From this day forth, I will accept no invitation or payment from this industry. I disown it. I decry it. I disdain it. I will

have nothing more to do with those who enrich themselves, who gorge themselves, on failure. With this announcement, which is irrevocable and which I swear to you all I shall never personally regret, I take my leave of your stage, and your chickenshit Festival."

I turned off the camera, withdrew it from its bracket and zipped it up in my jacket.

"Well done," I said. "And thank you."

She left a silence.

"You really don't get it, do you?..." She shook her mane of frizzed hair that she hadn't bothered to tie up for our river trip. "There are thousands like you. They hit me from all sides as soon as they gave me that prize. You can't see it. When things are already so unfair, you have to be a little bit unfair to make things a little less unfair."

"Let's move on to you."

"Oh god no! Please don't. Let's stop now. Let's go back. You've got what you wanted."

"You wrote an epistolary novel entitled, *Hello Mum.*"

"A novella. Sold more than one hundred thousand copies. And what have you done? Just by the way. Hmmn? Eh?"

"I have no such ambitions - not of any kind. I am too much in awe of what has already been achieved. But you. Oh no. You feel nothing like that. Not even respect. Maybe you don't even know what's already been done. Hence *Hello Mum*. Your '*Tyrone*'? Your '*Dexter*'? If a white man had written that book he would have been accused of stereotyping young black men as stupid thugs, drug-dealers, gangsters and killers, as gullible poseurs taken in by every status symbol handed out on TV. All your adult black men and women are faithless and feckless, copulating and reproducing mindlessly. Most British black people are nothing like that. Your book is racist."

She shook her head, wouldn't deign to reply, then said simply: "I tell it like it is."

Single-handedly I took out her Booker prize winning paperback from the haversack.

"It's not as bad as people say, but it is bad, unworthy of any prize, of any recognition."

That was too much.

"*Agh! Fuckyoufuckyoufuckyou! Haha-HA!*" She tried to fake-laugh off my attack. "So that's what all this is about. Bitter, white and jealous. And old. And failed. Just another Brit-Lit Loser."

I let the pages fan to my first marker on page 128.

"The first half is sex. Who is ogling, stroking or fucking whom. Just because it's lesbian sex doesn't make it any more interesting. Just sex. And hate speech, of course, and list after list of how people look or what they eat. No flair, no colour. Everything's surface. No subtextuality."

She sighed and tried to stay above it all. "So this is why I'm here. Cos you know I'd never listen otherwise. Never have to face your fuckwit opinions. Cos I'm too far above you now."

"Exactly so. Unless I had a gun, I knew you'd never listen. That's a measure of how far gone you are, how far gone everything is. Not me. I said it's not all bad but it's so lazy. You let your paragraphs drool and dribble all over the place. Who's taken in by that? Your book is not a poem, or a prose poem, or anything like that. Let's look - "

"No! Let's not look because - "

"At Carole and Bummi."

"NO! They're mine! Mine mine mine! And I love them! Hands off! I don't want you gobbing all over them! I've read your bullshit speech. I've heard enough about your life. You listen to me now and leave my work out of this!"

She was raising her voice again but at this time in the morning I wasn't worried. Apart from early-bird fishermen, and I'd seen none at this hour, rivercraft mainly came out in the afternoons, and most hirers had closed for the year now anyway.

"Page one hundred and twenty eight - "

"Shut it, stop it, for Christ's sake, old man. Have a care. Fucksake."

"Carole turns fourteen. It is a year since she was raped by Trey, a black guy with grey eyes, and then raped some more by Trey's friends. By the end of her thirteenth year Carole has recovered enough to return to her studies and excel at school because she doesn't want to be "forever scrambling down the side of sofas for change to feed the meter, like Mum", or "shopping in Poundland, like Mum", or "scrambling round markets at closing time for scrag-ends, like Mum". Remember?

"Nuff colour for you?"

"Carole is fourteen. But you tell us later, page one seventy - " fanning the pages single-handedly to my second marker - "that when her father, Augustine, died in her infancy, her mother Bummi started her own cleaning business. It quickly grew to employ seven other cleaners. So how come, ten years on, she's "'forever scrambling down the side of sofas for change to feed the meter"? You are saying she's both a successful entrepreneur and dead broke after ten years in the business. Makes no sense."

"You must have missed something."

"During Carole's school days there is no mention of Bummi's cleaning business, where her work is all nightshift, yet she cannot 'take the day off work', you tell us, to escort Carole to Oxford on her first day at university. You're making it up as you go along. None of it stacks up."

She didn't answer.

"Does it?"

"Pernicketyshit." She closed her eyes. Yawned in my face.

"On page one hundred and eighty-two, Kofi, the Ghanaian tailor, comes to work for Bummi's cleaning business to *'supplement his pension'*, you tell us. Because you must tell us everything. Nothing evolves from the characters themselves. So Kofi cleans nights for Bummi to supplement his pension, but what's this? He also has a time-share in Gran Canaria. He also owns a three bedroom house in Herne Hill. He had a skilled trade all his life, in one of the richest trades, but he still needs to supplement his pension on the nightshift cleaning offices. This is ham. This is not worthy of any prize at all."

I left a pause and she opened her eyes again.

"You are a very boring old man."

"The Nzinga-Dominique relationship - "

"Oh shut the fuck up, please!"

"On the wimmin's ranch in America is again just not

credible. How did Dominique even get a visa? But Nzinga is unbelievably dumb and heavy-handed in her manipulation, then Amma turns up again and starts - "

"*SHUT THE FUCK UP! STOP IT!*" She really bawled at me now, so the veins stood out in her neck. "Just what have you achieved? Ever? In your life? What? Tell me what? You bitter old albino turd!"

"As a matter of fact," I answered, really without thinking about it at all, "I used to manage the UK tour for Barry Manilow."

She was agape. Speechless.

"Barry Manilow? My God! Get me out of here! I'm gonna swim for it!"

"You have no choice."

"Only cos you've got a fucking gun!"

I continued taunting her: "Just compare, for a moment, your Nzinga's sexual jealousy with the subtlety of the Reverend Casaubon's codicil - "

"What the fuck are you talking about?"

"Listen to you. You're so profane. All the time. So inarticulate. Page two hundred and four. The first time LaTisha's pregnant she doesn't notice until she's seven months gone. Doesn't notice the missed periods or any other physical sign of pregnancy. Doesn't even suspect. For seven months. That would make her pregnancy one in two thousand, but you don't bother to create that special case for her in any way. The more pretentious of your white reviewers say your book is a series of *vignettes*. It isn't. It's snapshots. It's selfies, because you can't keep yourself out of it, your anger and hatred."

"My God! *My God!* Neither can you!"

"A vignette fades at the borders. Your borders don't fade. They overlap and blur but that doesn't cover up the mistakes, the blunders, the plot-holes."

And suddenly Ronnie came to mind, and her horrible portrait of me, which actually was a vignette, fading out all around, not only because she couldn't be bothered to complete the details, but also because she wanted my face out there, thrust forward from the stained wooden frame, a very plain frame (an "honest" frame, she called it), pushing out her physical revulsion with me into my own bedroom. Her distaste, her loathing, which she dressed up as her rejection of portraiture. 'There. That's done with.' It wasn't so much the peroxide whiteness she leant what's left of my hair, as its static quality, as if to touch it would be to touch something plastic; a new toilet brush pulled from its cellophane has more life in it than she gave my hair in that portrait. My lipless smile - worm lips, as Moos said - the slight exaggeration to my one-sided, thumbed over nose, would have been just about forgivable, but it was unforgivable to me, and to all real albinos, to make my grey eyes virtually pigmentless, eyes with the translucence of something man made, glass but not glassy, they had a cut crystal clarity, you went straight through the retina to a B movie ghoul.

The cough and putt-putt of an ancient outboard motor - I recognized a British Seagull or similar from my scuba diving, gravel pit days - sounded behind us, and that sound dragged me back too, weakened the will, reduced my heart-beat to that cough and putt-putt.

She looked over my shoulder, across the water. I could see she was about to shout. I put down her book and set the Browning on my knee, pointing up at her chest.

"You wouldn't," she said. "You're an old whitey gone soft in the head with bitterness and failure. A Wordsyworthy bitter old duffer, but you wouldn't do that."

To which I answered:

"Dame Tracey Emin?"

Her eyes widened.

"Oh Christ," she muttered in dismay. She glanced from me to the bank and back again, zigzagging the connections.

"Oh my god," she muttered to herself, looking down from me, into the bottom of the kayak, ".... Poor Trace..."

The boat with the outboard, a clinker-built rowing boat with a couple of fishing rods poking from the bow, a well varnished and cared for craft, came into my view and I put a hand up and waved to the smiling, grey-haired gent sitting in the stern, hand on the tiller of his Seagull outboard.

"Lovely morning to be out on the river!" I called.

"Isn't it just!" came a fruity reply. "Wish I had your hat now the sun's out!"

"Haha!" I replied, staring ahead at the President of the Royal Society of Literature. "A gift from my ladylove!"

"Oh yeah! I bet!" he called back, laughing. "Naughty naughty!"

And then his back was to us and the chance had passed, and she knew it.

"Actually," I said to her, shifting the rifle off my knee, "I am not a Wordsworth fan, but those lines about this river were chosen with care, and to set the taunting aside for a moment and tell you the truth I enjoyed your novella, and I could see the other had originality and possibilities, but you seem to have missed my point - "

I thought she had her hands under her buttocks for warmth and the attitude was one I found entirely unthreatening, but with a sudden bracing and locking of her elbows she lifted her torso, pivoted forward and kicked the Browning overboard - I caught the stock in time but then as I leant over to save it she kicked me as hard as he she could in the kidneys with both tight baseball boots and I had to let the rifle go to steady myself on the side with both hands, and a single kick brushed my face and dislodged my glasses. Now she was coming forward at me with both feet pummelling, and as I locked my knees to block my crotch she shunted further forward and moved up to my chest, trying to pivot me out of my seat and over the stern, but my weight in the berth held me locked in and I grabbed one foot in both hands and yanked it hard round, as I had with Loner, so she cried out in agony, and then I had both ankles and wrenched both to port - she shrieked, she screamed in pain! - so she had to roll over, where she had the advantage to shunt back at me, but I used my own feet then, locking my left on her hip and pushing hard while at the same time wrenching those thrusting ankles to the left until she cried out again in agony and slipped over the port side, into that water that could have been no more than eleven or twelve degrees. It took her breath away so she could not scream any more, though she did try, with her hands still clinging to the handle on the kayak side, her face crumpled up in pain - but she wasn't finished, she had guts, I'll give her that, because next she tried to capsize the kayak and land me in the Wye as well, knowing I couldn't possibly survive that cold if she couldn't - cold-blooded killer indeed! I leant to starboard, while she rocked the kayak, trying to force it over, and pulled the painter in and grabbed the mooring ring with my right hand, and with my left I leant over to get the paddle that was already in the water, snagged between the kayak and the other plinth. She seized that chance to push up, while my weight was all to one side, but her feet weren't on the riverbed, or it was too muddy to offer her any grip, or her ankles were too torn up, and I had the bright yellow paddle and straightened up and shunted it hard down the side so its toughened plastic tip ripped her fingers from the handle. She yelped and gave up the boat. She bobbed completely underwater. That gave me time to undo the painter but I didn't push off, I held onto the mooring ring, waiting for her to surface. Her hands came up and clasped the bow - nails torn, fingers bleeding - then her head came above the bow and the bow went down with her weight but not so much that it endangered buoyancy. She rested there a moment, clinging on to the bow, bleeding, catching shallow breaths, her teeth chattering. The wild thrust of her hair was soaked completely now and hung dark and lank about her face.

"Hold on," I said. "It's okay. I'll get you back in."

She shook her head, shut her eyes. "My fucking ankles!" she muttered. Her strong jaws made more noise than her voice, they chattered so in the freezing cold. "What you done to my fucking ankles! You cruel bastard!"

"Make your way along the side, hand over hand."

Again she shook her head.

"What's the point," she muttered. "What's the fucking point, you fucking, fucking … *man!* … You *brute!* You *dog*! … Christallfuckingmighty … " A long, agonized groan, all broken up by her snapping and chattering teeth, came out of her. " … Fought so hard, so hard, to get this far … Now what happens. Fucking kook tries to fucking drown me. What's next. What's fucking next … "

"I never tried to kill you, drown you. You're drowning in your own self-pity, in your own victimhood."

At that her eyes and face crumpled again and she

actually began to cry, and shake her head and shake those soaking, freezing dark lank locks. Her left hand was bleeding quite badly. The nail of her index finger was completely torn away.

"Make your way down the side, look, hand by hand, and I'll pull you on board."

"Nah ... Fuck you," she muttered, crying with her eyes shut, head shaking, jaws trembling uncontrollably now. It's impossible to render with punctuation how her words came out when she was in that freezing water. They were chopped up and hacked about by the chattering of her freezing jaws and the difficulty she had in breathing. "I don't fucking care any more," she said as flatly as she could, still with her eyes shut. "I'm done with you, you ugly old white dog." That's the nearest I can get to her hacked and panted insults. She opened her eyes. Her breath was still coming in tight gasps. "Who wants to share the world with the likes of you anyway?" It was a long and stringy and weedy question with no roots at all, but it was a preface to this next utterance, which she had to give breath to above all - "You - you - you - you - you have no idea, not the beginning of a fuckinginklingofanidea - " her hands knitted freezing white but bleeding red across the beige bow for this - "… what it is like … what it's like … to be … "

She sank. She surfaced ten feet downstream, doing a lurching swimming stroke, only with her arms, a kind of crawl but with her body sunk behind her, hardly keeping her head above water. There was still another twelve hundred metres at least before the town, in that freezing water. I knew she'd never make it. I thought of that poor suicide who came down here to drown himself in the Wye in February, how low he must have felt to do that, and how low I must have made her feel to swim away like this, so limpingly, with the agony of her ankles, with their ligaments twisted off the bone, her ankles trailing in the freezing water below.

A disenchantment set in straightaway when I played the video of her speech back in the Hymer. The sound was surprisingly good, despite the watery, breezy and leafy background noises, and my own movements in the kayak, which I had tried my utmost to suppress. The problem was with her manner: this was obviously a forced speech, a forced confession, and yet there was no evidence of any force or coercion. I had accidentally devised such a tranquil setting, so idyllic, really, and the weather had been on our side too, that - without any trace of fear on her part - the reading of my speech just seemed so half-hearted, something without consequence. Whether she had cunningly foreseen this and read it with this effect in mind, I don't know. All credit to her, if that were the case. Probably so, I suppose, for she was no fool. Even when she became angry, and I had thought this was the tone I needed, there was such a weakness to it. It was so ineffectual. Yapping away in the beige kayak. Any colour but beige! Oh, how I regretted my cheapness! She could have been at an amdram reading of a playscript, where she was the least enthusiastic member of the cast and sulky too about the part she'd been given. Or someone persuaded to read out the script for an ice-breaker at a business conference. I had to admit to myself that it had no bite, no appeal at all. On Youtube it would just look strange, come out backwards, with irony, as if she herself was playing a joke, having a laugh at her critics at the RSL.

It was a failure. She had died - I was sure that she would have died - for nothing.

I wiped the recording.

At the front of my mind, and I thought I could actually feel its thickness and softness inside the cranium vault, an overwhelming sense of fatigue hovered, waiting there, wanting to fall down upon my will and cover it up in a thick, grey, gelatinous dome, and I longed to lie down and let it fall, and seal, and suffocate, but knew I could not.

And there were many hours to go before dusk and what it held in store, with no decent bed to lie down on and forget about it all.

I knew I had to go back to the inlet and make a stab - literally a stab, into the cold dark water - to retrieve the rifle. Before I left the river, I had tried raking around with the yellow paddle, and I'd felt it, or thought I'd felt it, once or twice, but after several drags on the riverbed where the stream came in I was sure I was only burying it deeper in silt. I was struggling against the confluence of stream and river while trying to lever it up - hopeless.

Towards the end of that struggle I cast a glance downriver again but saw no sign of her.

I managed to force the kayak between the stone plinths and up the narrow stream far enough to find gravel shallows where I could go aground. After pulling it up the bank, I had made another camouflage hide for it and left it there.

I began to think the kayak would just have to stay there, and the Browning would have to stay at the bottom of the river too, I felt that low.

It had been a long walk, with the Tilley hat pulled down, to where I left the Hymer; all the way round into Hay-on-Wye and then across the bridge and another mile or so to where I had parked opposite The Warren. All that, on top of the exertions of the morning, which must include the exertion of acting out a role - never to be underestimated - all these demands had left me physically and mentally very low, and very hungry. I decided to drive up to Hereford and treat myself to lunch, with local ale, and see if that didn't lift the spirits. At the very least it would be much warmer in the driver's cab once on the move.

In the previous few days I had wanted to be seen in Hay-on-Wye as little as possible, and this morning I had been preoccupied with preparations, so I had not been keeping up with the newspapers. Instead, I had been listening to the news on Radio 4 day by day. There had been nothing more about the graffiti victims, Manilow or Tracey Emin.

In Hereford, I rounded up a gang of newspapers from three different stores, put the lot in a W.H.Smith carrier bag and treated them to lunch at *The Groom,* a shabby, out-of-place 1950s pub - tudor beams, pebbledash, its very own grey skies - clinging on to business at the fringes of the city's retail park. I ordered my All-day Breakfast (sans Lincolnshire sausages) and a pint of lime and lemonade and paid for it on trust, forgetting my earlier promise to myself to try the local ale, and not noticing I'd sailed by the buoy of low spirits.

Once back at my window seat, where the windows hadn't been cleaned for months, possibly years, I consulted the first of the papers, *The Daily Mail.*

Straightaway, on the second page, I found an Emin story. It had been nearly a week since her disappearance.

From my own research I thought the reputation of places like Beachy Head and the Dover Cliffs would drive the verdict of suicide for Emin. I wanted there to be the presumption, in some minds at least, that she did away with herself because she could no longer withstand the clamouring voices outside, and inside too, that told her she was a talentless fraud, despite the endless attempts to bolster her standing by those who had invested in her art and life for their own profit, with newspaper spreads, prizes, gallery interviews and grandstanding public accolades, such as a professorship of drawing at The Royal Academy, and the conferral of a damehood, so that she was now *Dame* Tracey Emin, if you please. These measures to prop her up against the growing tide of public incredulity were to my mind futile in the long term: she may as well have won a damehood from King Canute.

However, these were not the matters considered in the quarter-page article on page two of *The Daily Mail.*

The mystery of her disappearance was resolved in my favour, and the worst fears about what had happened - that she had taken her own life, for reasons unknown to her friends - were confirmed by the *Mail*. Her handbag, discovered, at last, intact, with phone and purse inside, by a walker, nestled as I had left it, in the weed clump at the cliff edge, near the Dover War Memorial, was the decisive evidence, and I felt something akin to pride that I'd had the wit to hide it in that way. But no broken body had turned up and there had been no reportings of suicidal persons along the Dover Cliffs in recent days, not even at the infamous Beachy Head, which averages a suicide every fortnight, and where a marked *Samaritans* 4X4 is on 24 hour patrol. Some human remains were discovered two mornings previously on the rocky beaches of Hastings by some hospice orderlies, escorting patients on a morning constitutional, which led to speculations that Emin's body had travelled some fifty miles south, but this was quickly dismissed by the coastguard service, whose responsibility it is to gather up broken bodies from the base of the cliffs whenever called for. Though much deteriorated, the remains were clearly of an elderly male of mixed race, later identified as one Frank Osmah, a car valet from north London.

There were some outpourings of grief from those close to Emin, including her agent, Jay Jopling, and someone from the Saatchi Gallery, and some provocative words from the Tate Modern's Sir Nicholas Serota, who speculated that although she had always been very strong in defending herself from public attacks, and here he couldn't resist referring obliquely to the late art critic of the London Standard, Brian Sewell, he, Sir Nicholas, personally had no doubt that over time such persistent prejudice and abuse must have had a corrosive effect on her psyche.

From there the reader was referred to her forthcoming obituary in *The Mail on Sunday*.

No mention of any possibility of foul play.

Jolly good.

Jolly bad. Again, my head-to-head with D.I. Know-All was postponed.

Before looking in the other dailies, I decided to enjoy my All-day Breakfast and return to the Hymer where I could read them in privacy.

More disappointment.

All the other papers carried the story, but none offered any more detail or speculation than the *Mail,* and most didn't bother with the earlier confusion over where and when or the fate of Frank Osmah. Some said misadventure was still a possibility.

The news made me feel strangely alone in the world, as if there were some deliberate attempt, a conspiracy, to blank me out of all this because no one wanted to see the monstrous fish, the kraken of the deep, that I was bringing to the surface. Manilow had started that. I had been with these people - the graffiti artists, the Savoy driver, the porter at The Palladium, Manilow, Emin, Evaristo - I had shared time with them and shared my life with their lives, counselled them and listened to them, and one way or another I had escorted them into the limelight or cued their exits. We'd been through some ordeals together, and many were no longer here: that was one form of aloneness. Simple. As if they were family, in a way. But the more complete sense of isolation came from knowing that everyone shared an understanding of how many of these people died, which, it seemed, almost by an effort of will, *actively excluded me*. Perhaps that comes closest to it. And that now drives this sense of terrible isolation and alienation, of not being part of the common lot, the common sense, the common truth, when that was exactly what I had been fighting to bring to the light of day all along.

To make matters worse, to intensify the notion of a conspiracy, when I got back into the driver's cab and started the engine, the radio came on, as it always did, and it was tuned automatically to the local station, Radio Herefordshire. A few rows from the car park exit, the phone-in programme currently airing, dealing with some heated opinions about sewage discharge into the River Wye - where responsibility lay, who should pay - was interrupted with the breaking news that the President of the Royal Society of Literature had been picked up from the river late that morning and rushed to hospital in an unconscious state. She was suffering from acute hypothermia but responding well to treatment and her prognosis was hopeful. There would be more news later and a statement from the police, once they'd had an opportunity to speak with her. The news flash finished by noting there had been two deaths from drowning in the Wye already this year, and it was very much hoped this would not be the third.

I slowed, pulled into a parking bay a few rows from the exit and cut the engine, and the radio.

So. What would she say? To the police. To the press.

Curiously, I found myself unalarmed. I had a strange intimation that, like Manilow, she would say nothing. She would deny me. I would be denied. Betrayed, in effect. Treated as worthless, as if I didn't exist. Even though she knew about Emin too, or would know shortly enough. Because to admit to any of it, to recount what had happened between us in the kayak, the speech, the quarrel, the physical fight, was to drag my cause into the limelight, and above all that must not happen, from her point of view, from their point of view. I would be Manilowed all over again. Thus each victim left me further and further away from the madding crowd, and as the victims were themselves forgotten - nothing at all in the news now about the graffiti artists or Barry Manilow - as the world moved on, I was losing my place in it - 'Men who are nothing, who allow themselves to become nothing, have no place in it.'

That must not be.

In no fit state to drive, I took the key from the ignition.

The Groom had no car park and I had parked in Hereford's retail park. That's three parks in one sentence without a blade of grass between them. I always chose such places if possible, for their size and anonymity, and they tended to have bigger bays too. I was facing west, a few empty rows from the broad service road, the other side of which were more garish retail outlets, facing the sun going down, with the driver's side under the straggling shade of a dying sapling. Across the service road, I watched a young family emerge from a veterinary store with bundles of supplies and head for their Ford Mondeo estate; immediately opposite, I watched a young man park and lock up his Nissan Leaf, and lope into the B&Q entrance, and come out again a moment later with a security guard, with whom he was in an argument about why he had to return to the car park to pick up and pay for a trolley.

"Just what's the fucking point?" he demanded, his head dipped to one shoulder. The security guard shrugged. "I mean, what's the fucking point of that? Why aren't they inside? For free?"

The guard shrugged again.

I have trained myself never to linger in a car, staring outward like this, but now that I actually live in a car, or van, it has become a more difficult rule to stick by. Despite the terrible sense of aloneness, the lives going on all around did not make me yearn to live out there beyond my windscreen. If I were to follow any of these lives back to their homes, into their homes, I knew what I would find there, the modes of entertainment, the modes of discourse, of familial affection and rejection, of waiting for a sibling to finish in the bathroom, or waiting for a jealous quarrel to end about some friend coming round. I knew all the routes into suburbia, the council housing, the executive dwellings, and knew the lives to which those routes led, and I did not want any part of any of them.

There had been a vague plan at the back of my mind to find my way down the service road, around and across to the B&Q store, and in there I would busy myself with working out how to make some apparatus, some kind of extendable rake, with which to drag the river bed - but what would be the good of that? Even if successful, the Browning might be ruined now, and then there was the risk of discovery while I was dragging the riverbed, and all the ensuing complications. Better by far just to leave things as they were. Let the kayak be some prize for an adventurous child poking about in the woods at the riverbank.

But in the end I did go back. Not for the kayak, which remained a treasure for that adventurous child. I had to go back for the rifle. Without it so many options closed down. I needed that mechanical violence, as Manilow had said, at my side, not least for the confidence it leant me. Physically, I posed no threat whatever to anyone. I would never get my way, have my say, and get away, without my gun.

Fetching it from the freezing depths turned out to be unexpectedly easy. I happened upon an extendable tree pruner in B&Q, more than three metres long, for about £50. I took it away unassembled in its shiny black sheath. In the back of the Hymer I removed the saw blade so that I could use the hook below to drag the mud at the stream estuary. I had a strike first time. It took three goes to get the barrel within reach of the bank but then I pulled it out, free of weed or root. The inflow from the stream must have kept the riverbed clean there. I was so pleased with the rescue I dismantled both rifle and tree pruner there and then in a blind but joyful hurry and rushed back to the Hymer with everything tied up in the black sheath, and the blue mood completely vanquished.

A dedicated evening's work lay ahead cleaning up the Browning, oiling it and polishing the stock.

To every peak a trough, but the wave pattern became more condensed and noisy now I was back in London, back among the urbanites. Horror, horror, and nothing in between. Such a notion had crossed my mind in a different way on the wild cliffs of Dover, but here was an altogether new horror creeping out from that bleak night a week ago.

The ghost of Dame Tracey Emin, on television.

At first sight I thought it was a recording, maybe connected with her recent death - a homage or retrospective, in the style of the old *Arena* programmes, perhaps. She looked so young and fresh and healthy and well-made up. But no no no: it was a news item, one of those slipped in at the end of the serious business.

I was watching her on TV in *The Woodman* in Muswell Hill - why do I always choose these places with the names of worthy and earnest tradesmen? *The Groom, The Woodman*, and last night it had been *The Carpenters' Arms,* in Kentish Town. I know why, well enough, and it haunts me so.

My life, my life, my torn down, torn up, torn ankled, wasted life.

The Woodman is at the junction of Archway Road and Muswell Hill Road, at the top of the hill. I had parked up in a cul-de-sac of Hampstead Garden Suburb, casually riding the kerb, as if the Hymer belonged to some Spanish friends a resident had made on holiday. I'd pulled all the blinds down, locked up and slipped away to treat myself to a pint and a microwaved meal somewhere … and here I was, watching Dame Tracey Emin on television.

Her commercial nous demanded total respect. She was taking advantage of her return from the dead to publicize what she had been working on, in secret, in her artist's hermitage, the private Annex of her LKE Studios in Margate. And here the work was, on TV. We were all to see it right now, for the very first time. Life had got far too busy lately, she said, and she'd had to create some private time and space for herself, hence her mischievous disappearance and that 'naughty trick', she said, with mock penitence, when 'a very special friend' planted her bag at the cliff edge for her.

This was an unmeetable horror.

To be used, robbed, cheated and then set aside, discarded in this way.

During the introductory voiceover, the news cameras circled her latest piece of Installation Art, publicizing to millions its every detail, promoting and legitimizing Emin's original talent and position at the very top of the hierarchy of successful modern artists. Offers of more than three million had come in already, it was announced. Given that her most famous installation art to date, *My Bed,* had fetched £2.5 million at Christie's nine years ago, in 2015, this was not in itself newsworthy, but they wanted these mad sums out there for those still in the dark ages - Jan van Eyck's age - about modern art.

Her interviewer was a swarthy, goateed friend, fan, fraud. A sexual frisson ran between them. She smiled coyly about the incipient bidding war.

"Money's not so important now," she responded, "if you know what I mean."

The presenter laughed, flattering her, and stumbled over his response. "I, for one, do not know what you mean, Dame Tracey!"

"I can't let it go," she said, looking at the new exhibit. "Not yet. Best thing I've done in years. Most original thing I've done in years. That's the point. The important bit."

"It is, if nothing else, extraordinarily original … " The interviewer said, shaking his head in awe at this new marvel. His smiles slipped in and out of his dark goatee as if they were his tongue.

Emin's private Annex must have been at least half the original building. A vast, white, pitched roof space, completely windowless, but with flush white garage doors whose seams were virtually invisible. Operated electrically, no doubt. The space was lit by dimmer spotlights - embedded glass studs in various colours, like bulging motorway cat's-eyes - from all corners and from all manner of angles, high and low in every wall, and in the rafters too. Because of the sheer whiteness it looked freezing cold, but Emin was dressed in her fisherman's smock, as she had been at the Dover cliffs a week ago, and stylish, loose white culottes. She'd installed underfloor heating, I concluded. Only the best.

In *The Woodman* I was chilly, sitting near the door, alone at a table for three, waiting for my basket meal from the microwave. There was not much interest in this tail-end news item in the crowded pub, except when the millions were mentioned.

For me, the art was unmeetable, as I have said.

In the middle of the vast white space, two cameras moved around an old VW camper van. Its sliding door was drawn back to bare domestic chaos and destruction inside. Not slovenliness and dissolution, as in *My Bed*, but total wreckage, as in *My Hymer*. The vehicle was on blocks. The wheels of the van were tyreless and around the wheel arches were massive scorch marks, as if the tyres had been burned away. Yet the rest of the paintwork was fresh. Crude strokes of white and cream and beige outlined a massive ice-cream wafer, taking up the full body of the vehicle, with the uppermost wafer starting at the roof gutter and extending into the raised concertina roof. Bloated drips of white paint denoted melting ice-cream from the centre of the wafer around the windows, which were scorched brown and black at the wheel arches. On the windscreen, fingered into a glued layer of dust, were five words in graffiti style loops - *Sun, Sand, Sex, And Death*. On the rear window, when that came into view, was Emin's signature, slashed into another layer of glued dust.

With a remote, Emin faded all the lights to dimness while the cameras withdrew to either end of the van. The wall lights on this side, the garage doors side, went out completely. Then, projected through the van, onto the flush garage doors, surrounded by sudden darkness, there appeared a backdrop of magnificent stars, a milky way, no less, above a deep swathe of grassy cliff, whose ragged, stony edges suggested an infinite abyss below. On the cliff edge, under a new spotlight to the left, two bald and naked shop manikins of indeterminable sex lay entwined in copulation. At the same time, a single light went up slowly on a neatly folded pile of clothes in the middle of the van, unnoticeable before, and a pair of knee-length boots that were gradually illuminated from top to bottom with fluorescent green. The camera at the bonnet moved round to capture the interior close up: the green pile of shiny clothes, the wrecked interior full of holes and dangling wires and broken bits and pieces. Now, through some trick of the spotlights on the upper walls, lights came up on the ice-cream wafer on the body of the vehicle either side of the sliding door, diminishing the stars and lightening the cliff edge in front, and the copulating manikins, and their surrounding darkness.

Emin was teasing her interviewer: he had to guess the title of this new work.

He looked genuinely at a loss.

"Come on, Dame Trace," he teased in return. "Give us a clue."

Emin giggled. "Summer pop songs. Early seventies."

"I wasn't born for another ten years!" The presenter laughed. "You were only a babe in arms yerself!"

"Nah. Real babe, I was, by then," Emin smirked.

"Still are!" declared the presenter.

An overweight cameraman with long grey hair in a ponytail stepped down from his platform and called out through cupped hands -

"Summer Holiday! Cliff Richard and The Shadows!" and he sang out loud, and danced The Twist, swinging and gyrating his chubby hips for all assembled, and for the viewers back home:

"We're all goin' on a summer holiday! ... "

Everyone laughed. Emin laughed harder than anyone else, bowing her head, flushed with laughter, in reverence to the fun of the cameraman's singing and twisting, and the dark joke at the octogenarian Cliff Richard's expense.

"You've gone back a whole bleedin' decade!" She laughed some more. "Would be good, though. But not the best. It's called - "

But I got there first, to the shock and astonishment of the crowded bar of *The Woodman*: no one was following this news item, but all of them now swung round, all of a piece, when I screamed, from the bottom of my soul:

"'The Death of Barry Manilow!'"

All stared at me agape, including the bar staff, but I was not looking at them. I was still staring above them, beyond them, at the screen, and I could hear her say clearly, seriously, in the ensuing silence:

"That's Barry Manilow's original outfit from his last performance at The London Palladium, in the middle of the floor there. He will never return. It is all we have left."

One of the bar staff, a slight, tall woman in her thirties, in a faintly patterned flowery blouse buttoned to the neck, with naturally curly, closely cut, sandy hair, and lightly mascaraed very striking blue eyes, leant forward over the bar, set her chin on her hands, and smiled and frowned at me. At Me. Me.

"Now how the fuck did you know that?"

And then it passed, my own moment in the spotlight, when I'd made an exhibit of myself, when I was of interest to everyone and to that woman in particular, and I had to leave without eating anything, taking away instead that intensely desirable image of an unattainable, smiling woman, half my age, in her every detail.

The sale of items from Sir Roger Moore's 'Personal Collection' at Bonhams Auction Rooms took place at 101 New Bond Street on 4th October 2024. An unnamed percentage from the proceeds went to registered charities and the rest was retained by Moore's executors. The sale was expected to raise about $500,000 but actually all 224 items - including old Biros, posters signed with those Biros, old programmes, doodlings, Roger Moore's old ski gloves, skis and ski jackets - were sold on the day for $1,117,300. More memorable items included the Cyril Castle Chesterfield overcoat worn by Moore during a taxi chase when making *A View to a Kill* in New York in 1985, and the morning suit he wore in the same film when visiting Royal Ascot. One major surprise for the organizers was the £57,000 paid for a fifty year old Omega watch that was expected to fetch just £20,000.

Raph Adams, Associate Specialist in the Popular Culture Department at Bonhams, headed up the sale.

Bond villains, terrorists, dictators and so on love to dress up their grievances in faith and ideology but at bottom it's always personal. Their original slights and insults, suffered in youth or boyhood, may seem trivial, even puerile, infantile, but in the victim's mind they burn like the mines of sulphur, until a sense of powerlessness must be traded for a sense of omnipotence.

To know Adams by sight definitively, I sent him a packet with an 007 instruction that he should leave 101 New Bond Street at 12 noon on Friday 11th October, with the packet I had sent under his arm, turn left and keep walking. That was all. He was to understand that once I knew him by face we could begin negotiations through a second communication.

Well, this is not how things fell out.

A short man, much younger than I expected, with a soft and pudgy face and horn-rim glasses, reddish hair gelled back from his forehead, came out of Bonhams at 12 noon, with the packet, as arranged, and looked up and down the street. Though it was not particularly cold, he was wearing a long, dark, winter coat, which had the effect of making him seem taller than he was. He had the packet tucked under his left arm in exactly the manner I had requested. He couldn't see me on the street because I was in Ésclot, the exclusive tailors opposite, feigning interest in a rack of woollen jackets near the open doorway. Adams, evidently a very cautious man, I thought at the time, again looked left and right and across New Bond Street, and may have focused on me in Ésclot for a moment, but I didn't see because - sensing his gaze returning - I stepped round the clothes rack to feel the cloth of a maroon jacket with huge lapels and square slate buttons, something I would never wear, designed for a different man of a different generation.

Adams did not walk off to the left, as instructed. I looked back across at the moment he stepped forward and dropped the packet into a shiny black metal bin bracketed to a lamppost in front of the auction rooms. This was no ordinary bin. On New Bond Street, outside Bonham's Auction Rooms, it had to be a shiny black bin with some fancy gold beading halfway up. Adams patted the packet down a few times before leaving it there and going back inside Bonhams.

My first thoughts were - *You should never have made a gesture that so exposed your arrogance, that so excited my revenge* ... and so on. The power of the Browning was solidly behind me now.

For where did his arrogance, his gelled and mounted red hair, his forbidding long black coat come from?

They came from his recent success in selling off a dead movie star's trash to his fellow urbanites, whose bits and pieces reflect their own vanity and self-importance, because for the urbanite the world is only mirrors and windows, nothing exists beyond self-reflections and adornments and fragments of the same; shards and bits and pieces that only signify other shards and bits and pieces are still missing, things needed in order to be special in some way, a need that nags at the imagination like a fly buzzing on glass, like an incessant conversation on a suburban bus or train about someone else that cannot be ignored. For the urbanite sees no landscapes or mountain ranges, no seascapes, rivers, lakes, woodlands or open heavens or eagles soaring, day by day, unto which his spirit may soar, beneath which he might feel some humility, he sees only walls, shops, alleys, malls, screens, and things to buy, and only these when he looks up from the dogshat pavement.

I didn't know at that moment of rejection by Raph Adams that he was far cleverer, and far more playful, than I am, and I was already outsmarted. Again. That Manilow refrain. That Emin pastiche. That Evaristo plot-hole. The possibility that the arrogant gesture of stuffing the packet into the bin was not, in fact, a rejection, but a lure - that possibility didn't cross my mind until I had left Ésclot full of temper and settled in McDonald's, in the West One Shopping Centre in Oxford Street. I had decided, on the way, to let the packet go. It was impossible to retrieve it without giving myself away, if Adams had a mind to turn me in. But once I had settled at a single table with a Filet-o-Fish and French fries and this new idea, that the packet (which, I realised, no longer contained what I had put in it anyway) was not bait to catch me but a lure both to draw me out, thereby gaining the upper hand, *and* to see what else was on offer - once that idea had occurred, I rushed the meal and returned to New Bond Street, quickening my pace and ducking and weaving as best I could on the crowded pavements, convinced I had hit upon the real Adams now. That image of him stuffing the packet into the black tin bin, with the phony gold beading, and then patting it farewell, replayed in my imagination again and again and each time I saw it as more dramatic, more a message from one who knew he was being watched. The thrust had caused his glasses to slip down his nose and when he pushed them back up he glanced again across the street into Ésclot, maybe because he had already picked me out there, maybe because he had seen me go into Ésclot and had watched me from inside the first floor at Bonham's for the quarter of an hour or more I had been there.

After all, he could easily have taken the packet to the police, if his intention had been to expose me.

I crossed New Bond Street to the Bonhams' entrance then started down that side of the street at an even pace back towards Oxford Street. Nothing happened until I got to Blenheim Street, outside L .K. Bennett's fashion store, where I stopped to cross again at the Belisha beacon. Then I heard his voice, close to my shoulder: it was a low voice, not gravelly but theatrically deep, theatrically trained, perhaps, not at all what I expected from his short stature and pudgy face.

"What else?"

I started to cross and replied over my shoulder.

"Everything he was wearing for his last performance."

"The Palladium." It was not a question.

"Yes," I answered. "At The London Palladium."

"But just last night Tracey Emin - "

"She faked it. That only adds. Think about it. That's why I'm here."

We had reached the other side and I turned to face him. I could see he had already processed why I had to move immediately to recover, and hopefully redouble, the value of the original material, which she did not possess.

Despite the long dark coat he was noticeably shorter than I had estimated from Ésclot. About the same height as Loner, in fact, which gave me a confidence that was undermined straightaway by the curl of his smile, now we were face to face. It was a one-sided, knowing and perceptive smile, in his round, pudgy, rather shapeless and colourless face; a smile which impressed me above all with its depth of cynicism. It exposed the edges of his glistening teeth and their expensive whitening treatment. His eyes, behind the horn-rim glasses, which I saw now were very expensive too, with glittering gold pins fixing their hinges - his eyes were what we call green when we mean a kind of light blueish grey. Eye colour is very particular to someone who is so often mistaken for albino. Now these eyes of his narrowed to carry through that smile of knowing and wry amusement and cynicism. My acting skills must have failed again because he saw straight through to my nervousness and uncertainty. And my heart sank further because I had already done this scene, as it were, and carried it off successfully with Tracey Emin in Margate, but against Raph Adams I couldn't manage it.

"Don't worry," he said, blinking. "I'm not going to ask you where you got them."

"Look," I said, trying to come across as business-like, in a hurry. "If I seem nervous about this it's because I am nervous. I know nothing about these things. I am just a go-between and a pretty poorly paid one at that."

"You're up to your fucking neck in it!" he replied loudly, publicly, and laughed. "Whatever you like to think, and whatever lies you're telling now! And all I have to do is go to the police and report you!" He laughed at me again. "You wouldn't get far if you made a run for it either. Look at you!" He not so much laughed as giggled at me now. A quick run of giggles to run away with how quickly I could run away.

"Be that as it may," I told him, lowering my voice and my head, "are you interested in these items or not? Both Sotheby's and Christie's have their own Popular Culture Departments, you'll be aware. In fact, Sotheby's is way ahead of you and has dealt in pop memorabilia for twenty years. Pictures of Twiggy, Mick Jagger in his twenties and so on." Why on earth did I bring that up? *Why*? Was I that desperate to impress him? "In short, I can go elsewhere."

"Be that as it may, in fact, in short, you are in deepest shit!" he rebuffed, looking away from me, down New Bond Street. "And you have no room to deal or manoeuvre *at all*."

"Very well." I had to draw things to a close. "Do you want to see the rest of the items, or not?"

"Yes," he said, deigning to slide a look into my eyes again. "Bring them in at about five-thirty - "

"Out of the question," I told him. "My terms. I'll send another note."

And with that I turned and walked back towards Oxford Street.

Again I had used Q-Park but I'd pre-booked this time with their VIP service. This event carried none of the complications of a second vehicle. The VIP section was a 3rd floor disappointment but there were no signs of the marauding thieves and troglodytes that haunted the Poland Street place.

I had given Adams only the location and the number of my bay, C-34. He was due at six o'clock.

At five to six he exited the lift and looked about, head high, to get his bearings. C Floor was poorly lit. In those seconds I had time enough to take in his appearance (same coat, same arrogant demeanour) and the fact that he was alone - this only struck me at this moment. I had not asked him to come alone. If he had come with a colleague, perhaps even his boss from the Popular Culture Department, I would have given up the plan and driven off to rethink. As he started down my row, I considered this a question of subconscious discernment on my part, rather than luck: Adams would never have shared this prospect with anyone. He wanted it all to himself. That aspect of his character I had understood intuitively, with no further 007 cloak and dagger directions. And anyway, given that he had already treated me so brusquely in public on the New Bond Street pavement, he would have no fear of meeting me down here in a public car park. That reflection, watching him come closer to the Hymer, brought the Browning to mind again. It was assembled, loaded, with the safety catch off, at my feet, lying along the base of the bench seat in the driver's cabin. The noise of it - for I felt sure I would have to use it to bring Adams into line - could be mistaken for a backfire or a door slam, if it were heard at all down here on the VIP floor, which was not crowded.

Our eyes met. He came to my driver's door, which was locked, and I shook my head, glanced over my shoulder to the sliding door, and pressed the door release.

In time with him drawing the door back, I slipped out with the rifle under a folded blanket. It was well hidden but an encumbrance. I left my door open.

I had set the boots on the new camping table and the rest of the outfit lay green and dark and mysterious, neatly folded in front of thc boots - my version of Emin's imitation of her own original work.

The lozenge lights had come on automatically with the door opening.

"What the fuck happened? … Aha. Wait a minute. Just like … "

But he didn't finish that, for some reason, and his hesitation gave me the two seconds I needed to draw the sliding door closed and stab the lock on my armrest. That provoked shouts and thumps at the sliding door, same as Emin, until I opened the rear doors.

He turned to face the Browning three metres away, out of reach.

"Quiet."

He chuckled. Stopped chuckling. Remained quite still.

"You've got to be kidding," he said softly.

Despite the rifle, I could sense his confidence, even his brusqueness on the rise.

Angling the barrel towards the ceiling I fired over his head.

The noise of it was far louder in the car park than I'd anticipated but it was also less like the sound of a lethal weapon. It was more the sound of a crack or split, as if a concrete joist had given way somewhere. The rip in the metal roof above him and the ricochet of the bullet above the van was enough to make Adams' jaw drop: he now realized, as others had realized before him, that the old man was indeed dangerous, could indeed be off the rails, someone unpredictable, deranged, unhinged. And there was the interior of the van, ripped apart in some desperate act: someone trying to escape, doing anything to escape, and failing to escape because the figure with the rifle at the door had prevailed, had thwarted the escape. And disposed of the victim. And there was the rifle itself, a live fire arm, supported loosely and pointing towards him virtually point-blank. I knew exactly what it would do to him at this range from what it had done to Shaft, when he'd been fool enough to try that stunt with the rock. Though, to be fair, that had been a team effort between him and Moos, and she was perhaps as much to blame for what happened as he was. The knowledge of what the bullet would do to Adams' stocky body from this range showed in my attitude at the back of the van, which was not grim and menacing, but light and focused and questioning, even challenging.

What can you do, now?

"You and I have to talk," I said.

"Okay," he replied. "Okay. No problem."

It was as if he had done the same course as Manilow. Stay calm. Acquiesce. Stall. *The Advantage Will Come! Believe!*

"But not here."

"Okay," he said again. "Where?"

"I need to know you'll cooperate. Stay quiet in the back here during the ride."

"Sure."

"Slide your phone across the floor. Hard as you can, so it gets here."

He took out his phone and knelt slowly. Too slowly. He was considering something. Just like Shaft.

"Don't," I told him. "They'll find your body in this

car park bay. Someone might back over it by accident."

He slid the phone very hard and I made no attempt to stop it. I let it fly out the back onto the concrete.

"We'll talk when we get there. About twenty minutes."

I withdrew the rifle, shut the rear door, locked it (this time), stamped on his phone, set it under the rear wheel for good measure, and returned to the driver's seat.

On our way once more.

No one was making any connections. Adding anything up. The only adding up anyone had done so far was by me, for the expenses of the trip, which were now well out of control. The original security I'd felt about my savings had shrivelled up. They diminished by the day. At the back of my mind I'd always had the notion I could sell the Hymer, but thanks to Tracey Emin's 'art work' I knew that was going to be complicated. It would involve questions I couldn't be bothered to compose answers to, and now there was the bullet hole in the roof too. More immediately pressing was that every time I needed to fill up, the fuel needle became a barometer of my spirits, sinking me into the red. The vehicle drank fuel, guzzled fuel. This was something I had not worried about at the outset of the journey from Andalucia, on my holiday trip north through all those ruined landscapes and seascapes. Back then I had even planned a diversion to surrealist country, with a visit to Dali's villa near Cadaqués, but once on the road, filling up every few hours, I calculated a detour east to the Catalan coast would cost more - particularly as I'd planned to treat myself to a night in a Parador Hotel - than the entire trip north through the Pyrenees.

Such were these pressures, and the daily frustration of seeing the work I had done so far just ignored, shrinking and disappearing without a trace in the news (there had been no mention of the deaths of the graffiti artists for weeks), such were these pressures that I knew I had to force the connections forward, even hand the case over on a plate, to generate interest.

These were the motives for returning to Stonebridge Lock with Raph Adams. To open the sluice gates, force the connections upstream.

But we had to talk first. There was so much to discuss and to organize.

Not dusk but night had fallen by the time we approached the reservoirs. It was far too chilly to lure any but the hardiest and poorest to undertake a narrow-boat trip in this cold snap, so the car park was deserted. From October it closed at 20.30 but there seemed to be scant vigilance to prevent our staying longer. I could have parked exactly where I had parked before, between the very same lines, but I felt superstitious about that and kept to the Watermead Way side of things, and this led to something fortuitous. At the far end of the car park was an electrical transformer box, about five feet high, on which the Hymer headlights lit up a piece of graffiti, or what its artist would prefer to call 'street art'. I aligned the Hymer so that the headlights gave full scope to the figure.

It was a representation, on the neat and even brick of the transformer box, of a swan's head, possibly, but with its neck in lurid purple, and with a chunk-arrow, yolk-yellow beak, mournfully or modestly retracted in an attitude of gross sentimentality. A tear almost fell from its glossy blue eye. Disney art. More Americana. At the top of the transformer box, on the grey weather seal, the graffitist had left her name in proud, even brazen, joined-up capitals.

The parking lights were sufficient to illuminate the figure and I left them on. Before getting out of the cabin I fetched up some parallel images on my phone in case I needed them for explanations and justifications in my discussions with Adams.

Outside, as I looked around and took stock, my breath rising in front of my face for the first time in 2024, I sensed a wintry chill in my feelings for Raph Adams and all he represented that stiffened resolve. A crosswind from the east, over the River Lea's navigable waterway and the low industrial estate beyond, caused the Hymer to sway, and the movement was reflected in a slight tilt of the grotesque 'street-art' in front of the bonnet, in the parking lights. Nothing, however, could imbue any life or depth into such an infantile and rudimentary thing, such a dead cartoon.

With the rifle under a folded blanket as before, I looked through the sliding door window. I could not see him at first but then discerned a crouched, humped figure, very dark in his overcoat, at the other end, where he was hidden in stealth, waiting for me to open the rear door. He took me for an idiot. I rapped on the sliding door several times and at last he stood and came down this end, stumbling over the camper fridge and stooping all the way even though someone of his squatness could stand up freely in the Hymer. He was protecting his high comb of off-reddish hair, gelled and brushed up to give the impression of greater height. Still that vanity, in the back of the broken-up Hymer.

I pointed to the bulwark separating cab from cabin.

"Stay there." I nodded. "Where I can see you."

I bobbed round to the rear doors and looked in through the mean, high window down there. He was visible enough, standing where I'd said, and there was no sign that he'd tried to sort out some weapon for himself either, some projectile to cut and maim me as soon as I opened up the rear door, no sign of Shaft's mortal foolishness.

Still watching him all the time for some giveaway movement, I unlocked the rear door, flipped down the step-ladder and climbed up, keeping the Browning level in front of me all the time. I felt for the handle behind me and closed the door.

"Sit."

He slid down the bulwark and settled on his crumpled overcoat with his stocky legs pointing out in a crude, defiant V.

I crouched and adjusted position so I was reasonably comfortable propped against the rear door, the rifle resting on one knee, the blanket set aside now. I would have liked to sort out the blanket as something to sit on but that was out of the question, far too awkward a manoeuvre with the rifle cocked, safety catch released. The wall of the toilet/shower was on my right and gave shoulder support and steadiness of aim.

"Saint Catherine's."

He frowned, nodded.

"An Oxonian."

"No one has used that word since Oscar Wilde."

"You read History of Art. A two-one."

"Okay, okay …" He was already weary of this. "So you've done your homework. What you don't know is that I missed a first by one mark. Sixty-nine. No jokes, please."

He shrugged and smiled after this detail. It was a different smile to the superior, knowing, deeply cynical and one-sided smile, that might almost have been a leer except there was no lust in it, with which he had tried to intimidate me in New Bond Street. There was more humility in this smile, despite his boast.

"For a history man - "

He interrupted - "I know where you're going and there's no point."

"I'll be the judge of that," I asserted. "You wrote a dissertation on the hoarding of mediaeval portraiture."

"Incipient capitalism. Interested me at the time."

"But now you're interested in the memorabilia of Roger Moore. The hoarding of his old postcards and Biros, his watches. His ancient skis."

He nodded. "Yep. One has to earn a living, does one not?" That 'Yep' was the first obvious sign of falsity, of him biding his time for an opportunity to attack, turn the tables. *The Advantage! It Will Come! Believe!*

Anyway, it was not an answer I could accept.

"When we were driving into this car park - "

Again an interruption, but a sudden explosion this time - "JUST WHERE THE FUCK AM I?"

That felt much more genuine.

"We are at Stonebridge Lock car park. Tottenham Marshes. No one can hear you."

"*What*? Where's that? What the fuck's that?"

"On clear roads, it's just fifteen minutes from central London. North east of Stamford Hill. South of Walthamstow Wetlands. Does any of this connect?"

"No."

"Not with anything you've read in the news?"

"No. Nothing connects at all. Maybe you've got the wrong man."

"That's a pity," I told him. "Because that's actually why you're here this evening. To make connections. Join the dots."

He shook his head and pursed his lips, as if resisting telling me again this was all wrong, all folly, and then he adjusted his horn-rim glasses and set his head back against the bulwark. The confidence was returning.

Already uncomfortable on the floor, I had to adjust my position and lean harder into the toilet/shower wall, which was only a plastic panel. I had been losing weight on account of the Hymer diet of processed foods and salad takeaways, but I could feel the feeble plastic sheeting bend inward under my shoulder and that worried me. Damage to that membrane meant bad smells leaking out, water leaking out, more prospects of dereliction.

"Stand up."

"Sit down! Stand up!" he mocked.

He sighed but did as he was told.

Then his manner changed. At first I read it wrong.

"I'm sorry," he said, "if I have offended you in any way."

More from Manilow's survival course, I thought - stay courteous, humane, human.

Standing now at his full height before the bulwark, he put his hands in his overcoat pockets. The coat looked very much like a Crombie, but of a modern cut, not straight down but waisted and double-breasted.

He continued in an altogether different tone, in a speech that became jerky and broken up in places with impatience and exasperation.

"I'm sorry I went to grammar school and to Oxford, and I'm sorry I'm young and fit and strong and in good health, and I'm in the black at the bank and I go out every week with old friends from Saint Cat's, and I'm sorry I have a good job in New Bond Street, and I'm sorry I have a promising future, and that I will, in good time, with some intelligence and a little cunning, maybe, ascend into the ranks of those who can make real money, solid capital, and that the capital will one day enable me to live wherever I like and do whatever I like - learn to fly, learn to scuba dive, sail a medium sized yacht, perhaps, and pay to eat in all the best restaurants, go to the opera, piss money away in casinos in Monte Carlo OR DO WHATEVER THE FUCK I LIKE - and escape forever the company of those such as yourself, the losers and left-behinds in their campervans, I'm so sorry that I am a walking, talking antagonism to you - BUT! - LISTEN TO ME! - you have no fucking right - NO FUCKING RIGHT WHATEVER! - to entrap me in this way or threaten me with that fucking firearm! … JUST LISTEN TO ME! If you let me go now, I will scuttle off back to the life you so despise and never breathe a word of what has happened here. My word of honour. Let me go before it is too late for both of us. I entreat you and I implore you, in the name of the supplicant to one with power over him simply because you have a fucking firearm, for Christ's sake let me go! NOW!"

Still crouched in my corner, my answer to all that was to raise the rifle so that it pointed directly above his head and fire a second round through the roof of the Hymer.

"Christ, man," he muttered, and he flapped his coat from its pockets. "What's the matter with you?"

That 'man' brought back Shaft and I knew I had to take the lead here and now.

"I'll show you what's the matter with me. I'll show you exactly what's the matter with me. Go to the window."

He did as he was told, but looked back at me warily because he was now side-on, to all intents and purposes with this back to me. Vaguely, he must have thought that if he was being asked to look out of the van, this may be the start, no matter how many diversions were ahead, to his exit from the van, to his hasty escape through the car park and onto Watermead Way, to flag a taxi or hitch a lift or just run run run.

"Draw the window back. Catch left side."

He found the catch and slid the window back halfway.

"All the way."

He obeyed.

"Look out the window to your left, to the front of the van."

He looked back at me again.

With great care and difficulty - pins and needles had set in all the way up one leg - I too rose to my feet, keeping the rifle vaguely pointing side-on at his stocky midriff.

"Look out of the window," I repeated. "To your left."

He did as he was told now. Swiftly as I could I approached and slid the window back so it closed on his neck, cutting off his wind. Frantically he tried to raise his right arm to release the window but each time he did so I struck down hard on his forearm or his fingers or his wrist with the barrel of the rifle. I waited until his movements weakened and drooped, then released the window. He withdrew his head, taking gulps and gasps of air, and fell to the floor. His face was swollen and flushed but his eyes were open and he was recovering quickly. He was a young man, after all, though overweight and unfit. It struck me at that moment that he had always been like that. Pudgy from infancy. There was a writhing movement on the floor during this recovery, an incongruously sexual writhing movement which did not suit his ungainly bulk at all. Eventually, the gasps began to quieten and the swelling around his eyes and mouth subsided but remained distinct. A curious swelling had also appeared above his eyes, causing a blue ridge there above his glasses, which were askew but still in place.

It was useless at this stage to ask him about what he'd seen out there. It was obvious he could not speak yet.

I stood over him with the rifle pointing at his chest but out of reach, in case he tried a desperate swipe of some kind, but his right arm, wrist and fingers were beaten and bruised, though not bleeding, and his left arm lay across his chest with the hand gripped on the forearm of his right arm, as if to comfort it.

By now he had recovered enough to answer some questions.

"What did you see?"

First a pant, then a word. "Where?"

"In front of the van. Directly in front of the van. In the lights."

He took several more breaths before answering, very unevenly.

"Some kind of electrical installation … Transformer? … Switchgear? …"

"And what was on it?"

"Nothing."

"Painted onto the box, onto the brick."

"Oh!" His face crumpled and he emitted something like a pant broken by an eruption of laughter, no sooner begun than stifled, and his left arm fell back at his side. "Street art."

"Street art. But what?"

"Fuck knows! Some shit. Some kind of bird."

I toed him in his fatty hips. "Stay focused."

His eyes shut and his head rolled on the dirty cabin floor.

"Would you like to see it again?" My menace was a touch too theatrical, reminding me at this moment, of all moments, why I'd given up that faltering acting career, once upon a time. Ghoul 14.

"NO!" He responded. It was the nearest he could get to a shout. He grunted and cleared his throat afterwards. Then, still without opening his eyes, he muttered, "No no no…"

"So what did you see?"

He groaned again. "It was just street art. Fucksake. I've seen it before, all over London. Her name's at the top - Frankie someone."

"Frankie Strand."

"She's all over the place. Underpasses. Bridges.

Tawdry sentiment. Infant art. Ghastly colours. Total shit."

Then he opened his eyes wide. He looked genuinely alarmed, as if he'd just let something slip or made some terrible mistake. He stared up at the roof a moment, at the two new holes there, then at me, then at the rifle barrel pointing at his chest.

"You didn't do it, did you?" he asked. "Paint that? You're not Frankie Strand?"

I shook my head and he closed his eyes.

"Thank god for that."

We weren't making much progress. My turn to sigh.

"It's actually much worse than you think," I said, in what I thought was a leading way.

"God … " He groaned again. "You'll have to explain. I don't understand! I just don't understand what you want me to say! What's going down here! I will try. I am not an idiot. But you need to give me more clues."

"Okay. Sit back against the bulwark."

When he had settled, I took out my phone and thumbed up the image I needed. It was from a nineties Camel cigarette advertisement.

Adams frowned at it.

"What's this?"

"Cover the eyes."

He covered the eyes in the picture with his thumb.

Then he nodded, slowly. "I see it now. Yeah."

"And the neck flesh. Puckered. Pubic."

"Yep." He nodded and pushed the phone back across the floor. "She's done the same thing but she doesn't realize it. Gross."

"And the purple."

"You're right. You're absolutely right."

That didn't seem part of the script he thought he might use to lull me and catch me unawares.

"So," he said, "she has plastered that image of drooping male genitalia all over London without realizing it, because she is so naive and has so little artistic talent and intelligence, insight, whatever. Clueless. Okay. She's made a fool of herself, maybe. But maybe not. Thought of that? Maybe she's leading everyone up the garden path. Including you. But in the end, so what?"

"You miss the point." I answered, putting away my phone. "The Camel advertisers knew exactly what they were doing. Subliminal advertising associating product warmth with being well-hung. Though the artist in question, Mike Salisbury, who created Joe Camel, denied all of this. He said people read what they wanted into it. But there are buttocks too, or breasts, if you like. There's cleavage."

He reached out and I took the phone from my pocket single-handedly and again thumbed up the image. I gave it back for a second viewing.

"Yeah," he said, frowning again, speaking to the image. "I see it. But the Camel art is … much better. Much subtler. More refined. No comparison." He pushed up his glasses and looked at me with the phone, the image, still in his hand. "But where's this leading? I mean, see it from my point of view, just for a moment - Here I am, on this filthy fucking floor, in the back of a busted up campervan, with two bullet holes in the roof, south of Walthamstow Wetlands - You say! - talking about street art and old fag ads. Where's this leading? I want to help you if I can, but I need to know what's going down here with you. You must admit it's strange. That you're … weird."

I smiled. "Maybe you'll sell copies of Joe Camel posters one day, or prints of Frankie Strand's street-art."

He risked an uncertain smile too. "Maybe. Does it matter? … A dollar and a cent, like I said."

My smile snapped shut.

"Yes it does matter - TO ME!" I shouted. "And it should matter - TO YOU! And I have the gun, and you don't! Remember that!" The anger and menace in my voice took me by surprise, as well as Adams. Now that it had surfaced, I let it flow. "It matters to me that this stupid woman has put her gross, infantile depictions of male genitalia all over the capital, without even realizing it. She feels entitled to do that. For nothing. At least the advertisers paid to have their hoardings up there, and they knew what they were about, and their art is subtle and well executed. It takes talent and intelligence to do what they did. She has neither, but gets away with ruining the urban landscape with this rubbish, and calling herself what you called her without flinching, without wincing - a 'street artist'. This kind of thing, all around me, all day and all night, has ruined my eyesight, the way I see things, ruined my mind, ruined my life."

He closed his eyes and sighed.

"Oh, wait a minute, wait a minute, man - "

"I can see you don't even care. So what? you say. Maybe, maybe not, you say. Does it matter? you say. You are part of it but you don't even care. With your first class education, you ask me if it matters? You are part of a force that is destroying culture, art, meaning - you are pushing it too, forcing it, the landslide of trash down on all of us. You have forsaken art, betrayed art for Roger Moore's old skis. You have betrayed history, all you knew and studied, for Roger Moore's old Biros."

"The old Biros sold well. Thousands of pounds."

Now I shouted at him again. Let him have it. "YOU ARE A TRASHETEER, MISTER!"

After a pause he spoke very calmly, and I knew I had lost ground, seemed unstable, maniacal, perhaps, for losing my temper, and I regretted it.

"I am a trasheteer. Nice neologism. Well, well. So here we are, as I say, in the back of your trashed up campervan, but I am, you say, a trasheteer. Not you, of course. Me. I'm the trashy one."

He said nothing more after that and we were both silent. I started edging, worming my way back to the rear door and settled down there again. I was feeling quite foggy. Maybe because I hadn't been eating well, just Hymer food, salads and takeaways, coupled with the sheer excitement of all that had happened since engaging with Adams in New Bond Street, just a few hours ago. And the urgency of that, after Emin's TV revelation. And my vigil from across the road in the Ésclot fashion house too - all that tension. A lot to take in for both of us but he seemed to be in better shape despite the way I had treated him, despite that jamming of his windpipe in the window and that smashing of his right arm. With the fogginess came that familiar sense of panic - What was I doing? *What was I doing*? - but it did not blast resolve so much this time around. I knew what I was doing all right. That said, the next moves, if anything, would be physically even more demanding, and I had to keep in mind Adams was of a different generation and much stronger than I was, despite his unfitness and the bruising I'd inflicted. This was not at all the same as handling Barry Manilow. I remembered ruefully, almost with nostalgia, the sense of superiority I had felt sitting opposite the octogenarian at the table, when there had been a table, and cushioned seats, when there had been cushioned seats, and cupboards and drawers and all the rest of it. The Hymer had represented something back then. A state of normality. A means to an end. A purpose. And that was all on my side with Manilow. But after Emin's trashing of the cabin it represented something altogether different: degradation, dereliction, destitution, dissolution, ruin. "What the fuck happened?" Raph Adams had asked, on entering, staring round the cabin. Somehow Emin's title, *The Death of Barry Manilow*, began to hold sway, to fill with meaning again, as it had last night in the TV interview. Adams had either seen it or read about it but he had said nothing more since he'd stepped inside the Hymer, for some reason of his own. He was holding back that connection, that card. Of course he was. In which case, if he was deceiving me about that - that he knew only too well where we were sitting - here, slumped here, in a second-class copy of her Installation Art - which was actually the original, which he could not know, but maybe somehow he did know that *as well!* - maybe he was already that far ahead of me, which filled me again with rising panic - *Thought of that? Maybe she's leading everyone up the garden path. Including you.* She - Frankie? Tracey? - *You didn't do it, did you? Paint that? You're not Frankie Strand?* I could not sustain it, this tableau. *Thought of that? Including you. Thought of that?* We had to move to a conclusion.

"Take off all your clothes."

Instead of astonishment and rebuff, Adams closed his eyes again and winced.

"So that's what it's all about."

"You're wrong. Absolutely wrong. I am not gay. Assume nothing. Don't stand up. You have to remove them from where you arc, from a sitting position."

"All the talk about street art, sexual imagery, old Camel ads, for fucksake … bringing me all the way out here. You certainly have a roundabout way of going about things, *mister*. You are weird, I'll give you that."

"That's all wrong. I don't want you that way. Just get undressed. You don't understand. Not yet."

He had the Crombie off now and started folding it neatly and setting it aside.

"Don't I," he said, without the interrogative tone but with a resigned, semi-disgusted and contemptuous tone instead. "Now I see why some poor bastard busted up your fucking van." He started undoing his tie.

"Wrong, wrong, and wrong again," I repeated. It was my turn to adopt a weary and cynical manner. "I told you earlier that you're here to make connections. That one is wrong. I need you to start making different connections. More imaginative connections. The first should be obvious enough."

"Don't worry." He stopped undoing his shirt and looked directly at me. "I've got that one now. Sorry it took so long."

"Yes?"

"Barry Manilow nearly died here. You have his clothes. The real thing."

"Well done. Straight to the top of the class ... And … ?"

"That doesn't mean I'm going to drown here, right?"

I nodded. "That wouldn't suit the purpose."

"Good." He half laughed and grunted as he had before, but it was such a short noise it wasn't a release of any kind. "Look, *Mister* … " He enjoyed repeating my excesses. "I've never been a great Quiz Show fan. Pub quiz man. TV junkie. Despite my dishonourable profession. I'm very happy for you to fill in some blankety-blanks. I won't find that humiliating at all. You can win every time."

"All right."

I was willing to cut much of what I had prepared for some quick progress.

"I'll give you some names, but you have to make the connections yourself. That's important. Because if you don't see the connection, the sacrifice of these people's lives will have been for nothing. It's important not just to me and to their families but - "

"To the whole fucking world." He nodded. "I know. Fire away."

"Here's the first name, then."

"I'm ready."

"Loner."

"That's the name?"

"I'm only giving you names. Like I said. Try to concentrate. If a name means anything, speak. If not, just shake your head. Again. Loner."

"You. You're a loner. That's you."

"No. Loner. Try again."

He shook his head.

"Shaft."

"Aha. Richard Roundtree. Seventies' TV series. First black secret agent. Black culture copying white trash. Died around this time last year aged eighty-four in Los Angeles. I'm Associate Specialist of Popular Culture at Bonhams, remember."

"That'll do. Arus."

He shook his head.

"Moos."

"A moose is a large - "

"Arthur Spencer Harris."

He shook his head.

"Rachel Allsop."

He shook his head again. I wasn't too bothered because these names hadn't been in the news for weeks. But it was important to work my way in from as far outside as possible, so that if one of these did connect, each connection thenceforth would be more resonant, meaningful, tumbling back and forward through the list.

"Tracey Emin."

"Aha. Back to her. She had a bedroom. You don't. That's controversial."

I nodded. "More."

Why wouldn't he connect with last night, when he had before? Now he only frowned, hesitated, keeping that back.

"It's all rubbish? You don't like it?"

I left a pause, then decided to play along, see where it led us. I nodded, pressed on.

"Evaristo."

"Bernadine. Bernadine Evaristo. Booker Prize Winner. Black writer."

I nodded. "Have you read her book?"

He scowled and looked down at the grubby floor. It was a pained expression, as if he didn't want to disparage the book but had to. "I tried. Couldn't read it. No real characters, no real plot .... So you think they're all rubbish? These people? Their art? That's it? And that gives you the right to kill them?"

I nodded.

"Evaristo nearly drowned the other day, in the river Wye, south Wales. She's okay now, though."

Back on track. I nodded again, said nothing, and there was a silence.

Very slowly, he shook his head just once. One way,

then the other.

"Oh no you didn't. You didn't really."

I took a deep breath through flared nostrils, something I hadn't done since *The Coffee Shed* with Dame Tracey.

"You did? You killed them? Tried to kill them? All of them?"

"No," I answered. "It wasn't like that." I looked him steadily in the eye, through those fancy horn-rim glasses. "When I confronted them with the truth about their art, they couldn't live with themselves. The shame was too intense. They took their own lives. Everasto tried to commit suicide, whatever she says now."

"It was just an accident, she said. She fell in the river. Slipped off a jetty, she said. Twisted her ankle."

Just as I suspected. So who was ahead now?

"She didn't," I told him. "It was a failed suicide."

Adams nodded thoughtfully, trying to cover his disbelief. His eyes focused a moment on the rifle barrel pointing somewhere between his groin and his midriff.

"I see," he said. Then he added, adjusting his glasses and looking up at me as directly as I had looked at him, as if searching for a pivotal moment here. "They were trasheteers too?"

"Yes."

"So we all must die? All the trasheteers must die?"

"Not you. I already told you - you must tell the story. You must tell the world why these people died. They must not have died for nothing. That would be wrong. Immoral. There is a punishment for you too but it is not death. You are the messenger. The prophet. You are important."

"Wait a minute."

Another connection had occurred to him, or he was trying to stall.

"If you tried to kill Barry Manilow here, a man with a bounty, a seventies superstar, a pop-culture icon - You know he was on TV with Michael Jackson at the American Music Awards, 1984? Did a tribute to Jackson? A long medley? - If you tried to kill him right here - "

"No." I shook my head at that. A definite denial. I didn't want and couldn't trust his diversions. He was holding back, playing games.

"I wasn't there."

"At the awards?"

"Not when his time came. It wasn't me. It was very dark. I told him his clothes were by Stonebridge Lock, and he went to look for them. As I say, it was dark and cold, and he was very old and frail, and he should have died. But he got lucky, as you'll know."

There was another pause, and Adams' frown tightened inward so much it looked painful, turning white the bluish ridge above his glasses.

"Then … what about those names at the start?"

"You remember, back in August, there was an incident where several graffiti artists died in France. All UK citizens."

"Yes. I remember that. One was shot."

I stroked the stock of the Browning.

"Now that you know everything," I told him, "you must continue to undress."

The original plan had been to escort Adams to the old Stonebridge Lock, the manually operated, disused one. It had emergency steps in the wall: he would take a cleansing, baptismal swim amid the weeds, bottles and polystyrene cold boxes that lie as surface details of the foul water beneath. When he came out, baptised in the drinking water of London's cultural trash, he would be ready to make his way back into the world to explain why so many had to die, and to publicly renounce and denounce his career as Associate Specialist in Popular Culture at Bonhams, and reject any further offer of such employment.

I lost appetite for all of that once Adams was ready to leave the van.

He acquiesced to all demands. Under my direction, naked, he took his shoes and clothes, except his shirt, to the far end of the van. Under my direction, back at the sliding door, he wound his tailored, faintly chequered blue shirt about his head and tied it tight by the sleeves for a blindfold. He bent down and blindly picked up Manilow's outfit, which I had placed before him, including the long green boots, and stood still with his precious reward clasped to his chest until I'd slid back the side door. After I had exited, I told him step by step where to put his feet so that he could leave the van without accident. I then walked behind him with my phone torch, guiding him across the car park towards the exit for the canal towpath, sometimes with the cold steel of the Browning barrel.

Before we reached the towpath we stopped for further instructions.

I explained clearly and frankly what I was going to do. After our walk, I was going back to the van and he was not to move until he heard the van start up. If he attempted to follow me back, he would leave me no choice but to use the rifle, not to kill him but to maim him, which I did not want to do.

"Don't force me to do that," I told him. "That would be on your head. Your fault."

He didn't respond.

In fact, all he complained about, after he understood the plan, shivering there at the towpath with his arms wrapped tight around his bounty, all he complained about was the cold. And he complained about that quite incessantly, but not too loudly, through moans and groans, violent shivers and shudders and curses. There were no desperate cries for help. He understood well enough that if I could escort him in this way there could be no one around. Twice he shuddered so violently that we had to stop to pick up an item of Manilow's outfit that had fallen onto the towpath. The second time this happened, when the glossy green jacket itself fell, I told him not to bother to pick it up and that he could come back for it later once he heard me drive away. The reason for leaving the jacket where it lay was that it had fallen in dogshit, and he had already trodden in the very same mess himself.

"Is that what I think it is?" he asked. The shit was old and the night chill kept the smell down.

"You can wipe it off on the clothes. I'll tell you if I

see any more, or any glass or anything like that ahead."

He managed a little sarcasm through chattering teeth. "Thank you so much."

Shortly after that incident we stopped for the second and last time.

"Stop here," I told him. "I'm going to leave you now. Do not remove the blindfold until you hear the van start."

He turned to face me, or face my voice, my torch, without my instruction. It seemed he had something to say. Below the chequered blue blindfold his jaw was trembling uncontrollably, lending him the jowls and dewlaps of an old man, and the fleshy white paps of his chest shook in the torchlight with every snatch of breath.

He did have something to say.

"Listen," he said.

"Okay," I replied, as if nothing he could say would shock or move me. "… I'm listening."

He had to take a breath and hold it to get these words out without shivering them to pieces.

"Emin's is better," he said. Then he repeated it. "Emin's is better … because Emin's better."

"Hah. Is that all?" I replied flatly, quickly, to show I knew he'd had that card all along and to suffer no loss of face. "Well, I look forward to reading the papers tomorrow."

Saying so, I turned and left him. I looked back a couple of times but he remained there, a short white body shivering in the night, with the shirt tight around his head and the green bundle held tight to his chest, nodding at me as I walked away, nodding and mouthing: 'Emin's is better because Emin's better.' Once the car park was in sight I quickened my pace and didn't look back again until I had started the Hymer.

On board *Mont St Michel* for the 23.30 crossing from Portsmouth to Caen.

No one but truckers. Car Deck One empty but for

a pair of shabby UK saloons near the front and a French customs vehicle at the back that must have been gathering dust for months. Officious French stevedores parked me opposite the UK saloons.

One would have thought the truckers would seize this opportunity to seek each other out for company and conversation, given the solitary nature of their working lives, but no: most were content to watch films or play games on their phones, both while they ate and afterwards, when they lay slack in recliners, the black sea a backdrop as immovable as their trucks below. A few stared out at the blackness, through the toughened glass, waiting for sleep to take them prisoner a few hours. Smokers went out on deck before turning in.

After an all-day breakfast blew me full of wind I went out there too.

For some solitude, some quiet, some peace of mind, I walked aft to avoid the smokers.

At the stern of the boat, on a whim, I decided to seek out the place where it all began, because Ronnie's accident was a mixed up business, and far too personal. Here I was again, before the heavy deck doors outside the Games Room, that poky afterthought, adjacent the kitchens. I pushed one door wide. I approached the rail, stopped halfway, then went right up to the very spot. I felt and stroked the rail. That sea-wind worn, storm-worn, hardwood rail. Tonight the touch of the wood was so much colder. It made me nervous to look over the side and down those five storeys to the grey churning sea, lit only by the cabins and the ship's lights. Somewhere down there, beneath all that, lay Loner, at rest, at peace. Enviable. Nothing could touch him now.

I turned to look back at those heavy deck doors, as he had done on that fateful dawn. "*Morning!*" he had called: I heard and saw again in my mind's eye that desperate plea for normality.

Again I turned back to the water and that five storey drop. The average depth of the channel is only about sixty metres. Just ten metres more than an Olympic swimming pool. Where did his body lie down there, amid the debris of this ferry route, traversed twice daily, year in and year out, by the *Mont St Michel*; where did he lie amid the cans and cartons and human filth at the bottom of this shallow sea? Had his broken frame been flipped from propeller to propeller, before sinking through the dark to the sea floor?

This was my work. What I had done.

I felt no remorse, nor any compulsion to explain to myself why I felt neither remorse nor shame. The last one, Raph Adams, had been a very different victim and the first to begin to share, in a crude way, some understanding of my point of view. He had declared without prompting - "I've seen that shit all over London!" - or something like that, words to that effect. But what he could not even begin to grasp was my imprisonment in that defilement, with those images force-fed into the consciousness through blighted senses, through an aesthetic sensibility fine as a jeweller's glass but crushed under the jackboots of popular culture, a life sentence without reprieve, parole, that had turned one's eyes, one's mind, inside out. He could not understand because he was part of it himself. A jailer, a guard, who'd trodden in the shit and without thinking, without remorse, to cleanse his sole, had smeared the path for others. At least I had left him without shoes.

These high and mighty reflections were brought down by a burly trucker, unshaven, his broad leather belt fastened low under a heavy paunch. In his fifties, maybe, but perhaps younger, this man of the road. The loss of much of his hair aged him, an empty motorway ahead, and what hair remained, long and lank on the hard shoulders, was dyed gypsy black. Stubbled jowls and jade earrings completed the effect. I found his appearance unprepossessing but his manner was immediately friendly and warm.

"Evening!" he declared, taking his place at the rail close by. He sounded Irish. I'm not sure from which part because I muddle north and southern accents. He wore an old blue club jacket over a Clydella shirt and vest.

"Aren't you cold?" I asked.

"Fuckin' freezin'!" he said, and laughed. "Only came out here to fart!"

Having said that, he let rip a loud blast, so powerful in force and stench that I caught it despite the crosswind and the mighty diesel fumes.

"Knew I should have left that broccoli alone!

Hahaha!"

He turned to me and laughed some more. He was gap-toothed. On both sides his remaining teeth parted in disarray with his laughter, ayes to the left, nays to the right.

I looked out into the darkness and thought again of Loner, just a swimming pool length below us, at rest, and of his forlorn attempts to leave his mark on the world in aerosol loops and twirls that carried no more artistry or meaning than this trucker's fart, or anyone else's fart, come to that. I thought, You're better off down there, my friend, I promise you that.

As loudly as I could manage, I farted myself.

The trucker laughed again. "Sounds like you should've left it alone too! Or is that the malt talkin'?"

"No," I replied, and turned away. "Eggs. Only eggs and beans."

"Goodnight!" he called, a touch forlorn to be alone again with only the rail and the sea.

"Goodnight!" I echoed, heaving open the heavy deck doors.

That was quite enough humanity for one evening. I tracked down the Purser's Office and paid for a cabin, which I hadn't intended to do, funds being so low now.

Keeping clear of the toll roads and stopping only for naps, fuel, coffee, sandwiches, I motored all the way from Caen back to Andalucia in under thirty-six hours. It was so cheering to feel the warmth of the sun again going south, each stop warmer than the last, it made me feel like singing. For some stretches, once I was south of Madrid, I had to use the air-conditioner, and thereabouts I bought sun-cream too. The Tilley hat was of no use once in Andalucia. I replaced it with a couple of cheap tourist straw hats with an *Espana!* band around the crown.

I cannot pass over one fateful incident on the journey down towards the end. I don't know exactly when it happened, night or day. I must have been asleep in the cab. I only noticed hundreds of kilometres later at a gasolinera south of Jaen, on the Granada road.

It looked like a team effort. On the right hand flank of the van, the side without the sliding door, was graffitied a mockery of the old *Kit-Kat* biscuit advertisement:

Have a Kwick Break!
Have a Kwick Krap!

A long run of bright brown, King Edward potato turds curled down from *Krap!* to finish at the release gate for toilet waste at the rear of the van.

Hey guys. Thanks guys.

If I had seen you, I would have shot you dead.

The lovely señorita filling up the van took an amused interest in the new look.

"¡Qué fea!" How ugly! Pointing to the garbled English, she asked "¿Qué significa eso?"

"Nada," I said. "Absolutamente nada."

"¿Que? ¿Por qué lo has hecho?"

The last twist of the knife.

Mid-afternoon, running on empty, I brought the Hymer to its final resting place in the Long Stay car park at Málaga airport. At least, I had to entertain the possibility that I was abandoning it there.

I caught the shuttle bus back to the airport, and from there took the train into Málaga. At *El Corte Ingles* I bought two light outfits of modest casual wear, a shaving kit, a flannel and liquid soap dispenser, two bath towels and a pair of expensive brown leather brogues; all of which I packed neatly into a showy Samsonite silver cabin bag. The Samsonite was a heavy investment. It gave me the appearance of a tourist with means, a tourist no security guard would look at twice in the milling crowds of the airport. Only when I had made full provision for myself in this way did I return to the airport to use the facilities there, the toilets, showers (more expense) and changing rooms.

When I left the ablutions in my brand new casual wear (leaving my old clothes, a discarded skin, on the changing room bench), when I left with my spare set of new clothes neatly folded in my Samsonite case, when I walked out onto the concourse wearing one of my *España!* hats, in my new brogues, I felt a surge in confidence that I could carry this off, that I could survive here, in the airport, for as long as necessary, as I had seen others here surviving - mainly British citizens in various stages of dissolution - whenever I passed through this airport. I vividly remembered the impression it had made on Rosaline when I explained to her that the person we had met in the car park lift on her arrival was actually a resident of the airport, that I'd seen him in lifts there twice before. "Christ," she'd muttered, without thinking, stopping and staring down at the car park floor, "there but for the grace of god…" He had been inside the lift when the doors opened: a tall and heavyset man, whose body would demand an expensive diet to keep upright. He was wearing a grubby fedora and leant wearily on his trolley of phony, tatty baggage. He pressed the button for us and lost no time in introducing himself as Claude. He'd had "a spot of bad luck" and "lawst" his wallet and BA ticket first class for Heathrow. "Bloody carteristas! Pickypockets!" he cursed. He only wanted thirty euros - twenty would do, in fact - so he could get the train home to Fuengirola and sort himself out.

I gave him nothing, said nothing in reply.

When we left the lift he stayed in there. All day.

Lord Claude, they called him. Claude the fraud.

Well, I would join his humble brotherhood and sisterhood but on my terms. I was not condemned to sleep every night in the airport as Claude and company were, because I could always take the Long Stay shuttle bus back to the Hymer if I chose, and, of course, I still had some survival funds of my own. No loitering in the lift for me. Not yet awhile.

On the journey down I had promised myself that I would provide for myself in this way, sort myself out first, to show some discipline and self-respect, some control over things, over my managed descent, before I bought a single newspaper or signed into the airport wi-fi to garner in all of Raph Adams' news from the last few days.

In the two great challenges of life - finding a mate and earning a living - there had been some measure of disappointment, shall we say. In courtship, there was Rosaline, the last great hope, after what is called these days an incel's life. I'm not at ease any more with 'single', 'singleton' or, God forbid, 'bachelor'. None tells half the story. As for earning a living, there were career setbacks in the seventies and eighties when I had found it impossible to make headway just because of the way I looked, which had been disheartening in the extreme.

On neither account had I ever felt the depth of disappointment I felt on my 70th birthday, scouring through the British press - all of it, even *The Financial Times* - for news of my crimes from Mr Raph Adams, MA, Oxon, Associate Specialist in Popular Culture at Bonhams' Auction Rooms, 101 New Bond Street. It would have been better if I could have riffled through the newspapers in their living form, one by one, at my leisure in the Hymer, as I had done before, in Margate, or in that godforsaken Hereford industrial estate, but I was dependent on the free airport wi-fi and what peace and quiet I could get at one of the shabby cafés in Departures, where I'd lashed out on a coffee and Danish to celebrate this moment, to enjoy all the different speculations and points of view. When I found nothing in the first paper - the *Daily Star* - I seriously thought of buying the cheapest return ticket I could find so that I might pass through Security and raid W.H.Smith's. But the complications and expense (I was down to thousands now, not tens of thousands) made me persevere with the Free Trials or navigate the paywalls of every single British national.

Nothing, nothing, and again, nothing.

Disappointment began to drain the psyche, as if a plug had been pulled and the fluids for motor functions seeped down through my scraggy neck, slight torso, bony shanks and narrow shins, to be filtered away among the sorry bones of my feet. On account of this watery feeling, and having too little concentration left to dam it up, an old nightmare image from youthful scuba diving days came to mind - of sinking through freezing brine down the one hundred foot darkness of the disused SETT ('Submariner's Escape Training Tower') in Gosport, Portsmouth. When submariners had used it, the water was heated to 32 degrees centigrade and there were lights all the way down the 100 foot water tower. When the PADI and BSAC groups rented it after decommissioning, the water was freezing brine and the lights cost extra. Our PADI instructor took us up the tower for what she called 'a little treat for her lads' because we'd done so well in the murk of her miserable gravel pits for far too long. She always talked in flirtatious ambiguities like that - 'a little treat for her lads' - and she always changed in and out of her wetsuit in front of us for our delight. Head down, she pulled that long frontal zip up slow and even from navel to chin, then looked up to see who was watching. There was a waiting list of men like me for her group, all incels, I suspected. A horrible ancient Slav, silver-haired and slab-faced, a veteran motor-cycling champion, or a champion of veteran motor-cycling - I can't remember now - with the manners of an ignoramus, played a vicious trick on me in the SETT. He was jealous of the instructor's introductory warmth towards me, which was quickly fading but he didn't seem to notice, and he wanted to put me in my place. Because I was the newbie, it was my 'treat' to go first. At the rim of the tank, the depth of still, freezing black brine, was terrifying to me, but worse, I saw some ripple come to the surface of that 100 foot well of darkness. "There's something in there!" I shouted, to derisive laughter. "Give me the lights!" The Slav grew impatient: "Get on with it," he muttered. "Sea's pitch, you fucking idiot. We have to practise without lights." But the instructor pulled down a lever, a huge three pronged shank, like something in a signal box for railway points, and the lights came on with a loud transformer hum.

"There's a fucking ray in there!" I screamed.

They all crowded round the rim to look. I was already backing out towards the lift. They were all laughing. The ancient Slav was looking at me, smiling, for the first time. The instructor called after me: "It's just a flounder! A

flatfish. A plaice!" But the lift doors were closing and I was finished with it all. I never went back. What was the point, when a flatfish scared me to death?

But it wasn't just the flatfish, of course, it was the terrible darkness and coldness of the 100 foot column of black brine. And though I never climbed into it, the nightmare image of sinking down through it, helpless to move against the weight of brine, sinking down further and further towards the unknown bottom, has awoken me with a start ever since. And it was something of that nightmare helplessness that took hold in the face of this fathomless disappointment, as I sat in the airport restaurant. I could no longer work out which arrow to press on the keyboard to move the newspaper text in the direction I needed.

Sitting back from the laptop, in the café, still with hardly any control over concentration, another memory found its way in, an attack from earlier still in my wretched youth. Trying to come to terms with abandoning my efforts at a stage career, I visited a psychologist at the Tavistock Clinic in Swiss Cottage (which had high standing at that time) with what I thought were the symptoms of clinical depression. A young, cold, self-important Canadian, with slicked black hair, wearing a dark suit with the broad lapels of that era, and a paisley tie on a pink shirt, listened to me for about five minutes, and then put up his right palm to interrupt, like a president about to swear on a bible. I stopped talking. He leant across his desk and knitted his hands. "What I have to tell you, you might find disturbing," he began, "but bear with me. You are not clinically depressed." He shook his head. "Oh no. No no no. Now look. Most of us are worried and discontent and frustrated most hours, most days, most of our lives. Some poor souls - all night long too. But, just because we're unhappy, we don't walk around with tears streaming down our faces, do we? That wouldn't get the job done, would it? Now this may not be a very helpful thing to say, but I can assure you that if you were clinically depressed you would not be here. The weight of your own worthlessness would be so dense, so immovable, you wouldn't be able to lift yourself out of bed. You would shit and piss where you lay. You wouldn't eat. You would become catatonic. You would feel suicidal but unable to do much about it. So, my friend, you are unhappy, disappointed with life, yes, but you are not depressed, and what I want you to do is stop feeling sorry for yourself, and get out of the Tavistock, and stop wasting our time."

From there, I had a life-long loathing of self-pity, and began to see it everywhere.

Had I been able to describe to that Young Turk what I was now feeling in the Departures lounge café, a lifetime later, to describe the sense of the life fluids draining out and motor functions shutting down, and the helpless floundering, sinking down the Escape Test Tower, he would have recognized the symptoms, I am sure. When I dared to lift my eyes from the screen to look around at the glum Brits at the ends of their holidays, and the lively, colourful, excited Spanish families, at the beginnings of theirs, the sense of alienation in the airport was complete, and I was sure panic back-lit my pale face under the *España!* hat, drawing all attention to me.

Yet no one looked at me at all, everyone passed me by, even knocked my chair and table carelessly with their bags without apologizing.

That unfathomable disappointment brought about a separation from everyone and everything around - the impatient waitress, the grubby table, the cold coffee, the stale Danish - a separation that must be the last feeling to accompany one when one knows one is dying, and slipping away from everyone and everything, sensing that one's senses are spreading thinner and further apart, diminishing and detaching themselves to release the soul, except there is no soul, only to release the identity one thought one had, and then nothing, nothing at all, except the unnameable oblivion.

It was when I was in the depths of this very static and vulnerable state, that a fellow airport resident was naturally drawn to me as parasite or predator. She was a woman I had seen before.

"I wonder if you can help me," she began, sitting down uninvited opposite. She drew her trolley of tatty, implausible baggage to her side.

I must have looked gormless, vacant.

"Oh ... Are you all right?"

I could not even shake my head.

"I know you're English," she said, and laughed. "Only the English or Dutch wear those hats!"

Her laughter exposed furry, neglected teeth.

Apart from your teeth, I thought, you have done a good job of keeping yourself presentable here, keeping body and soul together, and I felt a flimsy sense of encouragement no sooner felt than gone, that belonged to the former self, the one who had bought the new clothes and the silver Samsonite case. Her jet black hair, a wig, was brushed and neat, and hung in a straight helmet down the sides of her menopausal features, but on her forehead the fringe parted into dark kiss-curl curtains, reminiscent immediately to me of stage curtains, about to open on her finale. But they also took me to Marianne Stokes' 1908 painting, *Death and the Maiden*, where that well exploited theme was depicted at its most absurd, the massive black wings adorning Death were as monstrously fake as this resident's black wig. She wore no make-up at all, which for me is a good sign, but for her only signified beggardom.

"You see, I've got myself into a bit of a mess," she continued.

When I still did not respond in any way, she frowned and tried to look concerned.

"Are you sure you're alright, dear?" she asked, and then added, "I do care about you, you know."

She glanced around quickly, like a bird that has pulled a worm half out of the ground but cannot draw it out further; even so she must keep trying because she needs it not for herself but for the young in her nest.

"A pickpocket took my purse and my phone," she explained. "Bloody carteristas. Picketypockets! Luckily I still have my passport, look." She produced her worn, British passport, as if it were a seal of veracity and good faith. "I've missed my flight and now I've got to get myself home to sort things out, so I just need the taxi fare. Thirty euros should cover it. Can you help? You look like a good soul, a decent sort. A kind sort … Can you help?"

I continued to stare at her without any intention to unsettle her or threaten her in any way, and certainly without the slightest intention of giving her any money, but a threat of some kind must have been the effect, because she became nervous and her eyes flitted about the other tables again, other prospects, and then she looked behind her, guarding against the armed security patrols, with their cudgels and pistols, that were her enemy, my enemy, 24/7.

She remained torn between moving on and having one last go at extracting the worm.

"Can you help me, dear?"

Still I remained silent, but I was aware that my eyes had started to explore her clothes. I noted her man's navy blue cardigan, with knobbly leather buttons, not dissimilar to the trucker's club jacket on the *Mont St Michel* - her husband? - and then I stared down at her trolley of tatty, labelless, implausible baggage.

Who could mistake her for a bona fide passenger of any kind? It was plain proof of the laxity of security, despite their cudgels and pistols, but more importantly, of the success of my own disguise, as I sat there in my newish clothes, my *España!* straw hat, with the expensive Samsonite cabin bag drawn close to my chair. She took me for a real tourist, not one of her kind at all. I could have summoned a security guard to come and take her away and eject her from the airport, so that respectable passengers such as myself could get on with their coffee and Danish in peace.

"Just twenty euros would nearly get me home, and I could walk the rest."

I wanted to speak to her but could not: words would not come. They were sinking out of reach beneath me. I was actually in a far more vulnerable state than she could have imagined.

"Oh god," she said, standing up, sighing, giving up. "You're no use. Mr Gormless."

She wheeled her trolley beyond the plastic café fencing and resumed her meandering patrol.

So what had happened to Adams? Or, what had Adams done?

My first answers were innocent explanations of one kind or another - he had met with an accident, he had to spend time in hospital recovering from hypothermia - but these quickly gave way to more paranoid ideas that had more staying power.

Adams knew from my own account that only publicity could give what I had done any purpose, any meaning, and, like Manilow before him, like Emin after Manilow, like Evaristo after Emin, he had denied me that publicity, so that the graffiti slayings and all attempted slayings thereafter remained unconnected and meaningless, just flotsam and jetsam on the newsline shore. All that daring, that ingenuity and enterprise - all that expense! - all would be washed away and everything I had fought for and accomplished would remain unknown, or if known, in bits, indecipherable, absurd.

That was quite a punishment, Raph Adams, if that is what you had in mind. Far worse than what I did to you.

But after that low of my initial disappointment when no news came through, I made a determined recovery. No self-pity. I quickly established habits and patterns of behaviour designed to lift my spirits, and they were by and large successful.

For all names and anything related to them, I set up Google Alerts and only checked these once a day, last thing before sleep. Some nights I spent in the Long Stay car park, in the Hymer, despite the cold, so that my presence in the airport wasn't so noticeable. Every day I took the cheap C1 train into Málaga and spent the morning at museums and galleries: the Picasso Museum, or the magnificent Málaga Museum itself, in the old customs house, or the Museo Carmen Thyssen, where I could enjoy Rivas and Sorolla and the seascapes of Málaga and Cadiz, the Spain that had disappeared.

I suppose there was a noticeable and absurd aspect in some places, on some buses, about my appearance, with the Samsonite always in tow - I had to store it in security lockers at the galleries every time - but I didn't care. In the town centre itself the day was broken up with pleasant snacks in the street bistros for lunch, visits to the launderette, and sometimes in the afternoon bus rides out for long walks down to the docks, the marina, or along the brown beaches leading east out of town. Many afternoons I towed the Samsonite around the pedestrianised streets of the city's four storey elegant houses, and admired their ornate plasterwork and bowed rejas, and breathed deep the air of the crisp, autumnal, sometimes wintry afternoons - What joy! Genuine joy! To be amid such architectural beauty! - and on such afternoons all that I had done on my mad trip north in the Hymer began to recede.

In fact, during one afternoon that I spent at an archaeological site - they had discovered a Roman theatre near the Moorish castle, one of those amphitheatres built for minor games, whose history I found totally absorbing - that afternoon, as I wandered around the cordoned zones that were already open to the public, and whose paths were accessible with the Samsonite, my trip north began to take on an aura of pure fantasy, something that had never happened.

It didn't last. I knew what I had done. I knew the Hymer was in the Long Stay car park, that it was broken up inside and defiled outside, and that I might sleep there that very night.

Always, I had to return to the airport to use the ablutions and to sleep. The Checking Of The Alerts, that nightly ritual, was something to look forward to at close of day, a counter to the grim routine of inveigling my way into a seating area where I could lie down and sleep in relative comfort, or soldiering out on the two mile walk to the Long Stay for another freezing night in the cab. (I could only treat myself to the courtesy bus once a week, timing it with the change of drivers.) I suppose I must have been carrying on like this for about two months - from quite early on I had begun to lose track of dates and days - when an Alert for Bonhams Auctions came through that connected. I saw it by chance, not when I checked in at night, but as soon as it came through, when taking my morning coffee in Departures, before I caught the C1 into town.

Under the auspices of Bonhams' Popular Culture Department there would be an auction of the stage outfit worn by 'iconic popular music legend' Barry Manilow for his last performance at The London Palladium in September this year. On Bonham's website was a gallery of pictures of the green outfit, item by item, each of which you could hover over with the mouse in order to see several angles - there were six angles available for the boots alone! Those heels! - and alongside were action shots of Barry Manilow in full song with mic held high, head held high, and others of him in more tranquil pose at the piano, and in every shot the same green outfit glittered.

The auction would run online from 09.00 a.m. through to 09.00 p.m. on Saturday December 21st, GMT. Bids would be accepted internationally.

Raph Adams was heading up the sale.

Well, well ...

They'd wanted to push the sale as close to Christmas as possible.

'Bonhams' Popular Culture Department considers it to be in the public interest to allow this auction to go ahead for the benefit of Mr Manilow's fans worldwide and his legacy to popular music here in the UK

'The items pictured are certified by Barry Manilow's management as belonging to the popular music icon and composing legend, and it is further certified that Mr Manilow wore them during his last performance at The London Palladium on September 26th this year. Mr Manilow will not be returning to the UK. This is the only personal memorabilia from his final UK performance.

'Bonhams would like to take this opportunity to acknowledge publicly the role of Associate Specialist in the Popular Culture Department, Mr Raph Adams, who will be heading up the sale, in the recovery of these items. Our heartfelt thanks, Raph.'

Speculative details - the story of how Raph got home? Victim of a stag night prank, maybe? - were of no interest. They preoccupied me for no more than a day or so. Nor did the auction itself interest me. The date, the event, passed me by.

He had won.

I had known from the outset Raph Adams was smarter than me, and with his superior wit and cunning he had destroyed all I had achieved.

Bravo, bravo.

But I had one more move.

Today, on Christmas Day, there is a curious spectacle.

A very elderly choir, decked out in red and green, has assembled in Departures on a makeshift platform to sing Spanish carols - *villancicos* - to all the Christmas Day travellers. There are a dozen female singers, none less than sixty years old, some much older, on the raised back row, all in red and green, and in front of them is a mixed set of very elderly musicians, playing the traditional instruments for accompanying villancicos - zambombas, panderetas, cascabeles - with three elderly female guitarists strumming simple chords at the end of the line. The choir is led by an affable, portly, bespectacled, middle-aged professional on a soprano clarinet.

The elderly women in the choir take it in turns to offer solo refrains to each villancico. Each shakes a cascabel with vigour to introduce her refrain.

Now an ancient woman steps forward on the platform with her cascabel held high. Her short, thin grey hair is touched with clots of playful blue rinse, her thin and ancient frame clad in red robes, a holly green scarf adorns her withered neck, and baggy red trousers flap on her fleshless thighs. Her footwear is invisible behind the zambomba player sitting in front of her - a bald, puce-faced fellow pumping for all he's worth - but one suspects she wears ragged grey trainers. She delivers the bells of Bethlehem:

Belen, campanas de Belen!

Bethlehem, church bells of Bethlehem.

In each of the ancient women's faces the skull thrusts forth in earnest beneath the last layers of skin, and their movements are jerky, skeletal, graceless under their baggy uniform of cheap and gaudy Christmas garments, red and green only, far too hot, straight from a Chinese emporium, no doubt. Yet they sing and play with such gusto, such force and joy, the emotion is tangible and irresistible. Foreigners sway and nod and smile, the Spanish sing along out loud, boldly, without self-consciousness, and everyone gladly gives to the cause, which is to raise money for those who lost everything after torrential flooding in Valencia. This choir is singing and giving for their fellow Spanish citizens six hundred kilometres away.

Yet, they will not raise a fraction of what was paid for one of Manilow's boots.

Poor Moos would have loved this choir.

Maybe all of them would have loved this choir.

They died in vain. They are nothing now. Raph Adams saw to that. Our heartfelt thanks, Raph. He and his trasheteers.

I will not let them make me nothing too.

And another fraud will be defeated on Christmas Day: that airport resident, the British woman who tried to cheat me two months ago, the one with the black wig with its kiss-curl curtains, is heading out from the official money collectors into the crowd with a large Starbucks cup, the largest she could get - a *trenta.* As the choir sings on - *Campana sobre campana!* - the clarinetist spots her trick, tucks his instrument under his arm and comes forward, smiling, to collect what she has gained and pour it into the official red-robed collectors' hats. He sends her on her way with a push of the Starbucks cup in the small of her back. Out of the corner of my eye I see Lord Claude retreat now, with his trolley of phony baggage, and his own *trenta* Starbucks cup, without trying his luck.

The force of goodwill the choir arouses in everyone on Christmas Day is such that I have to leave. Its power and purity are too uncomfortable, too alienating, and the old anger returns, redoubles with its own futility, because it has nowhere to go any more. All is foiled, all has failed. I put the laptop back in the Samsonite among some dirty clothes - overdue at the launderette again - and leave.

In the late morning sun I cross the thoroughfare to the Express Car Park and cut through the milling travellers, Samsonite out in front, glinting in the sun, forging a way through, and I head for the station and my C1 train.

Only I never make it.

It is a warm, bright day. Plenty to see, to watch, from the train window, and in the city plenty of places still to go. Plenty to live for. But I head back to the Long Stay bus stop, ready now to make that last move.

An hour or so later, in the cabin of the stuffy Hymer, at the camping table, I open my laptop and begin.

Before dawn lifted its greasy lid on the Channel ...

Pablo Ruiz Picasso Airport, Málaga, spring 2025

www.ingramcontent.com/pod-product-compliance
Lightning Source LLC
Chambersburg PA
CBHW032126170626
46808CB00006B/2121
* 9 7 8 1 9 1 6 1 8 3 2 1 6 *